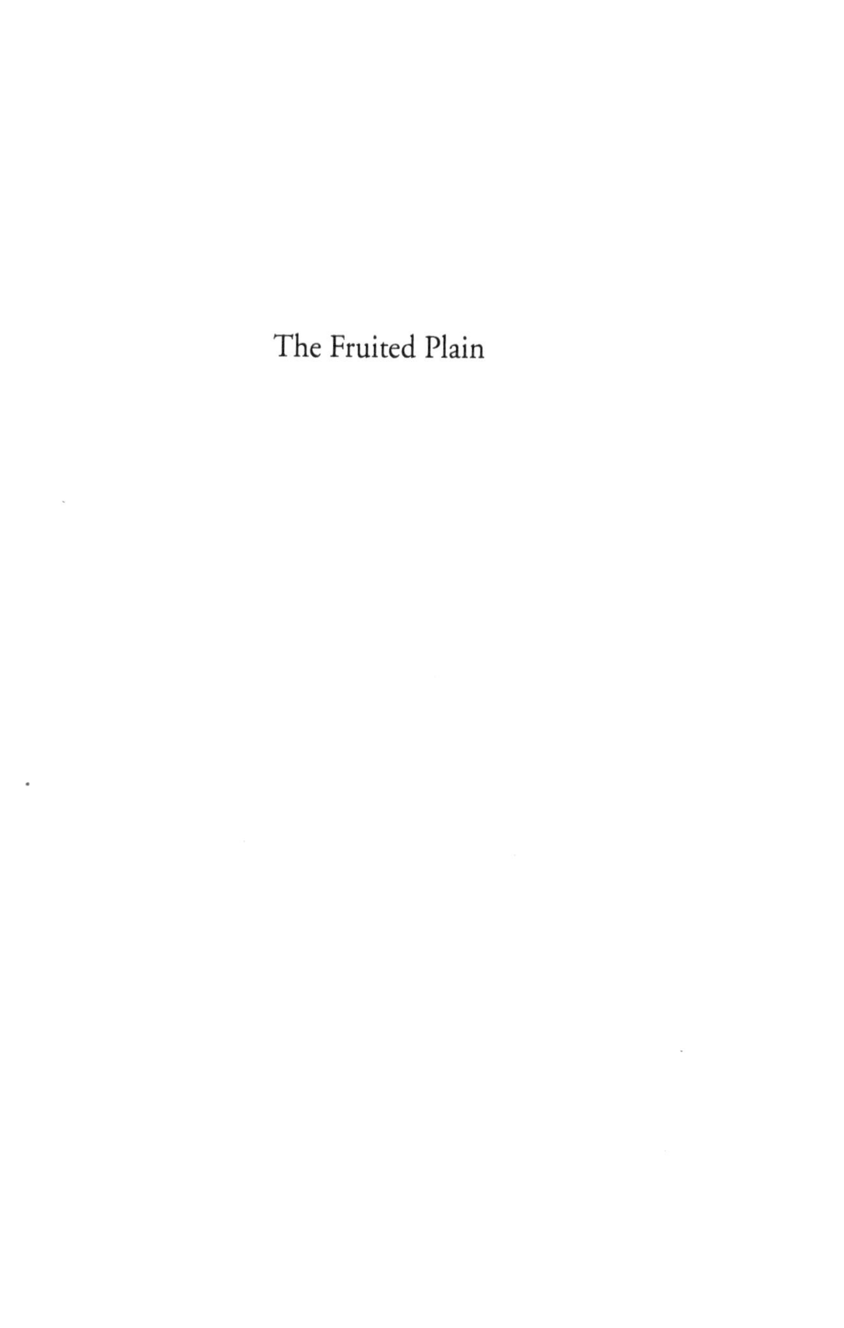

The Fruited Plain

The Fruited Plain

Fables for a Postmodern Democracy

ALVIN KERNAN

Yale University Press New Haven & London

Designed by Sonia L. Shannon.
Set in Adobe Garamond type
by Integrated Publishing Solutions,
Grand Rapids, Michigan.

Library of Congress Cataloging-in-Publication Data
Kernan, Alvin B.
The fruited plain : fables for a postmodern democracy / Alvin Kernan.

p. cm.
ISBN 978-0-300-09290-5
1. Humorous fiction, American. 2. Domestic fiction, American. 3. Satire, American. 4. Fables, American. I. Title.
PS3611.E76 F78 2002
813′.6—dc21
2001005847

A catalogue record for this book is available from the British Library.

O beautiful,
For spacious skies,
For amber waves of grain.
For purple mountain's majesty
Above the fruited plain.
America, America
God shed His grace on Thee
And crown thy good
With brotherhood
From sea to shining sea.

For Charles Kendrick Cannon
Old
Friend

Contents

Preface

The Fruited Plain sounds like, and is, the title of a celebration of the success of American agriculture. This is not that book. This is a rude satire of things gone wrong at the beginning of the third millennium C.E. in the central institutions of American democratic society. Democracy in America has always been an exuberant ideal with a tendency to a dangerous excess. There are in the land unscrupulous knaves who inflame and encourage this tendency of freedom to outgo itself because it opens opportunities to exploit America for their own ends. Freedom for them, as Voltaire said of truth, has left the heart to live on the lips, and it is they who are the targets of this satire, not the democratic people or their realistic hopes and fears.

Let it not be thought that I am an antidemocratic royalist or fascist authoritarian. Quite the contrary, I am a conservative of the stripe of John Adams and James Madison who believes that democracy has already made our land prosperous beyond belief, freeing us of priests and kings, and that it can do more in the future if it does not defeat itself by asking too much.

In normal times the pulpit, the courts, and the schools remind a democratic people that there is at least some restraining reality. But at the present these institutions are, as we shall see, among the chief offenders against good sense and honest truth. It is in times like these, when a glitzy scam of superdemocracy rules, that the muse of satire appears in the land and in plain words tells plain truths. Mark Twain, S. J. Perelman, Nathanael West, Tom Lehrer, Tom Wolfe, Joseph Heller, Don DeLillo—these are among the heroic names of American satire.

But satire is never welcome in optimistic America, where the constant cry is "boost, don't knock." As a result, American satire has always had to exaggerate—Gulliver among the giant Brobdingnagians, not the diminutive Lilliputians. English satire has a longer history than our own, but its characteristic understatement, as in the works of Evelyn Waugh, in my opinion the greatest satirist writing in English in the twentieth century, will not do for us. Overstatement has to run for all it is worth to keep up with our compatriots, and even then it will often fall far behind the reality. After a typical day of writing this book, exhausted from creating what I took to be telling exaggerations of American life, I would pour a martini and turn on the television evening news to learn that two schoolboys, armed to the teeth and maddened by killer electronic games and violent TV, had gunned down thirty of their fellows and that Congress had responded instantly by requiring a copy of the Ten Commandments to be prominently displayed in every schoolroom. Hit the remote control and there was the president of the United States (POTUS) telling us that the kind of oral service he had been enjoying, while on the telephone with other statesmen, and fiddling with a cigar, from a young volunteer working for him in the Oval Office did not, legally anyway, constitute "sex."

Ours is a land of extremes. The temperature rises to well over a hundred, and drops below minus forty. Wildfire and earthquakes, drought and flood, tornadoes and other ill winds race across it. It is a wild country. Cowboy and Indian land still, its inhabitants will never hear the rifle shots of understatement or even the Gatling gun of wit. Only the cannonballs of exaggeration will get the attention of real Americans, and then for only a moment as they ride, hell-for-leather, toward the horizon. Building Camelot, looking for the fountain of youth, California or bust, ending poverty and disease, making the lion and the lamb lie down together. "Forward ho" for Disneyland.

One
Merry Xmas from the Joads

Hi everyone,

Here it is Xmas of the year 2001, the first of the new millenium, and I have booted up my old PC to send all of you very special greetings from the Winfield Joads III, by e-mail. We all have so much to be thankful for, and specially us Okies whose parents and grandparents came out from the dustbowl in the 1930s to live here in California, the land of milk and honey. At first, I gather, it didn't seem like that, but things soon got better. They sure did for the Graves, my family, and the Joads, the family I married into, like they did for all hard-working, God-fearing Americans. Aunt Ruthie is the only one left of those who made the trip, and she still lives with us. She don't remember much anymore—Alzheimer's, Old Timers, Ha, Ha—but when all the family is in the same room with her you can just tell she knows she is among her own folks. She often thinks that she is back on the road coming out from the dustbowl, talking to her brother Tom about the police, and muttering about her sister, Rosasharn, doing something real bad in a barn with some poor old fellow. But you know all that, since the old Joads' adventures were written down in John Steinbeck's wonderful book *The Grapes of Wrath.*

I don't want to brag, but things have gone well for us this last year and I want you to share our good news. Our new house, in Upscale Chase, is part of a gated community—who would have ever thought the Joads would live in a gated community?—and has five bedrooms, one for almost every child, and a lot of amenities. Pa has a wine cellar, and we are looking forward to putting in a swimming pool next year.

I still work for the local government, supervising the care of some of our senior citizens, but Pa after many years at A-One Rockets decided to retire when the company was taken over by the Fortune 500 company American Nuts and Screws. He has been looking forward for many years to being able to start his own consulting business, and this gives him just the opportunity he needed.

The children are all well. The big news is that Calista will probably be married pretty soon. Earle, our oldest, is an electronic genius, and all the big-name schools are bidding for him. He thinks he wants one of the Ivys, but not Harvard, which he says is past its peak. The other kids all love school and just seem to flourish with the modern curriculum the new principal has put in place. Have It All Valley is on the cutting edge of everything, and we love being a part of this new, postmodern America. So exciting.

Merry Xmas and a Happy New Year, Everyone,
Elspeth Joad

Ruthie couldn't help sniggering aloud when she read the bit about the "gated community." The gates were only a pair of cement-block posts covered with stucco and cream paint. She may not have been as sharp as she once was, but she remembered very well how bad it was years ago when the family loaded up the old truck and left the Oklahoma dust bowl for California, where Tommy became a union organizer, but then he was killed with the marines at Tarawa, and Rosasharn was a Hollywood starlet, until she overdosed. Still the rest of the family made it, working at first in the wartime aircraft factories and then branching out all over the state. As she read on in the Xmas letter Elspeth had given her, to make her feel part of things, Ruthie couldn't help wondering if it hadn't been better in the old days, hard as they were, than the way they were now, not the way poor Elspeth described them, but the way they actually were. *I think that the bankers and politicians, and the lawyers and the doctors and businessmen, the fellows who write those slick ads, and the professors who run the schools, maybe they have really figured out how to make us folks do what they want by giving us what we want rather than telling us we can't have it, the way they did in the old days.* And with that thought, she nodded off.

Elspeth Joad had gone to Lone Tree Community College and majored in social work. She was the granddaughter of old Muley Graves, one of the Joads' neighbors back in Oklahoma. Grandpa Graves didn't come along when his family lit out for California because they didn't have anything to eat. Instead he hid out in the bushes and shot at the bulldozers that were tearing down the empty repossessed farmhouses, that is, he did until the FBI made him one of their most wanted and shot him with his girlfriend outside a bar in Tulsa. Elspeth married young Winfield Joad II, and they had six children. Earle was the oldest, and then there was Calista, and after her Somerset, always a trifle touchy, and Emerson, Thompson, and the baby, Triola.

The old Okies liked to tell one another how much things had changed from the old days. No more state police with blackjacks, strikebreakers with pick handles, and folks spitting and yelling, "Go back where you came from!" Everybody seemed to want to help folks now. "Only in America," as they say, and it was hard to remember the days when nobody gave people like the Joads anything, when they took everything from them, the land in Oklahoma and their work for a dollar a day in the San Fernando Valley picking cotton and fruit, and hit them over the head to boot.

But now, like the folks often say, it's just the opposite. Take the Joad house, for example. The Joads live in the suburbs, about forty miles out of Los Angeles, in Have It All Valley. They and their neighbors never thought they could own a house until a salesman came around and showed how the federal government would guarantee a mortgage, with only a thousand-dollar down payment—which the Joads paid using their Croesus & Freres Preferred Investors' Titanium Visa Card. Not only could they own a house, they could own a real tract mansion, with a butler's pantry, an exercise room, a sauna with a Jacuzzi, and, as a special gift from the builder, for signing on the dotted line right away, a billiard room. The Joads didn't have a pool table, but they found it nice to think that if they had one they would have a place to put it, just like in those stately homes you see on TV and in the movies. "Red in the corner pocket." The monthly payments came to 57 percent of their combined income, but the "Official Homeowners' Manual" that the bank gave away free to prospective buyers said it was okay to go as high as 60 percent.

It turned out of course that the thousand dollars down was only the beginning of it. There were the points to pay the bank for the mortgage, mortgage insurance, a lawyer to register the deed, homeowners' insurance—required by the bank—prepayment of taxes, and on and on. Before they were through at the closing, where there were about twenty people sitting around the table with their hands out, Pa Joad had to sign checks for every one of them. It took all their savings. Pa said,

"No wonder they call it Have It All Valley, with all those buzzards circling around and picking our carcass bare."

It was nice, though, out in the country, away from crime and the crowded and polluted streets, though it was a bit lonely at times because a lot of the houses were never finished, and the streets just petered out in the sagebrush and desert. Tumbleweeds as big as boxcars blew down the street once in a while, making the neighborhood look like a Clint Eastwood movie. Then, too, people moved out of a lot of the houses when the taxes went way up to pay for sewers, water lines, streets, and new schools for all the children that poured in. As the taxes rose, the value of the houses fell, and the mortgages got to be a lot bigger than the homes' market value, and so it made sense to load up the big Ford Excresence SUV, hoping it wouldn't blow out a tire and turn over at high speed—and move away, sort of like leaving Oklahoma all over again. Banker Brightgrin had said when he financed the mortgages in Upscale Chase that the value of all these houses was sure to go up, and when it did the owners would be able to take out a second mortgage and build a swimming pool, which they soon found they really needed in the summer, with the temperature around 105°. It was a dry heat, though.

But the Joads hung on to what they had learned to call "the good life," and like the plantation owners in *Piazza Days in the Old South,* on TV you know, they stood out in the evening on their front porch with the big pillars, looking at the Rattlesnake Mountains off in the distance. After a while they would go in and watch TV while sitting in the Jacuzzi. On a big night they would order some piping-hot pizza delivered right to their door by one of the local motorcycle gang, the Nazi Lowriders, a nice fellow, though that stud through his tongue made him really hard to understand.

Every night after work, Elspeth would come home and see the children's beaming faces gathered around the TV, watching *Divorce Court, Sally Jesse Raphael,* or *Oprah* getting folks to bring their big secrets out into the open, like spousal-abuse and incest, where everyone could understand and know them for what they really are. Seeing her kids learning so much about life made Elspeth feel that everything was all right, and she remembered old Grandma Joad saying proudly, "We're the people that live. They ain't gonna wipe us out. Why, we're the people—we go on."

But where they were going wasn't always so clear to the Joads as where they had been. *We do our best,* Elspeth would sometimes muse when she was a bit down, *we work and try hard to raise our children in the right ways, we believe in God and go to church every Sunday, we pay our debts—though we have fallen a bit behind on our credit cards—we vote at every election, and still things seem to fall apart. The president and the politicians say all the time that the family is the center of our country, but something seems to have gone wrong. Sometimes I think maybe we all want too much, want all the things they show us on TV. But it can't be that. All the things we buy keep the economy going, and the people who run things, and they ought to know, make credit real easy to get.*

Credit cards were a particularly good example of what worried her. Not a mail went by without an offer to the Joads for an unsolicited gold, platinum, or titanium credit card with a preapproved ten-thousand-dollar line of credit and a chance to win a free trip to Disneyland for the whole family. Every mail brought an offer of a new one—beryllium today, U-235 tomorrow—with a big credit line and an annual interest rate of 20+ percent, and the Joads, like other folks, had a wallet full of plastic. When they maxed one out, they would just pull out another to buy all those things they wanted, and really needed to have, like expensive Xmas presents for the kids—"they're only young once"—or paying the orthodontist to straighten Calista's teeth, or the down payment on the second car, a really safe Volvo, that Elspeth had to have to get to work, even to get to the supermarket, which was ten miles away. There weren't any sidewalks in Have It All Valley. Like all Americans, the Joads drove everywhere.

Television showed them how to live an upscale lifestyle, which meant having a big smile, lots of wavy hair, the latest fashions in clothes, and cars. Cars, wonderful cars, loaded with extras like AC, CD, TV, digital telephone, steel-belted radial tires, antilock brakes, moon roofs, Russian leather upholstery, "four on the floor," and simulated bird's-eye maple plastic dashboards. General Motors and Ford would actually give buyers money back when they signed the papers, sending a rebate greater than the down payment, and defer payments for months. If you had a big McMansion in Have it All Valley, you also had to have a big, I mean big, sports utility vehicle, tons of real "Amurrican iron," that would take the whole family to church or on educational trips to places like the Berry Farm or the Land o' Milk and Honey. *But then,* Elspeth thought, *if you have some trouble with a few little fender-benders—nobody got hurt real bad, though, my Gawd, how they yelled at me!!!—the insurance is canceled, which makes for quite a bind since you have to have insurance to drive, and even the school is seven miles away. Without a car you are not really an American, but I wish sometimes that I had that faithful old truck with all the extra tires hanging on it that the Joads drove to California and kept in the backyard for ever so long. It didn't look like much, but it only cost a few dollars, and it ran all the way out here.*

The Joads were not complainers, though, everybody hates a whiner, and TV was a cornucopia pouring riches into the household. The set was on all day long, like in most houses. The men watched sports all the time, and Elspeth's story, *Not Without Pain,* a medical soap opera, was probably the most exciting thing in her life. The little kids watched cartoons, and the older ones enjoyed the police stories and the sitcoms, and they all watched the news once in a while and felt good in comparison to all the poor folks in Africa, where the rebels cut their hands off, or Israel, where the Jews and the Arabs kissed each other and then blew up a school bus, or Northern Ireland, where the Catholics and the Protestants banged away at one another from morn till night. "Why can't they just live together in peace?" the Joads would say to one another, "There are sure Gawd enough problems in life without killing each other."

The children were the apples of the Joads' eyes, and no matter what, the sun rose and set on them. Take young Earle. He never took to school, played hooky a lot, and his grades were so bad that they were always threatening to throw him out of high school. But his mother insisted, "That boy is a real genius, a Tom Edison or a Henry Ford, when it comes to computers. He never says a word to us but sits up there in his room all day and all night and hammers away on his computer, with the radio on playing punk rock and nasta. I never go in there, though, because I don't ever know where his pet rattlesnake will be—it crawled into the Jacuzzi to get water one day. But we hear what he is up to sometimes. When the FBI came by the other day it turned out that somebody, and they thought it might be Earle, was 'penetrating' the codes of the computer system in the Pentagon. They seemed to think he was trying to find a way to fire some nuclear rockets at North Korea. But little Earle, he wouldn't do anything like that, he talks rough, but he really has a warm heart, like all the Joads."

His mother was dead right about Earle's skills as a hacker. He managed to break into the school computer system and change his low grades all to A+. The teachers never knew what was happening; once they put the grades in the computer they never looked at them again. And the school secretary simply printed out, stamped, and sent a transcript to anyone Earle requested, without ever looking at what she mailed. Though the teachers didn't suspect it, Earle had the highest grade-point average of anyone who had ever graduated from Have It All Valley High, and top schools like Ivy, Manatee, and Lemming were offering him "tuition plus" scholarships. He was determined to go to one of the big universities, probably Ivy. Filing his applications online, it was easy to write his own letters of recommendation from the principal and the football coach, as well as his math and English teachers. He had a tough time hacking into the Scholastic Achievement Test offices, though, they had all kinds of fantastic firewalls, but after failing to break into their system and change his low 400s scores, Earle figured out that he could tell the admissions offices that he refused to take an elitist test that victimized women, blacks, and the disadvantaged. He had heard that Ivy League admissions officers just roll over and beat their breasts with guilt when they hear that kind of thing, and he heard right. Little Earle will be okay, if his snake doesn't bite him someday when he is tormenting it.

Calista, who is fifteen now, is pregnant. This sounded bad to her parents, but they soon learned that like so many bad things nowadays, it was really a good thing once you understood it. At first, though, it really didn't sound so good. She came home one day and said in a happy voice, for once—usually she was pretty sullen—"I'm pregnant, the test I got from the drug store had a red ring."

Pa was a bit exasperated and lit into her right off. "What happened to the pill? And all those courses you took in school about the human reproductive system and protected sex? What about the free condoms the school nurse passed out to you and all the other kids to provide you with freedom of choice?"

"Those things did help a lot," said Calista, not quite getting it that Pa was being sarcastic, "but in the end it took a little recreational Mary Jane to loosen me up, that and the right boy."

Pa began to get red in the face when he saw his sarcasm wasn't taking. "Why couldn't you have stayed with foreplay or manual sex? You kids today are too big for your britches, and getting married at fifteen will be no joke, you'll find for sure."

"Married? Who said anything about gender exploitation? The local Women's Liberation Task Force has joined with the Gay Freedom Fighters to set up a marriage resistance brigade at Have It All Valley High, with Ms. Emma Pessary as subcommandante. They're raising everybody's consciousness about how you don't need to be different sexes in order to be married, and how you don't have to be married to have babies, so you don't have to live with some mean guy who's always drunk and dumping on you, the way you do on Ma. Women can make their own way these days, they don't even need men to have children, they can pick something up at a sperm bank, and in a few years we'll be able to clone our own babies."

"Who the hell is going to pay for all this?"

"Well, the school clinic has a government grant for supporting single mothers. There are lots of young girls like me who are going to have a baby, it turns out, but who don't have a husband and don't want one, so the government is subsidizing them as a part of a broad effort to offer a range of democratic alternatives to the nuclear family. Did you know that the birth mothers of over a quarter of white babies in this country are, like, single women? The black rate is even higher. While you're pregnant the government pays you a scholarship if you go to school, and after the baby's born they give aid to dependent children—there's a nursery right in the school—and preschool head-start programs that provide baby-sitters and keep the single moms from being victimized by being deprived of a good education."

"Who the hell devised this system?" Pa roared. "It must have been the general who said, 'Nuke 'em back to the Stone Age,' he must have had the family in mind. Who will take care of the children as they grow up, raise them and give 'em a sense of being human? Who will comfort them when they fail? Who will applaud them when they succeed? If you tickle them will they laugh? If you prick them will they bleed?"

"Pa's off, he's been watching PBS again," and everyone stared at the floor in embarrassment.

Elspeth tried to smooth things over by pointing out that it wasn't just ordinary people who had children "out of wedlock"—Calista tossed her pretty head at that old-fashioned term—"some of the best people are no longer marrying when they're pregnant. Marva St. Cloud and Judy Sincere, the big TV stars, have both announced that they are planning to cast off the chains of old ways and enter the brave new world of being single mothers. All the rock musicians and the rapsters have nothing good to say about the family, and they make a lot of money, almost as much as the football and baseball players. And what did Professor Fallopian, the big sex expert, say just the other day on the discussion of family depravity on Taffy Spreadeagle's show, 'The family is the American disease'? So, maybe Calista is into the coming thing and we ought to go along with it." Ma was really thinking that *running a family hasn't been a lot of fun most of the time if you're honest about it, and maybe it is time to give the whole idea a bit of a rest.*

"Well," said Pa, "we're going to go along with it all right, willy-nilly, but I don't have to like it. Have you thought of an abortion, there's our neighborhood abortion clinic now subsidized by another government agency that is trying to solve the overpopulation problem by reducing the birth rate to three infants per thousand women of child-bearing age."

"Oh, Pa, you sound like some reproduction expert. Reading magazines in the library has been making you think you really understand this kind of stuff. Besides, it's real dangerous trying to get into the abortion clinic run by Doc di Late and the Freedom of Choice people. The Right to Life people have chained themselves across the door, throwing red water on anybody who tries to go in to have an abortion, and holding up pictures of fetuses, uggh, like horrid."

"Why don't the police stop them, what kind of a country do we live in?"

"They did try but it seems that the pickets are just exercising their first-amendment rights of freedom of speech, and they've hired a lawyer to go to court and get an injunction against interfering with them. On top of that they're suing Have It All Valley township for the full amount of its annual tax base for punitive damages to compensate for police brutality. Oh, no, don't go near the Freedom of Choice clinic, somebody is likely to set off a bomb filled with nails or shoot one of the dedicated workers there who are donating their services so that women can exercise control over their own bodies and escape the reproductive slavery that men have kept them in for just thousands of years."

"Well," said Pa, who had been looking more and more pained as Calista explained things to him, "Is there any point in asking who the proud father is?"

Calista began to cry. "How can you be so mean, all of you, I'm not going to be like you, nasty minded and narrow, just like Subcommandante Pessary says you are, I'm going to be somebody and make something of myself, not bog down in some old marriage."

The yellow school bus dropped off the little kids just then and ended the quarrel for the moment. All four of the young ones had a big card hung around the neck that said, "I'm terrific," part of their self-esteem training. They were exhausted and headed straight for the television, having had a long day that began with being checked through the metal detectors, patted down, their knapsacks searched, to make sure no one pulled a knife or a gun inside the school. Then on that morning they had gone to a class where police officers talked about DARE (Drug Abuse Resistance Education) and showed them that the police are their friends, not their enemies. They also gave them SPD (Sexual Predator Defense) training, showing them how to avoid being picked up and molested by the sexual perverts who roamed the streets looking for victims. Half the houses were Safe Havens, but mostly it was a matter of not looking at anyone or talking to strangers, and it seemed to be working because all the Valley kids ran from old men who tried to pat them on the head, and even with people they knew, they looked away all the time and mumbled.

The kids particularly liked their Earth Day class, where

they did a ritual dance of saving the environment around a replica of the planet propped on a tripod as drums pounded in the background. As part of the new multicultural curriculum they also offered sacrifices to Tbongo's god Torque, or to the Hindu god with the long elephant's trunk. The kids liked getting to know about other folks' religious beliefs, but there were complaints by fundamentalist Christians in the community. "It is against the law," they said, "even to mention the name Jesus Christ in school, while they are at the same time setting up false gods before our children."

Then there was sensitivity training, learning to accept African-Americans, Latinos, and Asians as real people. "Two Daddies" and "Two Mommies" plays suppressed culturally induced homophobia and made the kids aware that there are many different kinds of families. But the newest and most controversial thing this year was a new social studies course in children's rights. The Joads like other parents spanked their children from time to time, and like most, they believed that a slap on the side of the head now and then was the only way to keep the kids from pinching one another and yelling all the time. But the teacher in the "Rights of Children" class told the kids that spanking was wrong and that it made them grow up to be a part of a violent society. All the parents were nervous about this course, though they didn't dare speak openly against it lest they be identified as child beaters, and there were rumors that some lawyers in Los Angeles were sending letters to the kids at school offering to sue their families for any harsh, authoritarian treatment.

The Have it All Valley School District nurse kept up on the latest in diseases that kids are likely to get these days. Somerset was diagnosed right off as dyslexic—his "p's" and "d's" were backwards—and they banged him right into special ed. along with half of his class. He *was* always a funny kind of kid, wetting the bed until eleven, and having terrible nightmares in which he dreamed about monsters with big teeth chasing him.

Triola, on the other hand, was found right off to have ADD, Attention Deficit Disorder, always jumping around from here to there, never staying put for long. But once they knew what was wrong, the school nurse ran her down and gave her a shot of Ritalin several times a day, and after that she behaved ever so well, just sitting quietly in the corner. Thompson and Ellsworth, the other two Joad kids, were really nice children and there didn't seem to be anything wrong with them yet, but you never know, and the school was keeping an eye out and giving them preemptive Prozac tranquilizers.

Have It All Valley really was, at all levels, K through 12, a student-centered, progressive school that adhered strictly to the century-old Columbia Teachers College educational science, preparing kids for actual life rather than teaching them things that nobody needed anymore. There was an American history course that taught how the Europeans came to the new land and murdered the natives and enslaved black Africans, how the colonists spread west to exterminate the Indians, how the Revolutionary War was fought to establish private property and disenfranchise the poor, and how the Industrial Revolution raped the land and impoverished the mid-European immigrants. The Joads were also taught the new math using base 13. They had some trouble in stores working dollars and cents into thirteens, but in the end they understood that the world made as much sense in thirteens as it did in tens. Numbers like 52 and 169 tended to crop up here and there in the local grafitti, to the confusion of the older inhabitants. English was taught with the same tolerance, namely, on the basis of equal respect for all the different ways of writing and speaking and spelling. Reading was taught by the whole-language method, which didn't work out too well, but then in the television age no one read much anyway.

If there was one central concept on which all the Have It All Valley teachers agreed, it was surely that students should not learn inert facts but should construct their own knowledge.

This principle governed the academic track classes that bright kids like Somerset were in as well as the "practical skills" track, where Emerson and Triola learned to repair vacuum cleaners and toasters.

Everybody soon got used to Calista being pregnant, and things seemed to be going all right, but just before Xmas, Pa came home to say that the factory where they make military rockets, and where he had worked for thirty years, had "downsized" him.

"What does that mean, 'downsized'?" Elspeth asked. "You look just as big as ever to me."

"Well, it means the same thing as 'made redundant.' They say they can't compete in the global market any longer paying union members high American wages and big benefits, specially with medical insurance going through the roof, so they're going to move the rocket division to Colombia, where labor's cheap, and though the natives don't have a lot of good old American know-how, the new robotized assembly lines controlled by computers don't need much skill anyway. All you have to do is put stuff in at one end and then haul the rockets away from the other. Besides, now that the Cold War is over and peace has broken out, the government don't need as many rockets as it used to, except for those they fire every month at Saddam Hussein, Osama bin Laden, and the Bongos and the Tongos in Tbongo, though they don't seem ever to land anywhere near any of those slippery rascals."

"Well, it's a good thing you have your pension. You're near retirement anyway, so with Social Security and the pension, and my job running the center for the homeless here in Have It All Valley, we ought to be okay, at least for a while."

"Well, there may be a little bit of a problem with the pension, too. It seems that the last time A-One Rockets was conglomerated in a leveraged buyout by American Nuts and Screws, looking for a diversified product base, the lever was our pension fund. Once it had control, American Nuts decided that A-One's pension account was overfunded, so they took a lot of money out, and what was left they invested in one of their subsidiaries, Liquidity Pumps Incorporated. This was great for a time and LPI boomed into the stratosphere, but a little later LPI went belly-up when its corporate executives sold big holdings of the stock at the top of the market, and the price fell like a rock."

"So the pension fund owns only a pile of worthless LPI stock?"

"Well, not quite, it's still worth thirty-seven cents a share."

"And what will your pension be, then?"

"Well, after paying off accumulated indebtedness to the big government agency that watchdogs pension funds, ERISA, they say I'll get about twelve dollars a month."

"And after a lifetime of hard work. Winfield," Elspeth said, "I don't see how we are going to make it. Your Social Security will pay a bit, even though there's getting to be something like ten golden-agers for every worker with a job paying into the fund, and the politicians long ago spent every dime that was held with the full faith and trust of the federal government in the Social Security surplus account, but it won't be enough to keep up the payments on the house or make the minimum payments on our credit cards, which are all maxed out. Calista is pregnant, and Earle won't take a job at minimum wage, which is all he can get around here. My own work taking care of those poor homeless folks at the Have It All Valley Care Center don't pay much more than that, and though we can live on food stamps and welfare, I don't see how we can keep the house.

"Well," Elspeth went on—a lot of sentences around the Joad house began with "Well"—"as long as the family holds together we will be all right."

They worried away for a time; but then Elspeth saw a TV ad for a law firm—Cease & Desist—saying that it specialized in problems like the Joads' and could help them declare a "Title 7 Come 11 Bankruptcy," which Congress had recently passed as a form of debtors' relief. This would allow them to keep their main assets, like the house and one car, without having to pay anybody a red cent on the mortgage or anything else so long as they were in bankruptcy.

At first, this idea didn't go down so well with Pa. "Bankruptcy. Never!!! The Joads have always been poor but ain't none of us ever refused to pay our debts. Why, we're the heart of America, we settled Oklahoma when the Indians were still there and not running gambling casinos all over, and before that we farmed cotton with slaves in Mississippi. Why, the Joads came over to Georgia with Oglethorpe. The Lord will provide and we will make it somehow. No bankruptcy!"

But after Elspeth called, lawyer Ellen Barratri came around from Cease & Desist, and once Pa looked at her miniskirt he began to see reason. Cease & Desist, she explained, would put the Joads into bankruptcy, and it would also file a criminal damage suit against the builder and the Brightgrin National Bank for not making the full terms of the Joads' mortgage obligation clear. "Likely they will settle out of court," she said, "and for enough to pay off your debts and have something left over as well."

Ms. Barratri was very determined and very sincere. "My firm will press this case in the courts of this land to ensure that you and plain, honest, hard-working people like you are no longer offered credit that you have no realistic chance of paying off. We will take the case to the Supreme Court if we have to, all on a contingency basis. If and when we win the case, and losing it is most unlikely with the legal talent that Cease & Desist will bring to bear, we will take no more than a mere 50 percent of the judgment, plus actual costs, at the usual rate of five hundred dollars per billable hour. You don't have to pay anything. If we should lose, which, frankly, is impossible, you will owe us nothing. It will be enough for us to have done our," the Joads thought she said something like *pro banana,* "duty to establish the inalienable rights of the people."

Ellen Barratri had a wonderful clear voice, and all the kids left the television and gathered around listening, and even Earle came downstairs, without his snake, to get a look at this lady lawyer with her high heels, her long legs in fine silk stockings, her miniskirt pinstripe suit, and her thin black lizard briefcase, just like Ally McBeal on TV. They followed her out to her car, a long Jaguar, jet black and shiny chrome, that glistened in the evening sun. Pa grinned all over when she sat on the side of the leather driver's seat with her legs hanging out, and he said that she had convinced them and that they would sign the papers as soon as they came in the mail. Both the girls, Calista with her round tummy, immediately said that they wanted to be lawyers when they grew up. And Elspeth was moved to exclaim, "I might have really made something out of myself if I had had a role model like Ms. Barratri, but I'm grateful to have a home, and I wouldn't trade my wonderful family for anything in the world. [brushing a tear from her eye] It is like old Grandma Joad said, more than once, in fact she was always sayin' it, 'We're the people that live. The ain't gonna wipe us out. Why, we're the people—we go on.'"

Two
Majoring in Deconstruction

To make your way, meaning to make a lot of money, in the modern world means going to college, the better the college the more money. After the breakup of the Joad family, it seemed more than ever necessary for Earle to carry out his plans for getting a first-rate education. He had given himself a new academic persona, complete with glowing letters of recommendation, by breaking into Have It All Valley High's database, and he had these sent to Ivy University. Yale was obviously out, too pastoral. Chicago was too trendy, and Stanford too rigorous. So, Ivy it was. Earle thought of pretending to be Latino to increase his chances for admission, but "Joad" had a kind of ineradicable Waspish sound, rhymes with "woad."

And now, here he was, a son of old Ivy, at last, one of the "climbers." He had a full scholarship, the Benedict Happenstance Fellowship, named after Ivy's distinguished graduate who had made a fortune from inventing a new cheese spread, "The Better Mousetrap," and lost most of it trying to corner gold. The campus was a bit of a shock, though. Years ago the students had struck and occupied the president's office to force him to adopt an "open arms for the homeless" policy. Those students had long ago graduated and departed, but the homeless had not, and the campus looked like a hobo jungle, with fires here and there in old oil drums, torn tents, broken stuffed chairs, portable toilets, and shacks made from odd pieces of plywood and galvanized tin roofing. The sweet smell of marijuana floated through the air, and here and there you could hear Ivy's "guests" grumbling about the heartless capitalist university refusing to let them eat for free in the dining halls and use the student toilets.

Indoctrination week was a real pisser. It used to be that you just went to college and took a tour of the library, but now there was a week of lectures and struggle groups run by a Multicultural Conflict Resolution Team. You had to pass a written test on these lectures to show that you had understood their main point that white, heterosexual males had always exploited and brutalized everyone else on the globe, and now the time had come for the big payback. If you didn't pass the test, your room assignment was canceled and you had to look for a room in town.

For days Earle listened as angry women scolded him or some furious South American denounced Uncle Sam as an imperialist pig and predicted that the Yanqui banana empire was about to collapse. Just about every militant group in the country had a shot at the freshpersons, except, of course, the FBI, CIA, and U.S. Army, Air Force, Navy, and Marines, all of which were banned from campus. On another part of the campus a three-day indoctrination familiarized the parents of freshpersons with how to relate to their children undergoing the stress of new life adjustments and becoming students at Ivy. Ma and Pa Joad would have liked to come, since all expenses were paid for those who had a below poverty-level income, established by your latest Form 1040, but Pa was in a horseshoe tournament at the nursing home, and Ma didn't want to come without Pa.

Using the student ratings of courses and instructors, Earle looked for courses that were known for being super-guts. Not that it made a lot of difference. No grades had been given at Ivy since the tuition passed forty thousand dollars a year. Who after all was willing to pay big bucks to get a C or be told that they didn't know how to write or think? But still you had to look for something that didn't require much reading and might pay off later. There was a lot to choose from these days when every teacher had a right to teach his or her own specialty. There was "Food Studies: food underwrites ongoing debates about the substance and boundaries of personhood." "The Slavic Vampire" sounded pretty good, too, and then there were "Pornography in Theory and Practice," "Soap Operas as an Art Form," "The Ghettoization of Queerdom," and a whole slew of useful courses in magic, witchcraft, and extraterrestrial life.

Earle was fascinated by "Handicapped Studies 1—The Body and Physical Difference: discourses on physical, mental, emotional, learning disabilities; nonvisible disabilities such as blindness and deafness." That was good stuff and counted as the prerequisite for Handicapped Studies 97, "Disabled Bodies in Literature and Culture: a focus on the disability novel as a genre." The course would study Attention Deficit Disorder (the disease his little sister Triola suffered from) in James Joyce's *Finnegans Wake*. There was another dynamite handicap course that focused on prosthetic devices like those of Captain Ahab and Long John Silver, and hunchbacks like Quasimodo and Richard III.

But it looked as if "Introduction to Women's Studies" might be a real winner. Women held all the important posts in the university and seemed more and more to be in charge of things everywhere. Besides, all the pretty girls would be in this class. The course description was maybe a bit heavy, but the actual course would probably be easier:

> *Introduction to Women's Studies, WS101,* is based on the fact that the suppression of the female has been a primary meaning of Western culture over a long time. This course identifies, documents, accounts for, and interprets this suppression via the forms it takes—many still concealed, clandestine, unexplored—and their counterforms, from early periods to the present. It goes on to identify and describe newly developing practices that counter masculine hegemony. Professor Ida Monorail and staff.

He hoped to find out what was behind all the fuss these days about men and women, but the course never worked for Earle. The teacher was suspicious from the start of a man in a class of women, and she was always getting at him some way or another. One day he ventured to say that a man would think of something differently from a woman.

"Pray tell, Mr. Joad, just how would a man think of it?"

"It's only my opinion, of course, Professor Monorail, but it seems to me that men think harder about things than women do. Just a habit, I suppose, but women seem content to look at a thing and let it go, while men are always worrying something until they get it right."

"So, Mr. Joad, you think women just want to gossip and socialize, while men do the real hard thinking, is that it?"

Earle knew he was on thin ice and tried desperately to recover.

"No, no, Professor Monorail, I don't think that men are any better thinkers in the long run than women, they just go about it in a different way, more directly, more exclusively, maybe, while women are happy to talk it over and find out what everybody has to say about the matter."

"Chattering like birds on a telephone wire, maybe, Mr. Joad?"

"Well, maybe you could put it like that, but women are

more interested in the short run, men in the long run. Women, that is, are more social, more willing to make the best of things at hand, like a house and family. Men are always looking for something, some big answer that will settle everything, or make everything work out. That's what I think, anyway."

Professor Monorail glowered, "Men like to make war and women like to have babies, that's just about what men like you have always thought, Mr. Joad, but it won't pass muster any longer, no sir, not for a minute more in the world or in this class."

Earle sank back into his seat and hoped she would forget about him, but she did not, and when Earle made his big mistake, she was waiting for him. He had found what he thought was a dynamite topic for his term paper, "How Women Are Biologically Programmed to Have Children," and with his expertise with computers he had quickly learned that the World Wide Web was filled with helpful information for aspiring students on topics like this. For 4.1015384/thirteens ($53.32 in tens, including state tax)—the Happenstance Fellowship included a computer fund—"A-Plus Term Papers of Jersey City dot-com" had made it possible for him to download a paper dealing with the genetic base for sexual identities, which had originally appeared, he later learned to his sorrow, in the *Christian Science Monitor*. A few small adjustments, and he was able to go to the Union and drink beer.

Ida Monorail usually didn't read the papers she received from her class—"Why bother when no grade was given?"—simply writing "some interesting ideas" at the top of every first page. But in moving Earle's paper from her inbox to her outbox, the receipt from "A-Plus Term Papers of Jersey City dot-com" dropped on the floor. Monorail thought of Earle's macho manner, and the fact that he read the newspaper sports section, turning the pages noisily, during class, and the thoughts stoked her latent dislike of this male idiot. She decided to charge Earle with something, and reading through the *College Handbook* she found to her surprise that college regulations absolutely required that any attempt by a student to pass off the writing of another as his/her own, something called "plagiarism," be reported to the dean. The administration either had never gotten around to excising this obsolete material from a handbook given to all new students or thought it so moribund an idea that there had seemed no need to change it. But, now, there it was, lying on the printed page like some old Viking helmet come to the surface in a long-closed barrow:

> We expect academic work presented by students to be the product of their own efforts, and the college will take whatever steps are necessary to preserve the integrity of the academic process. Any student or teacher observing plagiarism or cheating on exams is required, on threat of expulsion, to report such incidents to the dean.

The upshot was that Earle found himself summoned to appear before the Committee on Academic Standards. It seemed all wrong to Earle. To be charged with plagiarism in in the twenty-first century was like being accused of blasphemy or heresy. No one could any longer even define plagiarism. If you could copy anything on the Xerox, build up "hypertext" from the infinite resources of the World Wide Web, and download research papers from "A-Plus Term Papers of Jersey City dot-com" with the flick of a credit card, it was hard for Earle to see why he couldn't make a new hypertext out of material on the net. All the old writers said the same things over and over again, anyway, borrowing from one another all the time in the process, so plagiarism was and always had been the way of the world.

But what could you do? The faculty had it in for the students and would use any club to beat them with. The professors all protested frequently how much they loved students and how fulfilling it was to teach, but there had actually been proposals in faculty meetings that once a year, approximately at the spring equinox, the most unpopular student in the college—Earle was already a front-runner for this role—be turned loose inside the college walls and the faculty be allowed to hunt him down and kill him or her in any way that seemed most enjoyable. This would surely, it was always argued, release built-up tensions and make the end of the term more relaxed; but the wily dean, with an eye toward bad publicity, always declared the motion out of order or managed to table it for further study by a committee yet to be appointed.

Earle looked at his roommate, curled up in his usual fetal position, and, putting on his baseball cap backwards, went out the college gate, making sure to double lock it behind him. There had been a mugging and a nonconsensual sodomy in the quad already this year. He hurried through the gathering dusk, avoiding eye contact with the homeless, who were lounging about hoping to get in long philosophical arguments with the students about fate, free will, foreknowledge absolute, and other such matters. It was nearing a wintry dusk when he passed through the gothic doorway and entered the paneled room where so many solemn undergraduate disciplinary meetings had been held over the years. He took his seat on a leather-cushioned bench and stared out the window at the setting sun.

The Committee on Academic Standards filed in and sat at the table at the head of the room. It was led, in full academic dress, by Ralph Waldo Undone, the Fustian Professor of Anthropological Rhetoric, who had spent years in the field in Tbongo and had long been chair of the Committee on Academic Standards. He was known not only for his four score years and ten—mandatory retirement age, considered a form of discriminatory ageism, had long ago been made illegal by government fiat—but also for having been captured and nearly eaten—he was in the kettle—by some savages whose language he was abominably mispronouncing deep in the mountains of Africa. The experience had so traumatized him that from that day on he spoke only pidgin English. There were problems with his failure to speak the same language as his students, but not many, and there was considerable unease about his increasing tendency to pat the pert rears of attractive young co-eds, but somehow he always managed to beat the rap.

He looked briefly at Earle, who smiled in what he took for an ingratiating manner, and muttered something like "Me masta, bos, ples tambu" (Me boss of this holy place?). Earle was a bit put off by Professor Undone's strange words, but he was relieved to see that the makeup of the committee was proportional to the university's demographic mix. There was a huge black woman, Doctor Alice Dashiki, with tribal markings, dressed in batik robes and carrying a gourd filled with seeds that she rattled whenever she felt she had been affronted, which was often. She was one of the top professors at the university, having won the Pulitzer Prize for *Laboring Together* (Three-Holer Press), "the devastating story of black Siamese twins forced to pick cotton—two rows at once—in the Old South." Her close friend, Ida Monorail, sat next to her, her eyes just barely above the table. As the director of the Office of Social Justice and the chair of the largest department in Ivy University, the Department for the Study of Women, she was famous for erotic feminist books that, as her jacket copy put it, "incite readers to imagine a world in which desire has been dislodged from regulatory regimes." Her bulging eyes stared belligerently through her thin-rimmed gold glasses at Earle, and she tightened her lips even more thinly when he smiled diffidently at her.

There were others, some of the most distinguished members of the faculty: a coming young Irish poet—you have to be Irish these days to be a real poet, and every faculty has to have one—Liam Begorrah, with his shirt unbuttoned to the waist, who laughed a lot and loudly while he chatted with his friend, the philosopher of deconstruction, Pierre de Hors, who had recently stunned the intellectual world with his view that "deconstruction is not a method, not an ideology, not, heaven forbid, an academic discipline, it is—an experience."

De Hors was the most famous member of the committee. He was one of the European intellectuals who had now settled on the American campuses, where he interpreted the world for those who thought less clearly than he did. His stance toward modern, Western, capitalist society was adversarial, while his tolerance for the failings of second- and third-world countries was widely marveled at. He was seldom on campus, and his presence at this committee meeting was unusual enough to cause comment. De Hors was, in fact, there only because an airline strike had grounded him on his way to a conference in New Delhi on "Reparations for Colonized Nations." From there he was off to the Ivory Coast for "Huntsville, Texas, as the American Gulag." Then it was on to London for "The Necessity of Violence in Emerging Countries," to Moscow for "Communism, Democracy, and the Third Way," to Baghdad for "Electronic Democracy"—the only kind Saddam Hussein was willing to hear discussed—and finally to Rome for "The Sacraments On-Line." His research interests included everything from electronic cybernetics to science fiction. His most famous book, *How We Became Post Human: Virtual Bodies in Cybernetics, Literature, and Informatics* (Three-Holer Press), was considered "seminal" as well as "magisterial."

At the far end of the table, avoiding his bourgeois colleagues, was the fiery Mao-Marxist sociologist Ilya Redskievic, whose mots "Long Live Civil War" and "Let a Thousand Ideas Blossom from Rifle Barrels" had made his reputation on the talk shows, where he was known as the professor who could instantly turn a panel into a "struggle session." Marxism had imploded in the Soviet Union long before, but like other failed worldviews, it lived on in the American university, where class warfare was still the key to all social studies.

A deep sense of security filled Earle as his eyes moved around the room and saw there the famous Native American scholar Gemini Starsucker, who was said to be "making astrology a science"; the renowned acupuncturist Manfred I. Ching, from the medical school; and last and least, an unknown assistant professor of ancient history who was there to represent the junior faculty. This was the new American "open university" that replaced the old positivistic, meritocratic research university in the heroic revolutionary struggles of the 1960s and 1970s, in all its glory, all its equality, and all its diversity. *With people like these on the committee,* Earle quietly told himself, *what is to be feared?*

The Fustian Professor gaveled the meeting to order, very loudly because he had difficulty hearing, and looking with vague but still somehow angry eyes at Earle Joad, he shouted excitedly: "U fella mekim wanem meri gel, tuchum bokayis, luckim kan, jig-jig meri wanum, hevim seks longsam. Kokay no kam. Orait? No orait. Gumb bilong kokay." (You want woman, touch her cunt, look at her crotch. You want woman to fuck, have sex, your cock had no penis shield. OKAY? It not OKAY. No wear condom.) Earle had no idea what Undone said, but he gathered from the tone that he was being accused of something rather awful. The administrative secretary of the committee, Hans Untergang, who had necessarily learned a little pidgin, reached around Undone's chair and opened the agenda for the present meeting. "Ah so," said Undone, peering at the Joad file, "Longsam kopi jungle telegraph, boom-boom?" The secretary read the charge of plagiarism in English, and the chair responded gravely: "Yu mekim wanem, yupela savy universiti I stap we?" (What are you up to, don't you know this is a university?) Dashiki rattled her gourd angrily, and Undone, encouraged, pressed on with his denunciation. "Yu no stret, no stret fella. Stilim kago, Xerox, bihainim kago, orait? Yu mekim wanem, yu savy, me masta ples tambu." (You not honest, not honest man. Steal goods, copy goods, okay? What you do? You understand I run sacred place?)

It was up to Ida Monorail to detail Earle's sins, which she now did, *con gusto,* though she had had to read up on plagiarism in the on-line *Encyclopaedia Britannica* to get some sense of what it was all about. She was still not easy with the idea and could only present it in terms of an infringement of regulations: "This degenerate," pointing at Earle, "has broken college rule 3/7, buying his term paper for 'Introduction to Women's Studies, WS101' on-line. It is up to this committee to see that our rules are not flouted by making an example of this wretch Joad."

Doctor Dashiki, thinking of her considerable royalties, rattled her gourd loudly, but from the other side of the table came a roar, "All private property, as Proudhon long ago taught us, is theft, and there is no more reason why anyone should own anything written than they should own the water we drink or the air we breathe."

Smiling contemptuously at Redskievic's intellectual crudity, Pierre de Hors waited for silence and then rose, with a sneering Gallic smile, and reminded his colleagues that they lived in THE AGE OF INDETERMINACY and that "while all 'objective realities' exist under the rule of erasure, none is so ontologically empty as the conception of an actual text, solidly out there, the product of some single mind and the property of someone who spuriously claimed to have written it. How can the culprit Joad, who no doubt is still as miserable as he is charged with being, have plagiarized something that does not exist? All the world's a *texte*. Or, as Heidegger put it so perfectly, 'Language writes, not the author.' So how can Joad be tried for the theft of something that does not exist outside the fantasy realm of words and language?"

Earle listened to these golden words, his mouth agape. He was a quick study, and gone in an instant were his noble dreams of scholarly work in the feminist cause. In their place was a vision of VIRTUAL REALITY. It all came clear as de Hors talked on. "From top to bottom, everything is fake. The *Ding an Sich,* the essence, the layer of truth under the world of fleeting appearances—all are metaphysical illusions. Everyone sees different things from a different point of view. Every word rests on nothing more than another word. To define anything is to enter on an infinite regress." Earle had never been a dummy, his talents simply ran naturally athwart the grain of honesty and common sense, and he saw at once the very practical side of what de Hors described so brilliantly. With a concept like indeterminacy you could unpack the world, mock every ideal, devastate any argument, prove everyone, except yourself, of course, deluded and confused.

Not all the members of the Committee on Academic Standards were as perspicuous as Earle about the opportunities this new AGE OF INDETERMINACY offered, but all were relieved that someone had resolved their uneasy sense that they couldn't define plagiarism and had reassured them that there wasn't anything unusual or wrong about putting your name to something someone else had supposedly written.

At this point, the assistant professor of ancient history managed to take advantage of a moment of heavy silence to get the floor and began to talk with great passion.

"Stealing the words and ideas of another, and trying to pass them off as your own is the Original Sin of the academic and intellectual world. The power of knowledge is built on the authenticity of scholarly works; the surety that what is written and printed is the work of the individual who is named as author on the title page. Not only knowledge, but also civilization itself will wither and die if the writer's ownership of what is written is lost. The sacred principle of real property [here Redskievic snorted] itself is undermined if the right of intellectual property is diminished in any way."

Ida Monorail looked confused, and the other members of the committee whispered busily among themselves trying to identify this upstart, but no one knew him or understood what he had said. Eyes rolled up, and there was an embarrassed silence, until, there being no more discussion, the chair called for a vote, and the charges against Earle were dismissed summarily as being "nonreferential," de Hors's word. He was, however, put on probation for the remainder of the term for breaking college rules. Undone banged his gavel, and muttered, "Me masta, bos, ples tambu," and amid rattles and other small noises the committee fragmented, going its ways to resume the education of the future leaders of the country.

Breathless, Earle cornered Professor de Hors, who, carrying his travel bag and his laptop computer, was racing for the exit and the taxi to the airport.

"How can I major in deconstruction?"

"If you want to know more about decon, open the URL 'anomie dot edu.' Got to run."

After a few moments fruitlessly trying to get his roommate to get off the computer in their room, on which he was playing Academic Goniff, so that he could find out about anomie.edu, Earle thought he might as well go on over to the library and use one of the computers that had been installed where the old card catalog used to be. He opened "www.anomie.edu," and entered a brave new world:

> *The Department of Deconstruction. Deconstruction* is a highly contested term, defined on a broad continuum. Twentieth-century theory recognized the blurring of familiar boundaries and categories that demarcate cultures, disciplines, and discourses. Compartmentalizations of knowledge are inadequate. This understanding has created new paradigms and generated intellectual explorations as well as strategies as fluid as culture(s) and cultural expression. The Department of Deconstruction provides a forum for interrogating the meanings of hybridity and its limitless manifestations. In particular, we address the (de)construction of identities, languages, genres, and voices as well as paradigmatic intermingling and collapse. All course work in this subject is conducted on-line. A list of courses follows:

H101—Introduction to Hybridity: Illusions of the Self
H112—Gender Studies: The Infinity of Sexual Preferences
H113—Postcolonialism and the Tower of Babel
H223—Hybrid Rhetorics and Pedagogy
H281—Mimicry and Ambivalence
H349—Transculturation
H350—Identity Positions
H401—Honors Seminar: Identity Politics

Well, there was going to be a lot to learn here, or unlearn, Earle thought, and he was anxious to get started.

As he was leaving the library, he got turned around and found himself lost inside the stacks. It was warm and dark there, miles of shelves on floor after floor, millions of books, magazines, and manuscripts. They were all there, no one took books out anymore; not many students could read easily, and most of the old books were illegible, pages torn out, marked up with yellow and green hi-liter, underlined, and penciled-in, a legacy from the collapse of the Gutenberg era when students still read, but under protest. Books printed on acid paper were yellow, and the pages disintegrated when the book was opened. Even the computers located here and there for searching the catalog were abandoned. Everyone worked in their rooms now, when they bothered to be in residence at all. Since almost all academic exercises were conducted on-line, you could access your class just as well from Tbongo as from the Ivy campus. In the rare cases where someone needed an article or a book, they found it in some on-line virtual library. It was eerie, when you thought about it, an infinity of books, but no readers.

And then far down one otherwise empty aisle Earle saw a man walking along reading a book. He disappeared into a narrow space between two movable stacks, as if he were about to be squeezed out of existence, squeezed into a book. Earle got closer and saw that it was the professor of ancient history who had been on the discipline committee. He was holding Gibbons's *Decline and Fall of the Roman Empire.* Earle knew that the professor had voted to convict him, but he was a curious and a brash youth, and he wanted to know what made this strange fellow tick.

"Professor, excuse me, but my name is Earle Joad, and I heard someone at the discipline committee say that before Ivy U. abolished grades, you gave some less than average grades, grades like B+ and even B− or C."

"Ah, it's you, Joad, what in God's name are you doing in the library? Yes, it is true that I in my time have given even Ds and the obscene F. In fact, though the grading system is long gone, I still turn in grades for the few students I have in ancient history, even though the registrar no longer records them. It seems only fair to distinguish those who do the work and think about the subject from the lazy, the inept, and, yes, the stupid."

"But how do you get away with it, Professor? Don't the students complain? Professor de Hors has shown that there aren't any facts anymore, only interpretations, one of which is as good as another, so how can you mark an opinion, on a test or a paper, right or wrong?"

"Young man, I am an assistant professor of ancient history, of long standing, and in my field, perhaps because it deals with ancient times, there are lots of facts. The Athenians put Socrates to death for pursuing truth. The Christians died in the Coliseum for their faith. Rome declined and fell in the fifth century A.D. Whether these were good or bad things, or what caused them, these are matters of opinion, not fact, but some opinions accord with the known facts, while some do not, so it is reasonable to say that some views of morals and motives are still superior to others. That Greek and therefore Western civilization began in central Africa is an opinion boldly announced by Professor Lazarus of our African-American department, but it is a very poor opinion, a failing one even, since it accords so little with known facts.

"Expressing these positive views has brought me a great deal of grief and has kept me from advancement for many a year. They are about to cost me my job and my profession. The university press will not publish the book on Greek dialects of Asia Minor on which I have worked for years, my department will not recommend that I be rehired, no other university will touch me, and some of my colleagues have anonymously denounced me to the FBI as a dealer in stolen antiquities. My modest collection of old coins and artifacts, accumulated and fully paid for at great sacrifice over the years, is whispered to have been stolen from countries where I participated in various archaeological digs. Perhaps most painfully, my family and myself are shunned like lepers by other faculty, and the administration has not raised my wretched salary in years. The word 'Fascist' is chalked on my blackboard, and the mail brings death threats from the more zealous of the radicals."

"This is terrible, Professor. I can't condone your bias against Professor Lazarus, of course, and as a soon-to-be major in deconstruction I find your defense of fact somewhat offensive, as well as contrary to common sense. But I had thought that great universities like Ivy believed in intellectual freedom and not only allowed but defended the right of teachers to say whatever they could argue effectively."

"Well, think so still, Joad, until experience changes your mind. Your education has a long way to go, and it is likely that an immersion in the deconstruction major will darken your mind forever, but it is just possible, given your strange curiosity about one professor who still gives grades, that time may open your eyes to the fact that higher education in the humanities and social sciences has become a way of enforcing various political views and cultural bias, not an exploration of reality. What kind of university is it that gives no grades, that allows professors to teach no matter how old and senile they are, that does not believe in fact or truth, that admits its students and promotes its faculty on the basis of race, gender, and 'sexual preference,' that considers any intellectual view as good as another, that considers all statements to be political, and that charges more than the national median income for one year's tuition? Ponder these facts, Joad! Goodbye, and bon voyage."

The assistant professor of ancient history faded into the darkness of the stacks.

Earle was troubled and didn't quite know what to think as he made his way back through the empty library. Still, the future was bright, and he could hardly wait to get started on his deconstruction courses. When he got back to his dormitory his roomie was back on his bed in his customary fetal position and refused to rise to a discussion of whether the Red Sox or the Cubs would win the pennant this year. Since the computer was booted up but not being used, Earle though he might as well go ahead and sign up with the deconstruction department. So he opened anomie.edu, provided the necessary personal information, including his Social Security number, found out that there was room for him, and signed up for the intro course, which was the key to the major.

He had never taken a course entirely on-line before—the lectures, the readings, the papers, the exams—but when he brought up "Deconstruction 101" on the computer the next morning, he found himself plunged right into an anonymous opening lecture, both printed and voiced. "Professor Computer" was the voice he heard.

"Everyone thinks he is a 'self,' some impermeable, well-defined, isolated being, 'That which is within us but could be without us,' as old Sir Thomas Browne described it. But the self comes into being only through random experience and is composed of many hybrid pieces, a little memory here, some ideas there, a name, a job description, the entanglements of a family, and so on. No pattern, a real ragbag when you unpack it."

This was pretty much the gist of the argument as Earle recorded it in the notes he began to keep on the computer. All simple enough, but as Earle began to absorb the point of view of "Deconstruction 101" he found himself increasingly fragmented into a few odds and ends without any center or any coherent sense of the past or the future. He hadn't realized how much he had depended, without ever thinking much about it, without thinking about it at all, in fact, on the illusion of a nuclear self. Its loss proved quite inconvenient for a time. Earle was hard put to sign his name or decide what "he" wanted for lunch. In time, however, he got used to being no one and to thinking of each event in his life as a discrete occurrence or an undifferentiated response. But nothing really changed, life went on much the same without a self as it had with a self, and it was only when he thought about it that Earle realized, with a considerable sense of importance, that he was a self without a self.

Bright college years passed happily and quickly with these views, and as Earle progressed through the deconstruction curriculum he shed more and more of the ancient conceptions of a world filled with pigeonholes, categories, classes, unities, and other such metaphysical concepts. Now everything was barely differentiated from everything else and nothing was but what was not. Sex? A million possibilities flowing without distinction from one object to another. Pain? How could you separate it from pleasure or a million other nervous states? Truth? Nowhere did defining boundaries collapse more easily or more completely.

From the outside Earle looked much the same. He preferred french-fried potatoes to green vegetables, he went to the dentist when his tooth ached, he was desperately in love with Robin Nicely and fondled her large brown nipples with very distinct feelings, and he wrote, once in a while, to Ma Joad in the nursing home, and sent his best to Pa. In short, he acted as if he moved in a world of differences. But his education in one of the most exclusive and expensive universities in the country had taught him to recognize all these seemingly discrete entities, nipples and french fries, as mere illusion in a hybrid world where everything was ultimately like everything else, and like nothing else, a big bowl of mush.

Graduation found the campus afroth with activity and excitement. Honorary degrees were to be given to the arch-minister the Right Reverend C. Beecher Retrofit, the head of Religion USA, Professor Leroy Lazarus of the Ivy faculty, and the great psychiatrist Dr. Toussaint Transférans, manifesting the university's commitment to religion, culture, and science. None of the Joads could make it, though Somerset sent a prayer book and Calista a genuine work of art, which looked like, but couldn't be, a little red wagon filled with plastic dog turds. Earle, dressed in a rented tuxedo, and his new girlfriend, Chancie Ill-will, had too many glasses of champagne at one of the celebratory proms and found themselves in bed together in his dorm room, pledging eternal love and determination to fight to rid the world of poverty, pain, and hatred. Fortunately, Chancie was on the pill, so there was probably nothing to worry about from their slip into unprotected sex, but the Age of Indeterminacy was also the age of AIDS, and they were nervous all the same.

Graduation day itself dawned bright and clear. The bells ringing backwards, a longstanding Ivy tradition, the band blaring out the college anthem, "In Time the Ivy Cracks the Stone," and the black-gowned, mortar-boarded students scurrying past the statue of Benedict Happenstance on the central green. The administrators and the faculty—there was Doctor Dashiki with her gourds, and farther back Ilya Redskievic was defiantly waving a red flag with hammer and sickle—in their bright-colored robes from many universities formed up in a procession led by the official college mace bearer, none other than the Fustian Professor Ralph Waldo Undone, the senior faculty member. From long and painful experience Ivy had learned to let no one speak at commencement, and so except for an opening prayer by the Right Reverend Doctor Retrofit, the ceremony consisted mainly of calling out names and handing out diplomas. There were a few unseemly disturbances when the comptroller and his hirelings physically prevented certain students from going up on the stage because they owed thousands in back tuition, but on the whole it went well, and Earle and his classmates soon found themselves bachelors of art of Ivy University.

Having shone in his college major, Earle went on to graduate school at Manatee Institute of Social Technology, one of the cutting edges of deconstruction studies, with a government-sponsored Title XXXI fellowship, to put a technical finish on his command of hybridization. There he polished theory and modes of analysis that removed him even further from the stubbornly distinctive world of differences. In the Manatee seminars, the very word *difference* was undercut and translated into the French *différance,* which erased difference by putting it in an endless process of "deferral," one concept constantly being defined only by another concept, one word by another.

Earle still functioned, but he was beginning to be a bit weird, and people began to avoid him. Chancie had gone to San Francisco, where she was living in a commune with a group of hippies, and even Ma wrote less and less frequently about how the Joads were the people who would keep the world going. It took Earle a long time, ten years, to write his dissertation on "Political Deconstruction in Israel and Bosnia: A Comparative Study in Consciousness," mostly because he spent so much time teaching undergraduates. The Manatee Department of Deconstruction was as peripatetic as the Ivy faculty, and since they were always at one conference or another, or on leave every other year, the graduate students did most of the undergraduate teaching. Because they were paid so little for their work, most had to hold second jobs, and Earle had fortunately found work at Colonel Kaintuck's Chow Mein and Tamale Ranch, where he wore a big ten-gallon hat, chaps, and cowboy boots with jingling spurs, on which he tripped every now and then while running out of the kitchen to sing "Happy Birthday" to some celebrating customer.

Manatee eventually told him there was a limit to the time he could remain an enrolled graduate student, with medical insurance and subsidized housing, and Earle was forced, along with two times thirteen colleagues in his year, to go on the market and look for a job. It was not a bad year, there were four jobs advertised in the *Journal of Hybrid Studies,* two of them tenure-ladder jobs, and when he went to the annual meeting of his professional association in Milwaukee and hung out at the Cultural Studies cash bar, he heard rumors of other possibilities. It certainly helped that his dissertation had been accepted for "publication" on the Internet by the Deconstruction Association of America, and anyone could download it to disk or print it simply by opening www.textandcontext.edu. It had three "hits" in the first 12/13 months it was on-line, which was about average.

The size of the regular faculties had been shrinking over the years as the professional administrators who increasingly ran the academies found it both cheaper and more convenient to hire part-time teachers on short-term contracts. This had not only capped the faculty budget, it had almost put an end to faculty whining about higher salaries, more benefits, fewer teaching hours, paid leaves, and other privileges, for the adjunct teachers had none of these. There were still a few regular professors, some of them even tenured with named chairs, stars like Professor de Hors, the Derrida Professor of Anomie, but they were few and most often in the sciences and the professional schools. So few, in fact, that administrations no longer bothered to consult professors on policy matters or hold faculty meetings.

Universities and colleges were now big capitalist enterprises, concentrating on the main business of democratic America, the bottom line. Teachers could be hired and fired at will, subjects added or dropped according to enrollment figures, the curriculum designed to meet the trends of the marketplace, tuition raised to any level the traffic would bear. In other words, efficient at last, and the growth of Manatee's endowment, fifty billion dollars, and change, and without counting the value of the art collection in the Sunshine Museum, demonstrated just what realistic, hard-headed, know-how business management could make of what once had been Ivory Towers.

Departments of Deconstruction were everywhere now, and there was one at old Lone Tree, the community college where Ma Joad had gone but which was now a big state school, Lone Tree State University. Lone Tree State was one of the few schools that advertised a deconstruction job that year, part-time and totally off the tenure ladder, but still a job, and it offered Earle the position.

Dear Dr. Earle Joad:

I am pleased to inform you that the administration of Lone Tree State University, on the advice of the Department of Deconstruction, is willing to offer you a one-year contract, renewable, though not guaranteed, for five years, as a part-time lecturer, to teach two sections each trimester, one to be the introductory deconstruction course, and one in business writing, enrollment not to exceed 60 students in the latter. After the introductory meetings the deconstruction course will be taught on-line, in the usual manner, but the business writing course requires your presence in the classroom at stated hours. Payment will be a generous $2,000 for each course, which means you can make a maximum of $12,000 a year, which is, unfortunately, but necessarily, below the level at which any benefits such as medical insurance and parking rights begin.

I enclose a copy of the *Faculty Handbook,* which will tell you of your rights and responsibilities, and a form to apply for a mainframe computer hook-up at a nominal fee of $600 per year. You may also apply to rent a University Gardens apartment at the rate of $15,000 per annum. As a part-time lecturer you will not be eligible to join the union that the university runs for its employees.

Will you be so kind as to let me know within the week whether you will accept this offer? We hope, of course, that you will, but we have a long list of highly qualified applicants for this prestigious and rewarding post, so don't delay.

Yours sincerely,
Barbara Heavy Thinker
Dean of Personnel Resources

Earle was overjoyed at this vote of confidence in his scholarly potential and teaching abilities. He regretted that he would not be able to afford one of the faculty apartments, since the rent was higher than his salary, and that he could not join the union. But twelve thousand dollars a year, even after deducting federal, state, county, and city income taxes, plus Social Security, would be more than he had seen for years. By scrimping and saving here and there he was certain he could make ends meet and at long last launch his scholarly career at the comparatively young age of thirty-three.

The world was all before him, bliss was it in that time to be alive. The dropping leaves of fall found him at Lone Tree State, making his way through the many construction sites that filled the campus with the sound of the jackhammer, the wood chipper, the pile driver, and the back-up beeper of numerous bulldozers and front loaders. Through the noise and dust he found his way to his temporary trailer classroom filled with bright faces and minds thirsting for knowledge.

"Welcome to Decon I. You probably think that it is possible to discriminate between objects, between men and women, for example [professorial chuckle], but before the term is over I can assure you that you will be educated men and women who will have abandoned such quaint old-fashioned ideas, and no longer know right from wrong, or up from down." The students bent earnestly over their desks and typed Earle's words into their laptops.

But his job didn't last for long. Enrollments plunged in deconstruction the next year and Lone Tree State cut back on its offerings in this field. Earle was part of the "downsize," but he applied for and got a job as a temporary acting assistant dean in the office of the undergraduate college when the former acting assistant dean left town a few days after the beginning of fall classes. With the job went a desk and computer in a small office in the basement of the administration building, where Earle was expected to hear appeals and make placement decisions about new students who had been admitted with low math and writing scores to Lone Tree State because of the university's enlightened policy of open admissions. It was Earle's job to decide whether these students should be placed in the standard introductory courses or in remedial courses. Full tuition was charged for the remedial courses, but they carried no credits toward graduation and were for this and other reasons distinctly unpopular.

Most of the business of the office was conducted by e-mail, and it was by this means that Earle first heard of Ralph Dungan, senior and junior.

Dear Dean Joad,

You will soon be visited by Ralph Dungan, Student Identification Number 6543–21–012, one of my freshperson orientation advisees, who has been admitted to the Lone Tree Class of 2025. His parents will accompany Dungan. Ralph scored @ Level 0 in English, Level 0 in Math, and 82 on the Crockett-Alamo Test, and was therefore placed in remedial courses—Math 00101 and English 00101. He is appealing these placements.

Dungan's father is a graduate of Lone Tree College, though not a contributor to the Alumni Fund, and at my meeting with Ralph, both Mr. and Mrs. Dungan expressed strong dissatisfaction with admissions/testing/developmental course policies @ Lone Tree. Mr. Dungan said that as an alumnus and a taxpayer, he will be contacting his state representative and an attorney to protest that we did not provide young Dungan with the options needed to bypass remedial-level course work. Dungan Senior is a spirited man and is, I think it fair to say, quite agitated about having paid tuition for courses that will carry no credit toward the degree.

Please let me know if I can be of any further help in this matter.

Yours sincerely,
Judith Holofernes
Dean of Counseling and University
Harassment Officer

Dear Dean Holofernes:

You have very thoughtfully expressed many of the things I would agree with about placement issues referred to by your recent e-mail. I appreciate having information of this kind, and I appreciate your taking the time to prepare the detailed message sharing the information about the student and his parents and their complaint.

I also appreciate the care with which advisers like you can clarify for students and parents the proper ways to challenge a W099 placement. They are expected, as you know, to study more and then retake the math and reading tests, or to present sample papers showing improvement, before petitioning the Dean of Remedial Placement. W099 appeals, I don't need to tell you, are a very positive process for the student, since the student has the experience of discussing three or four samples of his or her past work with his/her adviser in detail in light of the various challenges of college writing that are ahead.

Yours with the wish for a quiet and productive weekend,
Earle Joad
Temporary Acting Assistant Dean of Remedial Placement
cc: Director of Training and Development, Freshperson Year

Dear Dean Joad:

Recently a Mr. Michael Dungan visited my office, without appointment, to complain about the placement of his son, Ralph Jr., 6543–21–012 SID, a member of the new class at Lone Tree, in remedial classes on the basis of his test scores. "A principle is at stake," the father said, very angrily, "I have paid $27,500 for non-credit-bearing courses, and my son lost $2,500 in summer wages when he could not work because he was meeting M023 & W069 requirements during SSII."

I tried to explain to Mr. Dungan that placement in remedial courses was not in the province of my office, but rather of yours. This seemed to enrage him, and shouting incoherently something about "run-around," he tried to shake me by the throat, and would have too except for the intervention of my faithful secretary, Muriel Allaround.

While I'm not sure what level the Dungan concerns will ultimately reach, I deemed them significant enough to make you aware, since you are the first court of appeal on remedial placement, and the College expects you to perform these duties. If you have any questions, let me know.

Hope you have a safe, relaxing holiday weekend, and that your hernia operation goes well!

Kenneth Afterthought
Director of Training and Development,
Freshperson Year

Dear Professor Xuare Root Tew:

I write to you as the head of the math department to tell you that I have recommended to a concerned parent, Mr. Michael Dungan, an old Lone Tree man, much concerned with educational issues, that he consult you about his son's placement in a remedial math course 00101 and about the great advantages of W099. As a noted mathematician yourself you will have no difficulty in explaining to Mr. Dungan why it is better for young Ralph to take remedial non-credit math during his first year of study.

Let me know if I can be of any assistance.

Earle Joad
Temporary Acting Assistant Dean of
Remedial Placement
cc: Ichabod Waffle, Dean of Lone Tree State
College

Dear Dean Waffle:

It has never been a good feeling for me, over the years, watching so many incoming students be enrolled in developmental math classes. My colleagues and I wish all students start at least at introductory college math classes, succeed, advance in their disciplines, and graduate in a timely fashion. But what can we do when some students are not ready and do not have sufficient math background? They must be put into W099 remedial courses by the responsible people in administration who have been appointed to handle these matters, like the estimable Dean Joad, who sent a most difficult parent to see me about this important matter.

With thanks and heartfelt appreciation to all involved.

Xuare Root Tew
Dingle Professor of Theoretical Mathematics
bcc: Director of Training and Development, Freshperson Year
Dean of Counseling and University Harassment Officer
Dean of Personnel Resources

Dear Dean Joad:

Professor Tew in his recent good letter has made me aware of your efforts on the part of young Ralph Dungan, SID 6543–21–012. The skill with which you have taken to university administration has been noted by everyone, and I want you to know that this office is fully aware of what you are doing.

The master Enrollment Management Plan tells me, however, that should Ralph Dungan drop out because he is not allowed to take pre-calculus and quantum physics, the loss of his tuition would negatively affect our enrollment/income figures. By this e-mail I am asking my Associate Dean, Arthur Blowbye, to call a policy committee meeting, including you of course, to consider this important matter.

With the hope that you are finding your Lone Tree administration experience enjoyable, and that your health is improving under our generous medical plan, I am, faithfully yours,

Ichabod Waffle
Dean of Lone Tree State College
cc: Arthur Blowbye, Associate Dean for Bottom-Line Affairs

Dear Dean Waffle:

A reassessment of Ralph Dungan's test scores by the policy committee has made it clear that young Dungan, SID 6543–21–012, has progressed remarkably in math and English over the last few months. It now appears that while he is not quite fully ready for admission to the regular college courses in these fields, he is sufficiently advanced to be granted credit toward his degree for his remedial courses. I have so advised the concerned departments. I have also asked Dean Joad to send Dungan, copy to his father, the needed forms M086 & W069, which will allow him to claim credit for these courses.

Sincerely yours,
Arthur Blowbye
Associate Dean for Bottom-Line Affairs

Dear Dean Waffle:

I write to protest the recent decision by Dean Blowby to allow Ralph Dungan, SID 6543–21–012, to be granted credit for the remedial course he is taking, English 00101. This course is designed for students who read at or below the ninth-grade level, and it is most difficult to see how any work they do at this level, like reading some advanced comic books, can count toward a university degree. I remain completely unconvinced by Dean Joad's argument that these courses should be thought of as "the subbasement of the house of intellect," and therefore an honorable part of the entire academic structure.

If the committee decision stands, I do not feel that I can responsibly teach 00101 English any longer, and the department will have to find a substitute at this late date. Why not try Joad?

Sincerely yours,
D. Philoon Harding
Lecturer in English

Dear Philoon:

So good of you to let me have your opinions about a question which so vitally affects our policy of open enrollments and its corollary, the right to take credit-bearing courses. Free and open discussion remains the lifeblood of the academic enterprise. Our Enrollment Management Plan, as I am sure you are aware, is case sensitive to these issues, a matter that always comes up when we have to consider the reappointment of lecturers with term appointments for the coming year. Earle Joad seems to understand these matters intuitively, and having the greatest confidence in his judgment, I suggest that you discuss your concerns with him at your and his convenience.

Sincerely yours,
Ichabod Waffle
Dean of Lone Tree State College

Three

Religion USA

Among the weary walking life's road, one day came a much-troubled Somerset Joad. He had always been a sensitive and impressionable youth, diagnosed at school as having dyslexia, and in his last years at home he had retreated into watching television nearly all day and well into the night. As he watched he began to notice more and more teeth. Teeth had frightened him since childhood, and on TV everyone had big white teeth, and when they smiled, which was all the time, their mouths opened so far back on their cheeks that you could see nothing but sharp, bright teeth. As Somerset looked, longer and longer, the pictures on the screen blurred and the components fell apart like an old photograph that had been torn in pieces. The individual bits were still there, but they were somehow empty of meaning, almost did not exist, certainly did not cohere. Only one thing was real, the teeth, and they, perfect, white, and plenteous, were supersaturated with meaning, had achieved what Mad Ave. reaching for the absolute called "icon status." For Somerset, the teeth lived with the intensity of the waving wheat and the shining sun in the paintings of Van Gogh, but though the actors on TV spoke of love, and kindness, and the necessity of using deodorant if you wanted a good life, their teeth, long and sharp, glistening white, filled him with dread.

At first the dread was pointless, just dread, but as it intensified Somerset began to fear that the teeth would tear and rend his own feeble parts. He kept this diabolic epiphany to himself, hoping that it would go away, but in time it spread from television to life around him, and whenever he looked at a teacher, or a doctor, his mother or father, his girlfriend and his skateboard gang, he saw only teeth that wanted to bite and devour him. He moved among the tattered scenes of awareness without bumping into anything, but the only real reality was the teeth. At night with the covers over his head he dreamed of teeth as big as skyscrapers and as bright as the sun, snapping violently at anything that tried to sneak by them or through them.

In fear he retreated more and more into himself, and his nightmares began to disturb the household. Doctor Malpractice, the HMO physician, could make nothing of it, and suggested that Somerset go see a young psychiatrist who had been given an honorary degree only recently at Lone Tree State University and had had much success with bizarre cases. Doctor Toussaint Transférans had been educated in Haiti and done his early medical work among the schizophrenics of the New World Bedlam Hospital in Jamaica, where after a time he had begun to believe that the patients were the only sane people in the place. His colleagues found this idea less than amusing and drove Transférans out of the Caribbean Psychiatric Association. Without a valid license, he bounced like a pinball from post to post in the States, with bells ringing and whistles blowing, to end at last in the lower Southwest, the tilt corner of America, where many of the country's more interesting neuroses had reached epidemic status.

There he began to mix Dr. Freud with Doctor Samedi, blending cognitive Freudianism with a little voodoo. He found that voodoo explained the very odd actions of some of Freud's patients, like Rat Man, who otherwise made no sense. *Where did those rats come from?* Or, *Why, Oedipal-wise,* he often asked himself, *would a son ever want to kill his father and marry his mother?* Freud offered him no final answers, but voodoo did. *Someone hit Oedipus with the evil eye and gave him a love potion.* With his views of psychic motivation firmly based, Transférans's practice turned out to be a very superior mousetrap; sex and magic were a potent mix in Southern California. A pathway was soon beaten to his door, up which someone walked one day and left on his front porch a turkey carcass gnawed bare. Somerset found it a little later coming to visit the doctor. With his teeth obsession the bare bones surprised him not at all, and he picked them up and handed them to Transférans, who blanched and was obviously distraught, yet still smiled his huge smile.

In spite of the doctor's piano keyboard of teeth, Somerset found it easy to talk to him, and his difficulties came tumbling out, as confused as he was: "The world doesn't make sense anymore. Only teeth are real. People all seem to want to bite everything, to bite the flesh from the bone. Like that carcass on your step."

"Please, not to mention that dreadful thing. I have enemies, bad enemies."

"People are not normal, like most people think, they are cannibals, and even when they smile at you they are getting ready to eat you. It's all so obvious, if you stare hard enough. Look at TV, a cave of teeth, where people snap at one another and tear each other apart all day and all night. All those teeth grinning at you, why they're just trying to get at you and force you to buy something from them, or to obey them and admire them. Politicians' teeth are maybe the worst, the mouths smile brightly, like Banker Brightgrin's, who is running for the U.S. Senate, and they seem to care for you so much, and they promise they will solve all your problems, but they only really want to eat up your vote, and your money, and swallow you alive. It's like that in the rest of the world, too. Even the girls who seem so nice really just want, as they say, 'to eat you up.' The motorcycle gangs roar up and down the freeway to kill one another, the schoolteachers don't want to teach you anything, they just want to dominate you; and every get-together is a free-for-all in which everyone tries to beat up on everyone else. The whites hate the blacks and the Protestants hate the Jews and the Latinos hate the Anglos."

"Somerset," the good doctor replied, "you have found your way through an abnormal fear to what Doctor Samedi used to tell us in Haiti: 'Man is a killer, watch out for him as you do for the snake in the grass.'" Having set the scene with this voodoo wisdom, Transférans applied a simple Freudian maneuver to Somerset:

"Why, mon, these teeth are not really teeth, they are symbols, disguised representations of what is really troubling you. Let us explore your unconscious mind, mon, opening it up like a conch with a hammer, and at the center we will find what the teeth really mean. And once we have found the truth at the center of the conch, then you will feel better and be able to go out into the world fit and strong again. When you look at people you see only teeth. Serious, yes, but I can *help* you. What are these teeth?"

"Teeth?"

"Now listen carefully, Somerset. As they grow up people pass through several stages, the anal, the oral, and finally the genital." He pronounced English with a syncopated steel-band beat, so what he said, to Somerset's ear, sounded something like,

> Never suppressss the instinct-u-al,
> Anal, Oral, and Geen-ee-tal.

"Now to get hung up on the anal or the oral is bad business, mon, since we need all of us to wurrk our way through to the geeneetal. Now these teeth of yours are clearly a sign that you are arrested in the oral stage, someone or something put a spell on you. You want to eat a lot, you want to suck on things, you love words and want to talk, all primary indications of an arrested orality."

"No, no, Dr. Transférans, I never eat much, and they taught me at school never to talk to strangers, I've told you more than I have ever told anyone else."

"Now, now, lad, these little secrets come tumbling out no matter how much you want to hide them. There is a trifle of abreaction, perhaps even a dislocated ontology here, the teeth are probably overdetermined, probably your father's teeth, too, threatening to eat you, like Doctor Samedi ate all his offspring to keep them from revealing his secrets. Perhaps you even dream of running with a primal horde and giving a primal scream while you chase down and kill the old man who is blocking your way to your mother. You threaten your father, probably you once saw the primal scene and he got very angry when you began to cry and interrupted his pleasure. No doubt his anger is what mired you in the oral condition."

"No, no, Pa's not like that at all, he's real easygoing. And Ma's real churchy about everything, specially sex. You don't seem to understand, Doctor. This doesn't have anything to do with sex, this is really serious. I'm losing my mind, of all the things in the world, only teeth have any *Dasein* [a word Somerset had picked up on PBS], and they scare the hell out of me."

"Well [jovially], we got to the bottom of that in no time at all, your symbols are so classic they can be read right out of Freud's good book. You are no longer sick but healthy, so get out of here, go back to Have It All Valley, move on to the geen-e-tal, screw all the girls, forget the teeth, and live the good life that America makes possible. You are too tense, perhaps you need to relax a bit. Prozac will soon take care of that. Here is a prescription. Don't forget to give your health insurance card to the nurse on the way out."

In spite of the wonders of modern psychiatry, Somerset remained terrified, seeing not people but teeth everywhere. And when the Joads lost their house in Have It All Valley, and the family broke up, he struck out on his own, hitchhiking from town to town, begging, living under bridges, and going to jail for short periods of time when the cops rounded up the homeless. In one lockup where he spent a longer-than-usual sentence, he even took a few extension courses taught by teachers from the local community college. Somerset liked particularly a satire course given by Professor Kernan, who, it was said, had once taught in the Ivy League before trying, without success, to exchange grades for sex and taking to drinking Holland gin. The old Greek Aristophanes, the Romans Horace and Juvenal, Ben Jonson, Molière, Alexander Pope, Voltaire, Gogol, Evelyn Waugh, and our own American Nathanael West. Best of all, Somerset thought, was the old Englishman, Jonathan Swift—"all the world is knaves and fools." He particularly liked Swift's dying words, something like, "They had better have left it alone." That man really had seen the teeth, though he didn't look his horses in the mouth. Satire eased Somerset's mind a bit by making him aware that he was not alone in his perception that things were dangerous and badly wrong, but he still saw the teeth.

He got to know the chaplain in the jail well enough to tell him about the teeth, and the chaplain told him that he thought that he had been possessed by the devil. He ought to go, Father Rugby Portface said, to Religion USA, an extraordinary religious community quite near his old home in Have It All Valley. The central cathedral was ecumenical, and the biggest religious mall in the world surrounded it, filled not only with stores but also with chapels of a vast number of the many religions of the world, where various relics and services were on sale. One of the chapels, Portface went on, was run by Father Sean O'Banshee,

S.J., who had been seconded to Religion USA from the Vatican to cast out the evil spirits who flew about Southern California as thick as Mediterranean fruit flies.

And so, one day in Chicago when the temperature was below zero and every icicle was a saber tooth, Somerset decided to see whether religion could help where psychology, satire, and wandering had failed. After some time in a frigid boxcar, he came at last to Religion USA and the soaring gothic cathedral that had been started years earlier by an old hermit possessed by a great vision. Rising out of the desert, the work, by now of many hands, was cruciform, with ambulatories, spires, gargoyles, and flying buttresses built entirely of empty beer cans, old tires, odds and ends from the local dump, old school-bus bodies, and worn-out military aircraft and armored vehicles that had been abandoned at a nearby storage lot. In time a generous bequest from the eccentric billionaire Benedict Happenstance covered the original materials with pure white plaster, although the details always retained traces of their original shape. A soaring groin would remind you of a B-29 on its way to firebomb Japan, while the baptismal font still somehow seemed something like a Sears and Roebuck washing machine.

A stained-glass rose window behind the altar was the pride of the cathedral, and people came from all over the world to look at it, amazed that it could have been wrought by human hand. There was, in fact, a mystery about the window, for when the cathedral was being built, a bearded stranger came one day out of the desert and offered to make a wondrous stained-glass window in return for the right to be buried in front of the altar when he died. His art was based entirely on old bottles, which he gathered in area dumps. Sometimes he used the actual glass, at other times he reproduced the colors of the liquids left in the old bottles. Embedded in cement, which he applied by the dripping handfuls, the beautifully colored glass—flaming reds, yellows, deep blues, bright greens—ran wild inside the circle of the enormous window. In one corner the Gadarene Swine in Budweiser brown rooted around for acorns on the forest floor, and look, over there, Lot and his wife fled from the burning ruins of Sodom and Gomorrah in tail-light reflector red. Christ reading to the Pharisees in the temple was warm in Pepto-Bismol pink. Eden Garden, green as the bottles of Heineken beer of which it was made, was at the center. Noah's ark bobbed merrily on waves of Phillips' Milk of Magnesia blue, and all humanity formed a long line up to the seat of God on Judgment Day against a sky of Italian wine-bottle azure. The artist was a wizard, and colors as red as the residues of tomato ketchup and as black as Smith Bros. cough drops, gave fear to Hell, whose flames swirled fiercely just inside the periphery of the great circle, as if they could barely be contained.

One wild and stormy night, lightning flashed along the heavens, one great cloud banged thunderously on the next, and when the morning came the window was finished, and below it lay a huge basalt gravestone carrying the strange words "Hic et Ubique."

The great flagship cathedral was finished and expanded, and the biggest religious mall and factory outlet in the world grew up around it. In one of the satellite chapels, Father O'Banshee exorcised devils with Latin spells, crucifixes, keening, and buckets of cold holy water. The elfin O'Banshee was rumored to have himself once entered into a pact with the devil, an exchange of his soul for all the women he desired, and he looked the part, small, twisted, leering, as red of nose as of biretta. Surfeited with sex, he had broken his contract with the devil, it was said, by the simple act of cutting Old Nick dead on a street in the Vatican one day and refusing thereafter to have any intercourse with him. Satan complained to the Holy Father and to the cardinals of the consistory about the sacredness of contract, but the pope issued a bull, *Obscurus obscurorum* (Explain the dark with the darker), declaring that since all dealings with the infernal regions were unlawful and a sin against the Holy Ghost, benefits from said dealings could safely accrue only to Holy Mother the Church.

O'Banshee immediately became a Vatican personage and, dressed in the cowl and gown of a Dominican monk, was put in charge of the Office of Infernal Authority, where with one assistant and a worn-out mimeograph machine that smudged all his handouts, he identified for the world the forms in which "auld reekie" appeared, and offered for a small fee to provide certain surefire spells for dealing with him out of hand. The discovery of a numbered Swiss bank account into which these fees had flowed brought him eventually under a dark cloud in the Vatican hierarchy, which then seconded him to the Chapel Perilous of the Possessed in the mall of Religion USA, where he developed a passion for the American junk food sold in the nearby Taco Bell, Colonel Kaintuck's, and Burger King.

As he searched for what the directory listed as "Exorcism Center, All Major Credit Cards Accepted," Somerset Joad saw Dr. Toussaint Transférans giving a Visa card to a clerk in the "Baron Samedi Voodoo Franchise Chain, Gifts and Curios, *Ici en parle français.*" Transférans didn't see him, however, and Somerset hastened on without a greeting.

For once his listener was not surprised. O'Banshee had heard it all, so to speak, and knew just what to do. He immediately doused Somerset with icy holy water, made the sign of the cross over him thirteen times, and gave him a purge that soon had him vomiting large amounts of some bright Day-Glo-green goo. The goo may well have been the devil in one of his many forms, but when Somerset looked at the priest he still saw only teeth, and O'Banshee lost all interest in Somerset when a large tour group of men and women who had all been kidnapped in flying saucers and penetrated in the most remarkable ways by aliens from outer space came into the chapel. In the face of this technological challenge to the science of Holy Mother the Church, Somerset became only a tiresome and penurious youth without a major, or even a minor, credit card who stubbornly persisted in seeing nothing but teeth.

Somerset wandered through the mall fascinated with the strange sights and busy crowds that thronged the many passageways of THE BIGGEST MALL IN THE WORLD. Not only a vast number of chapels but a large number of stores dedicated to the sale of worldly goods—very upscale, Gucci, Neiman Marcus, Tiffany, Brooks Brothers, BMW—had grown up around the cathedral. The shops and outlets had been a godsend, for their rent made the nut for the entire operation and at the same time enabled those who wished, and, yea, they were many, to spend some of their long-term capital gains and pick up some indulgence coupons with a bit of worship.

Among these sanctified outlets, the number of "chapels" became so extensive that they constituted a Religionland dedicated to the worship of the Almighty. Those who fancied fundamentalism could find a chapel with a fiery preacher threatening hellfire and railing against abortion, dancing, tobacco, purple Teletubby dolls, Harry Potter, alcohol, and extramarital sex. This was a troublesome group, these born-again, fundamentalist Xtians, for they were not always content with running a satellite sideshow in the Mall of the World's Religions. From time to time they were likely when filled with the spirit to pour out into the corridors and run down the mall, armed with their second-amendment assault weapons, to smite the Philistines hip and thigh. Religion USA had a militant arm, a SWAT team run by a former chief of the LAPD, who had himself been born again during a police scandal, Deacon Fredson Ananias, to suppress these and other overly sanctified folks. And though it took some broken heads and threats of charges of heresy, the fundamentalists were always stuffed back into their chapels.

Hedonism ran too strong in Southern California for ecstatic zeal to appeal to most people—but between shopping for new shoes or going to the movies, they would happily stop in and watch some of the Lord's elect handling serpents or speaking in tongues. If they wanted something more established, across the mall jolly Episcopalians like Father Rugby Portface, who had followed the advice about going west that he gave to Somerset in the Manatee hoosegow, wearing the full regalia his church so loved, his red cassock, his purple vest, his black gaiters, his broad-brimmed black hat, and his big gold pectoral cross, for a small fee consecrated, amid clouds of incense, women, homoerotics, and others as ministers.

At the far edges of the mall, chickens and lambs, even goats, were sometimes sacrificed in dark, forbidden rites, but the screams of the dying animals and the smell of blood disturbed the rest of the mall so much that the management team was trying to get the voodoo priests and the animists out of the place. Hindu, Muslim, Catholic, Protestant, Confucians, and Buddhists—here was God's plenty from which all could take their choice. Only one sect held out. There was no synagogue, not even Reformed, to the great disappointment of the Right Reverend C. Beecher Retrofit, the shepherd of the cathedral, who longed for an ark of the covenant and a silver Torah scroll, the solemnities of the numerous high holy days, the sorrow-laden chant of the kaddish echoing down the mall; but the Jews remained stiff-necked as ever in the face of all the prime locations he offered them for the lowest of rents.

The control center of God's Bazaar, as it was sometimes called, was the Cathedral of Light, the flagship church of Religion USA, presided over by the Right Reverend Retrofit, who had been called from an African mission some years ago to become the exegete of Religion USA. Whatever might go on out in the reaches of the mall, tomato juice had long ago replaced the blood of the Lamb at cathedral communion, and Religion USA was one-hundred-and-ten percent progressive in its rituals and in its theology. The mall provided rusty spikes and bloody whips if you liked that sort of thing, but in the cathedral itself the goodness of mankind, and of womankind, too, it went without saying, was stressed. Not for Religion USA the old Calvinist doctrines that considered the heart of man so corrupt that out of it no good could proceed. "Original Goodness," not "Original Sin," were the words over the cathedral pulpit, and "Original Goodness" was the message broadcast daily to the world from the cathedral on the Religion USA radio and TV programs.

On occasion the young and comely women, golden groined and high breasted, of the Religion USA modern dance troupe danced naked in all their God-given beauty in the chancel. There had been a big surge in membership when true Christian love, as in "God is Love," was retrofitted as sexual love. Who could possibly imagine, the "Doctrine of Love" from Religion USA explained, that Jesus was referring to what people felt for the sick and the poor, or for members of their own families, when he spoke of the overwhelming power of love to bind the world together? But realize that sexual love was being referred to and Jesus' word was clear in an instant to those who earlier had had difficulty with his doctrine. Most of the Religion USA flock took to this idea like ducks to water, and from that time on the cathedral services were as full as its coffers.

In addition to spreading the gospel of love and reassurance, the cathedral provided lots of spin-off services to its parishioners. Their pets—slavering Great Danes and sinuous anacondas, spirited Arabian stallions and bleating llamas—were blessed in the aisles and at the altar on Saint Francis's Day. (The ecclesiastical calendar was ecumenical.) At the beginning of the boating season, all the parishioners who went down to the sea in ships went down to Long Beach, where, as of old, the priests prayed for the power squadron, the sailboats, the PWVs (personal water vehicles), the sailboards, and all other vessels in peril on the sea. A priest, and often a high priestess, for Religion USA was an equal opportunity employer in all ways, would sanctify in holy matrimony union between any living things. If a woman wanted to be married to the Pekinese who was dearer to her than any man or woman in the world, what harm was there in giving her a little joy in her latter days?

But people kept coming up with the damnedest ideas. If two people can be married, why not three? Or four? Or any number? There had once even been a scandalous attempt to marry the animate with the inanimate—one of the church's six-figure benefactors, old Benedict Happenstance, the cheese king, had wanted to be married to his Rolls-Royce. Religion USA wanted to oblige, but there were objectors, and the question was tabled for a time while the Institute of Advanced Theology, a tax-exempt, freestanding entity attached to the cathedral, argued over what the staff casuists decided was a variety of the ancient quarrel between Unitarians and Trinitarians. The Unitarian theologians with their Monophysite inclinations argued that only living creatures could be married to one another, but the Trinitarians, with their environmentalist-green and multicultural allies, interpreted the doctrine of three persons in one god to mean that all things, sticks and stones as well as animals, are holy, and can therefore be married.

The Trinitarians got a government grant to run a computerized frequency check of inanimate objects in Holy Scripture and found that there were many thousands of references to inanimate objects, such as "tents" and "rocks," which proved, they said, the holiness of inanimate as well as animate things. The Unitarians, however, resisted this kind of proof, arguing that statistical reasoning was not of the spirit but of the flesh, and therefore its conclusions were unacceptable. No hurry, a resolution was not crucial, and while the debate dragged on, the church kept uniting in holy matrimony any two or three things that appeared together in the nave.

In the quiet of the evening, as the angelus rang from the baptistry made out of an obsolescent Titan ICBM, Somerset looked up at the famous rose east window, hoping to find release at last from the multitude of teeth that beset him sorely. But as he looked, he began to realize that the artist had played a monstrous joke on the simple, trusting folk who built the church. He must have been not only an atheist but a cynic, with limitless contempt for religion and all other human institutions. His scenes did not come from Genesis and Revelation or from anywhere in the Holy Bible, as was thought, but were clever substitutions from the world's great satires. Noah's ark was really Lemuel Gulliver sailing to the land of the Houyhnhnms, you could see them trotting along on the horizon. Adam and Eve in Eden Garden were really Candide and Cunegonde working "to make their garden grow" in retreat from "the best of all possible worlds." He recognized the old woman with the missing buttock, eaten at the siege of Azov, working among the vines. The Gadarene Swine were actually the pigs of George Orwell's *Animal Farm,* Snowball and Napoleon, proclaiming that while all animals are equal some are more equal than others. The people fleeing the cities of the plain, Sodom and Gomorrah, were in fact the mob of people "who came to California to die" in Nathanael West's *Day of the Locust* and, tired of orange juice and sunshine, were burning Los Angeles for kicks.

And so it went. The artist had constructed brilliant images, not of Christ teaching in the temple, but of Waugh's Tony Last reading Dickens's novels about the goodness of the human heart to Mr. Todd, who held him prisoner in the depths of the Amazonian jungle. What resembled the Last Judgment when viewed quickly proved on closer examination to be Pope's dunces—"busy, bold, laborious, pert, and blind"—marching through London on the lord mayor's day in a vast throng toward the universal darkness that covers all. The Last Supper was Trimalchio's Roman banquet-orgy in *The Satyricon* of Petronius Arbiter. And all this was made the more eerie for being rendered in a style that was a strangely eclectic mixture of Goya with Thurber.

Never looking too scrupulously at the window, the elders of the church had remained blissfully unaware of the colossal hoax that the artist had pulled on them before disappearing into his grave. The circle of many-colored glass that stained the white radiance in their cathedral was, verily, a black hair combed out of the tail of the Antichrist, verily, the cloven hoof of the Beast. Since few Americans, nourished on television, had read either the Bible or any literary satire, had indeed read little of anything, the pilgrims had never tumbled to what was going on above them as they prayed.

Somerset was horrified and tried to make the hoax known to the militant arm of Religion USA, the goodly archdeacon Fredson Ananias, who was checking to see that no homeless people were sleeping in the pews. But he only looked suspiciously at Somerset, and said, "Get thee behind me, Satan, for thou art an offense unto me," thus ending the matter.

Yet Somerset's revelation of the presence of evil in even the most sacred ground seemed to seep through the church. Original Goodness appealed less and less, and there were Manichean mutterings among the faithful about evil having a real presence and power in the world. It all came to a head one Sunday morning when the high priestess, Ginger Clitterhouse, dressed in her most alluring velvet gown, orange with black stripes, slit revealingly up the side to her pert bottom, and with a daring little scarlet "A" below the starched white clerical collar, was expounding the Song of Songs, dwelling on the sweetness of breath like apples, breasts like goblets, and necks like towers of ivory.

Somerset Joad, now a minor acolyte, was slumped in a pew, trying not to see the immense number of teeth that filled the church to bursting. Instead of being comforted by all this talk of flagons and apples, he began to get more and more agitated. Perhaps it was too hot, perhaps the teeth became too menacing, but he thought that he recognized the man with deep-sunken eyes and tangled hair sitting next to him and slowly getting to his feet. It had to be, it was, Jim Casy, the old hellfire preacher who came west with the original Joads and was supposedly killed by strikebreakers. He had turned up once in

Have It All Valley, where he talked sadly about the old days when he had lain with girls he'd earlier filled with Holy Spirit, but now he complained, "the sperit ain't in me no more." His sulfurous religion was too much for the modern Joads, and after baptizing a few sinners in the Jacuzzi, he went off and, they heard, built a little church way out in the desert, beyond the Rattlesnake Mountains, near Scorpion Springs, where he prayed for the souls of all humanity. The Joads thought maybe he had died, though his chapel had become famous—but here he was in Cathedral USA speaking in a loud, prophetic voice.

"What about sin, all you mealy-mouthed suckers? What about the pain and suffering that you visit upon your fellow man? What about the poverty and sorrow that walk the streets and sleep on your sidewalks until your policemen move them along? And what most of all about the stench of death and eternal damnation with which the Lord Jesus Christ will punish the rich for indifference to the poor, and for your beds of lust? You rejoice in your own goodness and praise the hypocrite for virtue. But what really goes on in this world of yours where men delight in torturing their fellow man?"

Here and there there was a timid, "Amen, Brother," but Casy was up and rolling and nothing could stop his litany of evils. "Chairman Mao slaughtered the innocents in his charge in the name of perpetual revolution, the Tongo and the Bongo daily kill one another for no better reason than that they are Tongo and Bongo. Yea, gulag and concentration camp have swallowed up whole generations, and still the dictators cram with dirt the mouths that cry out unto them for pity. Slobbo Milosevich utters the abomination 'ethnic cleansing.' In Cambodia old Pol Pot killed millions of his own people and walked away to become a hypochondriac whining about how sick he was. Look a bit back at Hitler and the Holocaust, at Stalin starving millions of Russians and sending them to Siberia to freeze and die. Is America free of these terrors? Blacks being dragged by whites with chains behind pickup trucks, gang wars on the street, and armed children smiting their schoolmates hip and thigh. Our lawyers and teachers mock us. The mouths of our politicians are cesspits that stink with lies. The jails groan with the desperate, and the streets cry out with the hopeless. Surely, man is vile, so vile that out of him no good can proceed. Where is goodness to be found? Not in mankind, whose very efforts to do good result in evil, man, whose days are filled with vanity and whose greed is insatiable."

The priestess was struck dumb, ran her finger around inside her clerical collar, raised her twenty-four-carat gold pectoral cross as if to ward off the terrible vision of Casy's words. The choir could manage only a weak "Alleluia" and a sonorous "Amen," which brought the service to a hasty end. The flock, many of whom had never heard obscene words like *sin* and *damnation* before, were astounded, and their mouths gaped open unto them. Deacon Ananias was so angry that he smote his short crosier—it concealed a can of pepper spray—on the baptismal font, revealing the name "Sears and Roebuck."

The face of the archpriest, the Right Reverend C. Beecher Retrofit, remained smooth, but in his breast was turmoil. He had labored long in the vineyard to assure his sheep that their gated communities, their Mercedes automobiles, their winter vacations in the Caribbean, their abortion on demand, their long-term capital gains, and their gourmet cuisine were all in the Christian mainline, approved by the three persons of the Trinity, or the one—however it might turn out—and backed up by all the blessed. Assured that they were both rich *and* holy, the flock had grown fat and produced thick coats of wool, which were regularly sheared by the church, while assuring them as they baaed away that truly it could be said of them without profanation that they were beloved in the sight of God.

The *pastor agnorum* was particularly worried about the effect of the old madman's blasphemy on the man they all affectionately called Mr. Bigbucks, otherwise Benedict Happenstance, who at this very moment was prancing around in the nave bellowing some nonsense about sin and death. Bigbucks had been targeted for a seven-figure tithe—in a nonrevocable trust for the lifetime of the giver to produce the maximum tax benefit—to fund a new amusement park, the Land o' Milk and Honey, with nearby luxury hotel and prepaid all-inclusive tours.

The mere thought of losing this boon to salvation caused the good C. Beecher Retrofit to fall to the floor in a trance, as he sometimes did, where he lay and communed for a time with the world beyond the visible world. The Land o' Milk and Honey filled his vision. *There will be an ark, of course, at the center of a water playground, the Sea of Galilee, where John the Baptist serves as lifeguard, and a plastic nonskid walkway just under the surface will allow the faithful to walk on water. A modern passion play in which Jesus and Mary Magdalene, dressed in only a few rags, very seemly still, everything in good taste, discover that love is, as it is propagated by Religion USA, deliciously sensual. A little risky, but perhaps a crucifixion experience in which for a small payment there could be some time on a cross—Velcro, not nails, of course—complete with Roman soldiers. There will be a picnic Garden of Eden, sans serpent, but with a curvaceous Eve and a muscular Adam. Raise Lazarus from the dead for the edification of the faithful, but no scourging, no crown of thorns, no apocalypse and all those other unwholesome scenes that produce gloomy thoughts and undermine the good life. Get into that kind of thing and the first thing you know you will be dispensing poison Kool-Aid in anticipation of the Second Coming, or practicing flagellation, like some of those kooks far out in the booths in the mall. That way, and before you can say Jack Robinson, the attorney general will be sending the FBI in with tear gas and tanks to see what is going on in the cathedral. Of course, they won't find anything. There is nothing wrong going on here. Maybe the acolytes do play around with the priestesses a bit, and the dancing in the nave sometimes gets a bit steamy when the jazz, the real American sacred music, gets hot, but on the whole we run a very decent enterprise that is in step with postmodern America and its liberal, democratic principles. The books are audited every year by Cook and Fiscal. No, no, everything is fine, but we must do something about that wretched Joad. There has been trouble ever since he arrived. Call him in, give him a good talking to, and explain to him that religion has always been based solidly on giving people what they want, not on some primitive millenarian writings or some wild metaphysics. No sir, real religion is for the here and now, not for the distant and the imaginary.*

Greatly refreshed, the shepherd rose to his feet from his trip, only to find that there persisted in the breasts of his flock not only some suspicion that there was a dark as well as a bright side to things but an actual hunger, ancient and deep, for the existence of depravity and, nay, let it not be denied, hell and devils. Jim Casy's words had brought all these long-suppressed feelings to the surface, and instead of trotting meekly out the door of the church on a bright summer morning to enjoy a Bloody Mary before brunch, the flock moved aimlessly about the nave, baaing confusedly of wickedness, days of atonement and reckoning, hellfire, damnation, angels of darkness, predestination, original sin, and the need for imputed salvation.

Casy had disappeared somewhere, but as the hub and the bub increased, Somerset Joad, who had been transformed by the preacher's words, appeared at the head of a line, dancing, making up new words as they went to the "The Old Rugged Cross."

Cross, Cross, Double Cross
It's the devil's sad loss,
When he pitchforks the sinners,
They become born aginers,
And they give him the finger,
When he tries hard to linger
On the mountain of Calvary with its old rugged
cross.

"Yeah! Hit it again." Somerset's eyes shone with an unnatural light, his body twisted and turned as his circuits were hit by great jolts of religious voltage. He clapped his hands in ecstasy. He was filled with the voice of ancient prophecy, at long last fulfilled, "Hit it, brothers and sisters, let's hear it one more time for sin and death." The flock followed him, stripping off their clothing as they went, casting money clips, wallets, gold jewelry, and diamonds aside, confessing their sins to all and everyone. At the end of their third gyre through the ambulatories, Somerset led them out of the church, onto Apollyon Drive, and thence onto Route 666 toward Casy's weather-beaten old church in the desert, the Chapel of Lost Spirit, surrounded with crutches and bedpans, prostheses and motorized wheelchairs, Viagra™ containers and Jack Daniel's sourmash bottles left by the afflicted who had there been cured.

Somerset's mental vision opened up on vast spaces. Gone were the grinning and savage teeth, in their place the serenity of truth known at last, of joy achieved, of vistas of eternity. At last the world made sense. It was going somewhere, not just being gnawed away by the cruel teeth of time. True, people still were no more than savage animals rending one another for love, fame, money, power. But now, even now, he knew with absolute certainty for the first time that they were moving through suffering to redemption. The day was at hand when a great ship from outer space would arrive in the tail of a comet and gather into Abraham's bosom all those who had trembled at the name of the Lord, blasting off into everlasting galactic light. Though Casy had vanished, his Scorpion Springs chapel was the place, Somerset now knew, where the spaceship would come for them, and it was there, reunited with all the blessed, who will have cast off the integuments of the tomb, that the faithful would cross over the river and rest under the trees at last.

The long procession stopped traffic everywhere as it wended its way toward Beulah Land, gathering up in its progress all the heartsore and weary, all the heavy sinners, of greater Los Angeles. Portly legislators stripped off their cashmere jackets and sobbed as they told of paybacks and mulcting welfare funds. Wealthy stockbrokers exited their stretch limousines to cry out that they had made profits on insider trading. Police officers' truncheons remained raised in the air over prostrate perpetrators. Judges in black robes babbled of sending the innocent to jail and rewarding the guilty. Hollywood stars told of fornication in its most depraved forms. Drug sellers threw their murderous merchandise down street drains and prayed for forgiveness. All the great blooming plain of America was shaking in the wind, dropping its full-blown fruit, dancing toward old Casy's chapel, chanting of evil, suffering, death, and repentance. "Cross, Cross, Double Cross."

Later, there was muttering when the skies remained empty and no spaceship had let down on the bare desert. The portable toilets donated by the chamber of commerce were overflowing, everything was covered with dust churned up by thousands of ecstatic feet, water was scarce in the burning heat, and swarms of flies covered the remains of the numberless pizzas consumed like manna in the desert by the faithful. "Suffering," cried some, but only some, "is making itself felt, Alleluia."

The blessed had not burst forth renewed from the grave, but most of the living remained sure that the great day of release was at hand, and Somerset counseled his followers to keep their faith that they were on their way to a brave new world. Yet there was considerable slippage by the third day, when a number of limousines with darkened windows picked up exhausted people and returned them to their Beverly Hills mansions. And by the fourth day, the flock had begun noticeably to break up as tired men and women stole away in all directions muttering that they hoped never to hear the word *suffering* again. People began to cast dark looks on Somerset, and some of the angrier ones even ventured to spit on him. He began to see teeth again, everywhere, even among the devout on their knees praying for deliverance. The sly old archpriest, who had bided his time, moved easily among the sheep, greeting old friends with bright smiles and joyful hosannas that the day was at last come when the weary could lay down their burdens and the sick would at last be healed. But now, a fresh Diet Pepsi in one hand, ice cold by courtesy of the local distributor, his crosier in the other, he eased up to Somerset.

"Well, my son, I think there has been a slight mix-up. I had a vision last night, and I saw not the dry desert but a green jungle land, rich in water, where hosts of sheep grazed contentedly and moved toward a great fleet of flying saucers that were landing one after another like the jet planes at LAX on a busy day. As each pulled up to the ramp the sheep trotted aboard, baaing something that sounded like, 'suffering good, pleasure bad,' and the ramps were pulled up after them, and the saucers spun away into the distant stars at the speed of light. Do you think, O thrice-blessed Somerset, that this could have any meaning for what is happening here?"

"Could it be, oh most Reverend Retrofit, that I have the wrong place out here in the desert? That at some other place in this great world the spaceships are waiting to take us all to Beulah Land? Did you by any chance see the name of this place in your vision?"

"Well, just by chance my eyes fell on the sign above the airport, and though some of the letters were missing, I could make out 'Idi Amin International Airport,' which is located in the African rain forest, somewhere near the indefinite boundaries between the noble Tongo and Bongo tribes, on the banks of the mighty Tbongo River. It is most fortunate that Religion USA just happens to support a foreign mission in that area, where I myself once humbly labored in the Lord's vineyard, and it so happens that the office of *pastor agnorum* there is at present held by an incompetent, and the sheep are running wild. It is in that place, my vision tells me, that the 'Third Going,' Noah's ark being the first, the departure from Egypt the second, that you so devoutly anticipate will finally occur."

"How right you are! Oh, if I could only go there with the flock and wait for the spaceships to arrive."

"That can be managed. Here is your official appointment as *pastor agnorum* in Tbongo, duly signed and sealed by all the deacons of Religion USA, and here is an all-expenses-paid, nonrefundable first-class ticket on the Sonic Boom from LAX to IAIA, leaving within the hour."

"But what about all these good folk who have followed me here and wait to be taken up into the heavens?"

"Have no fear for them. I will lead them back to the cathedral, while you speed in a stretched limo to LAX and points beyond, *infinitely beyond, I hope,* and in time, when the flock is rested and repaired, I will send them on to join you in Tbongo."

The dust from the stretched limo still hung in the air when the Right Reverend C. Beecher Retrofit gathered his flock again and had them trotting back to the cathedral, where he would send them home to warm showers and cold drinks to reflect on the strange experiences they had passed through. In time, when they had recovered from their odd fit of religious enthusiasm, he would again assemble them and instruct them with gentle voice about human goodness and the pleasures those who follow the right path can enjoy in this world. *Once more the high priestess, that adorable Ginger Clitterhouse, will lead her troupe in the nave among the choir stalls doing the exotic dances of all faiths, once again the pets will lie down in peace together, and the Religion USA folksingers will appear on national network TV on Thursday evening to bring the voice of the Lord to all.*

As he entered the manse attached to Cathedral USA, C. Beecher Retrofit sighed with satisfaction thinking about the quiet days to come, and he lighted up a big Castro Corona in anticipation of sitting in his red plastic Lay-Z-Boy, the ex cathedra model, drinking an icy Tanqueray double martini straight up, and looking at the sun setting peacefully in the Pacific Ocean. God in his heaven, where he belonged, all right with the world.

Could it possibly be, God in heaven, yes, it is that wretch Joad, who by now should be at thirty-five thousand feet flying faster than the speed of sound toward the green hell of central

Africa. I told *him his ticket was nonrefundable.* "Well, well, dear boy, how good it is to see you here sitting in my favorite chair looking so relaxed. But what happened to interfere with your mission to Tbongo? Did you miss the plane? Are you perhaps troubled once more by those awful teeth? I have always had sensitive teeth myself, so I can feel for you."

"The teeth are gone, Doc. It was not the road to Damascus but the road to Santa Monica, so to speak. As my powerful stretch limo hurtled down the freeway, I looked to the left, and again to the right, and there I saw the warm sunshine, the palm trees, the pastel stucco of upscale stores and gracious homes, the green lawns, the shiny cars, and . . . and the nearly naked, long-legged, big-breasted beautiful women produced by California's plenitude of God's sunshine and orange juice. They spoke to me, Doc, they spoke to me in a distinct voice that said, 'Somerset, baby, the world may not be for aye, but it sure is for here and now, and it is here to be enjoyed to the fullest. Here you are, already at a young age a saint, nay, a martyr, who has had visions of hell and of eternity. Your experience is worth a lot, and you could with a little help write a book, a best-seller, about your nightmare experience, titled something like *Looking Death in the Mouth* or *The Teeth of Hell.*' And there could be lecture tours, and highly paid feature articles on the nature of the devil and the meaning of suffering. I can even see a movie, with Brad Pitt playing me and Laura Dern as Ginger Clitterhouse. Peripherals would be fabulous, T-shirts, sweatshirts, candy bars, and, best of all, a little pin of three front teeth and the simple words beneath, 'Take a Bite Out of Life.' Not for me, I'm afraid, the sweat-soaked ardors of the foreign mission in the lands of the unblinking Tongos and Bongos."

The archpriest relaxed more and more with every word Somerset spoke. *It will be okay. No more of those dreadful teeth, no more nonsense about sin, death, and repentance. No, sir, this fellow is not going to make any more trouble. Maybe he would do as the manager of the Land o' Milk and Honey? No, he doesn't really have managerial talents. Something a little more in his range? A religious booth, mystic visions, out in the mall where he can sell dental relics, administer high colonic irrigation, find lost jewelry and silverware, and dispense advice on which drugs will produce the best religious trips.*

The archpriest threw his arm over Somerset's shoulders, "Yes, yes, dear boy, Religion USA has a lot of experience in helping young men like yourself find their way through this world of oh-so-many temptations. The Career Planning Office will make available all its expertise to start you on your way tomorrow toward a life of true service to the godly, but now if you will hand me that big green bottle labeled 'gin,' you and I might share a little drink to cement a relationship that I am sure will be mutually profitable."

FOUR
Art Lets It All Hang Out

As the plane came down over the great city, Calista Joad was filled with joy at arriving at long last in Gotham and its avant-garde art scene. The state had put little Lowrider in a foster home, said she was a poor mother, where he had lots of other nice kids to play with. *Why not, it takes a town, or was it a village, to raise a child, doesn't it?*

But that was all in the past, and below her she saw the city's deep shadowy canyons, its teeming streets, and its skyscraper tops reflecting light high in the sun. The great architects of the time, Paul Cubit, Philip Buttress, Isamo Notsoguchi, and others, had covered Manhattan with cloud-breaking buildings in eclectic styles without right angles or straight lines that plunged and soared, floated and rolled. Shingle Style, Las Vegas Classical, Route-One Electric, neo-Log Cabin, Trash Pharaonic, the great structures sprawled over block after block. Corinthian marble columns rose to join gray cement architraves, and neo-brutalistic brownstone was relieved with flashing neon.

Few people lived there any longer, but true art still centered in the Big Apple, and it was art that Calista had dedicated her life to. On the flight she had been reading a *New York Smirk* editorial about the cultural importance of arts and artists, words that expressed perfectly just how important great art and its divine creators are to the world:

> Art is more than a piece of property that some one or some institution owns. . . . In some real way art works belong to no one because they belong to all of us. They are among the most salient examples of the breadth and depth and complexity of human nature. Throughout time, our species has used the arts—this rich set of symbols that only humans have devised—to transmit the heritage of people and to express most profoundly their deepest human joys, sorrows, and intuitions.

True, true, how could it have been better put? Calista thought. *What a privilege it is going to be to live in a city where you can read a newspaper every day with high-class editorials like that.*

She noted that *The Smirk* had focused on the materiality of "physical, tangible, visual art," and she had read with pleasure in the arts section of the same paper of a particularly tangible site-specific work of art, Sergei Knockoff's *Batterer 2* was a sixteen-ton oeuvre, measuring seventeen by fourteen by three feet of solid cupro-nickle, which had toppled off the jacks in a SoHo gallery, killing a worker, pinning two men to the floor, knocking down several supports in the building, and causing several walls to crack, floors to sag, and a standpipe to break and flood the building. *A human tragedy, yes,* Calista ruminated, *but how well it speaks to the power of great art.*

Calista had an interview for a job picking the weeds and grass shoots out of the prime exhibit of the Art in Your Face Museum, a large glass room filled entirely with dirt titled *Room*

Filled with Dirt. This "anti-eco art" work was priceless, but it required constant sterilizing to keep nature from invading culture with seeds that grew, expanded, and threatened to break down the confining walls. Calista felt honored to have landed this critical job, so central to the arts, which she had found on the AYFM WWWEBsite, even at minimum wages. The job itself, however menial, would be a stepping-stone to becoming a full-fledged art critic in the New York art scene, which was her goal in life. But first Calista was faced with the practical problem of getting from La Guardia to the museum in Chelsea.

"Hey, sister, want a taxi to the city?"

"How much?"

"Two."

"Dollars? That's cheap."

"Hundred."

"Is there a bus?"

"Fuckin' fugeddaboudit."

Arrived in Greenwich Village at last, Calista found getting about through the traffic difficult. Tired, her feet aching from high heels on hot pavement, her miniskirt riding up her thighs, a twist in her undies, she sat down at a sidewalk café, ordered a Diet Coke, and listened eagerly to two bearded men, wearing berets, sitting near her talking about, what else? art.

"I hear Fifi La Pelt has won her case and the National Endowment for the Arts has to pay punitive damages for refusing her a grant to buy liquid chocolate, symbolizing the menstrual slavery that the patriarchy has imposed on women, to drip on her when she dances naked."

"Fuckin'-A right, performance art is really where it's at. Next thing you know, old what's-his-name will be getting a grant to produce stronger piss to float his crucifixes. Or the African guy to buy more elephant dung to smear on religious images. Some people really have genius."

"Well, it's a good time to be an artist. I just read in *The New York Smirk,* this big paper here [rattling the pages] that prints all the news that's fit to print, that the governor and the legislature up in Albany just passed a new law, 'One Percent for Art.'"

"No shit?"

"Yeah! A percent of the construction costs for new building is going to have to be spent on art, such as statues, murals, fountains, chandeliers, and other crap with aesthetic value."

"Well, that's going to be real helpful. I've had trouble lately trying to sell some of my stabiles to Rodney Uncas, one of the few real Mohicans left. His tribal name is Na-Ha-Po-Pie, translated that comes to 'He Who Rolls Snake Eyes.' The tribe claims to be a sovereign nation that was genocided by the Pilgrims, and now they're getting reparations in the form of tax-free enclaves and the right to build gambling casinos. I've been trying to persuade Uncas to buy some of my work to give class to their big, new gambling wigwam, make it something more than just another tepee. But the chiefs have been holding out, and they are going to be really pissed off when they find out that the law is going to make them shell out big wampum for freeform paleface art."

"Well, the prisons may be still a better bet. Since millions of people are now convicted of breaking the thousands of laws the legislatures have been passing, there are lockups going up all over the place, and the new law means they are going to have to have murals, classical music, statues, and all kinds of shit in the cellblocks. Some right-wing creeps have questioned whether prisons need art, whether the prisoners deserve it, or even if it will improve them in any quantifiable way. But those fellows on *The New York Smirk* editorial page aren't having any of that bull. [reading] 'Only Philistines think that people who are emotionally or mentally disturbed don't need and want art. Put art in the prisons,' *The Smirk* says, 'and the level of violence will go down and the guards can rehabilitate the perpetrators and get them ready a lot sooner to re-enter society as useful citizens.'"

"That's telling them, so long as the media, the courts, and the government support us, art is going to be okay."

Calista took her bag and ran. It was all too much for her. *Are those real artists? those crude louts who thought only of making money and getting the government to give them a handout? Art had long ago declared its independence from patrons, and the romantic artists had willingly died from TB and starved in garrets, like in* La Bohème, *to follow their own imaginations to whatever heights they led them. Great modern works of the creative imagination like Attila Bobo's* Sick Girl Petting Her Dead Rat *or Mark Supertwine's* crossing bicycle tracks #23 *are pure works of art, pandering to the interests of no effete aristocrats, no tasteless bourgeois swine, no hypocritical priests. But now, she could hardly believe it, it sounded as if government—ugh, all those lying politicians—had emerged as a new patron of the arts, and aesthetics was now a legal issue.*

When the job at AYFM didn't work out—the curator told her to wear only her high heels and glasses while he checked her suitability for the job—she decided to look for some other way to break into the art world. But first she had to find a place to live. Rents for the few vacant apartments were astounding, over a thousand a month for the cheapest slum walkup, but she had heard that the personals in *The Village Vice,* men looking for women, and vice versa, were the place to look for a pad if you were willing to share.

"BMPA [black male performance artist], fifty-some, buns of steel, wonderful sense of humor and love of fine cheeses, seeks H$SFLWF [hard-working, well-to-do, single fun-loving white female] to keep house."

"SWF without any kinky hang-ups, into leather, whips, etc., but no spurs, looks for long-term submissive partner, any sex."

"Handsome, witty, well-endowed, college-educated, sensitive painter, no egghead, loves to dance, walk, listen to music, visit country inns, try anything. Life dedicated to art. Wants tall, slim Ivy-League, big boobs, $50k eggs. Share water-view flat, Cross Bronx Expressway."

This last sounded best, though Calista sure wasn't Ivy League and didn't know what "$50k eggs" were. *Something dirty probably.* And besides she was almost flat chested, but probably the guy had only been to high school and was short.

The A train was quite an experience. Around the turn of the millennium the city seemed to have won its battle against graffiti, and the subway stations, as well as the cars, were decorated only with tasteful advertisements. "Can't Sleep? Gasz Pains?" But with the explosion of all kinds of art in the twenty-first century, subway graffiti had flourished again in ways they had never done before. For a time tour groups, mostly senior citizens from the many nursing homes that somehow remained in the city, eager for a day's outing of any kind, came to wonder at these modern masterpieces, shuffling from one to another while being lectured by volunteer docents in the aesthetics of postmodernism. The cement and tile made a wonderful surface for Day-Glo spray paint, and after a time imaginative graffiti like "FUCK THE WORLD," illustrated by a globe with a gaping vagina, or "UP THE REVOLUTION," showing Marianne with her red cap bent over and being reamed doggy-style, and "KILL ALL THE LAWYERS," illustrated with all kinds of fantastic torture executions, covered every inch of the subway walls. So violent and vivid did the sentiments and the drawings become that they frightened the tourists away, but then the great Ivy historian of urban architecture, Vincent Gouache, published his magisterial book, *True Art Lets It All Hang Out* (Three-Holer Press, Four-Holer Editions), proving that graffiti are a great New York vernacular art form, growing, as true art always does, out of resistance to the capitalistic state by the underclass, in this case the local gangs who roamed the cement jungle of the subways at night with spray cans and razor blades.

Then the graffiti became once more what the tourists came to see, and there were tours once again that went around on special trains, led by docents from the Art in Your Face Museum, who identified the different painterly styles, though the artists remained unknown, that could be distinguished in this wilderness of color. "Eclectrobang" did explicit pedophilic sex scenes with a full palette and big blocky masses of huge penises and children, male and female, with dark circles under their eyes, shrinking away from the focal point. "Sadismo" used Day-Glo green hi-liters with a fine line to show women in exquisite agonies and hyperperspective being tortured by the mayor, the chief of police, and the head of the city council. "Marauder" painted crucifixions and other weird versions of the more violent and erotic biblical scenes in a strange blending of the styles of Goya and Thurber.

After Calista had passed through these tunnels of assault graffiti, the Cross Bronx Expressway, filled with unmoving trucks and cars, didn't look so bad, nor did the "water-view," which turned out to be the debris-filled Harlem River. At least they belonged to the familiar world above the consciousness line. The smog did make seeing, let alone breathing, difficult, but "Hey, this is New York," and the climb was only seven floors. Breathing heavily, she knocked on the door. "I saw your personal in the paper . . . ."

His brow was low, his stature lower, and his morals probably lower still. Maybe you wouldn't exactly call him a dwarf, but he sure was upwardly challenged. His single mother, an aging flower child from an immigrant Italian family, thought it a good joke to call him "I. Nano," and he bore the name with some pride after he learned that it meant "the dwarf."

Calista laughed when he said, "Hi, come on in and take off your clothes—only kidding—you're not exactly what I had in mind, but they taught us at Lemming College that you have to wag your tail if you want to run with the pack." Nano's views of art were as old-fashioned as his pictures. He had never been to art school, and so talked still of perspective, of brushwork, of composition, of color, of meaning, and of beauty. He revered the great American painters in the realistic tradition, Benjamin West, John Trumbull, and George Caleb Bingham. He had for a time imitated their successors, Thomas Eakins, Reginald Marsh, Edward Hopper, and Thomas Hart Benton. He spent a lot of time going to avant-garde lectures and heckling the new art intellectuals and postmodern theorists.

Unfortunately, Nano had read recently that a couple of Russians had worked out statistically that America's favorite painting would be "executed in a modified Hudson River style and perhaps something more than 44 percent blue, show a riverbank with George Washington, a typical American family in outdoor clothing, and some animals, including a hippopotamus." Desperate to pay the rent, he had now filled his studio with studies and variations on this theme—sometimes a hippo, sometimes an allegory; sometimes Franklin Pierce or Martin Van Buren—and though he hadn't sold any pictures yet, he was sure that he would find the right combination and make it big any day now. At the moment De Witt Clinton, hands behind his back, looking at a rhinoceros bathing in a waterfall in the Catskills, was on his easel, in heroic scale.

Nano's bright spirit so endeared him to Calista that she moved in right away and began to look for work in a studio or gallery. Anything to get started in the art world. After weeks of pounding the pavement, Calista began to realize that what she had overheard in the café conversation was true. The law and government had coiled around art like the sea serpents around Laocoön and his children. What the Medici palazzo and the Vatican had once been, the foundation, law office, courtroom, and legislature now were to art, and the result had been the near disappearance of the art work itself. If you wanted to work in the arts you didn't paint pictures anymore, or write books, you got an agent, sued someone on a contingency basis, applied for a grant from some agency, or looked up earlier art cases in Lexis-Nexis hoping to find an angle.

And so she found herself filling out an application as a legal assistant to Ellen Barratri, called to the New York bar after a brush with the California authorities, and now one of the leading legal lights in Pegasus, Parnassus & Culpable, a firm specializing in art law. Ms. Barratri almost seemed to remember Calista, at least she smiled at her, and put her to work right away doing research on *Retrofit v. Puss.* The Pegasus client, *Puss,* was the first full-frontal zine that had dared show nothing in its pages but enlarged images of the female primary sexual organ. It didn't seem at first as if this would be a big seller, but it turned out that there was nothing the American male between eight and eighty enjoyed more than looking at pictures of a vulva, turning them for hours this way and that, hoping to be able to see further inside. The owner and editor of *Puss,* Alphonse DaGunto, had earlier been shot and paralyzed by a defrocked Episcopal priest, one Father Rugby Portface, who called him the greatest danger to public morals since Nero and the Marquis de Sade. Condemned to spend his life printing pictures of what he could no longer enjoy, DaGunto became paranoid about clerics and ordered that the saintly Right Reverend C. Beecher Retrofit, the leading religious figure in the country, be portrayed in *Puss* as an hermaphrodite, and displayed a purported picture of him with an enormous dong and a gaping vagina. An accompanying interview with Nails Inhouse, who claimed to have been in a juvenile prison with Retrofit, said that he used to display his gifts to anyone who was interested and said further that he had worked as a freak in a sideshow where he was advertised as the purest of the original three human sexes described by the ancient Greek philosopher Aristophanes. It was further charged that Retrofit's great success at Cathedral USA was the result of his ability to perform AC-DC for his parishioners, participating in whatever unnatural sexual combinations they might wish to construct. An outraged and spluttering Retrofit went to law.

First-amendment rights of free speech were certainly involved, and when Calista searched the legal database, she discovered that remarks that would ordinarily be considered libelous and indecent could be defended, if done with the right style of exaggeration, on the grounds that they were art, specifically the art of satire. As an ancient art form that makes outsized attacks, satire had long been generally and legally understood to be not a statement of fact, or a direct imitation of reality, but an artistic exaggeration, like a caricature, blown up to reveal not the wickedness of individuals but the real dangers to society of their actions. There are always vicious men and women of such brazen high authority and power that the normal workings of society are unable to restrain or correct them. There are also widespread harmful ways of thinking and acting that are so deep-rooted that the usual correctives, such as religion or the law, cannot touch them. In these cases, satire had in the past been considered society's last line of defense against these dangerous forces and was therefore protected in this function by society. Satire had thus been given a social license to attack vice because it served the high social purpose of ferreting out the hypocritical and whipping those too powerful to be shamed by any other means. Aristophanes, Calista was happy to point out, was himself a satirist notorious for outrageous attacks on the Athenian establishment.

Judge Anthony Momus was delighted to get *Retrofit v. Puss*. As an undergraduate at Harvard, he had studied in its English department, widely known for being totally given over to the high reaches of literary theory. While making a fortune defending oil companies from suits about spills that had devastated beaches from Alaska to Kuwait, Judge Momus had retained a passionate interest in aesthetics and published frequently on the subject in learned journals. There was, he boasted, not a play, poem, or novel in his entire library, only critical theory, as befitted a man accustomed to the pure reasoning of the law. And now he had a chance to display from the bench his knowledge of hermeneutics and reception aesthetics on such long-argued literary controversies as "Is satire literature?" and "Does satire really harm those it attacks?" The case was to be heard without jury, and Momus knew that lawyers and literary critics alike would read his judgment for centuries to come!

The defense said from the beginning that it would rest its case if Retrofit would simply take his pants down in court, but the prosecution refused on the grounds of dignity and the right to privacy.

The trial began with a group of literary critics from the University of Chicago, brought in by the prosecution, who argued that since it was impossible to reconcile the great variety of views about how deep the satiric harpoon could legally penetrate, it was necessary to go over the history of the disagreement, which they proceeded to do at great length, without, of course, reaching any conclusion. "Teach the argument" was their motto. Deconstructive critics from Duke, paid by the defense, sneered at this banal historicism and supported *Puss*'s case by arguing that language is nonrepresentational and always conflicted. An interpretation was offered to show that the *Puss* article could be read as praising the Right Reverend Retrofit for his Christian tolerance of variety. Besides, it would be a vulgar error to identify the target of the *Puss* attack with Retrofit, because he could not himself be said to be a coherent and consistent entity.

"Satire," lawyer Barratri summed up for the defense, leaning over in her low-cut dress, "can't really harm anyone, it is all in good fun, and besides in this particular case where the exaggeration is obvious—who would ever believe for an instant that a distinguished cleric like the Right Reverend Doctor Retrofit would really offer his parishioners a variety of sexual services?—the article would instantly be recognized by a reader as satiric exaggeration, not mistaken for fact. Therefore Retrofit has not been harmed and my client should be declared innocent, and awarded costs."

Momus began his decision weightily by quoting the Roman satirist Horace (*Sermones* 2.1): "Who writes evil things against some other person must himself by rights be prepared to be sued for redress of grievance." He pointed out, however, that Horace was simply setting the audience up for a defense of satire and intended that the statement be taken as ironic. Frequently referring to Quintus Horatius Flaccus, Momus delivered a long history of satire and how it has been allowed to tear, burn, rend, firk, swinge, lie, and in general bedevil any poor wretch the satirist may take a dislike to. He ended by quoting Horace again, "the case is dismissed," adding that it was clear that *Puss* intended to call attention to a serious danger in our society, hermaphroditism, and that it had, in the manner of classical satire, attacked the vice, not the man. He delivered a stern lecture on keeping literary genres straight to the Right Reverend Doctor Retrofit, who kept angry eyes fixed on the ground, and assessed him the full costs of the case.

Calista was right, in New York, Art City USA, art was far more alive in the courts than in the studios. She was digging out precedents for PP&C on the "Son-of-Sam law." Son of Sam was a loner who liked to spy on lovers in isolated cars and then kill them. After several murders he was caught and explained to the police that it was okay for him to shoot people because he was the Son of Sam, Sam being the name of a neighbor's barking dog that gave him orders to kill. His explanation failed to convince the jury, and he had gone up the river for a long time. He had later wanted to write a book about his exploits, and the New York State Legislature, alarmed at the thought of murderers profiting from their crimes, passed a Son-of-Sam law requiring that all royalties from such descriptions of a crime should go to the victims of the crime or, if they did not survive, to their heirs and assigns, not to the criminal.

Somewhat later a dancer in a topless nightclub, Ginger Clitterhouse, was convicted for attempting to kill her lover, one Fredson Ananias, whom she had known earlier in California, when he threatened to abandon her. With many idle days on her hands after she had been incarcerated, she had taken an extension course in expository writing, part of the Art for Prisoners Program, and begun to write a book telling of how she had been victimized by a number of men, beginning with her father and including the noted ecclesiastic, C. Beecher Retrofit, to whom she had been briefly married after she accused him of raping her when she was under the age of consent. In writing this memoir she had been assisted by Forked-Tongue Publishers, Inc., which had supplied her with the help of one of its free-lance writers, Richard Savage (a sodden wretch who claimed to be the illegitimate, unacknowledged, and unsupported son of Norman Mailer and Lillian Hellman) to help her with some of the difficult points of English grammar. The Son-of-Sam law came into play at this point, since Ginger's big scene was the shooting of Ananias, but Forked-Tongue, still intent on furthering the public weal, hired Elmore Culpable, who promptly put Calista to work looking for grounds on which to challenge the Son-of-Sam law.

On Calista's advice, Culpable argued that the Son-of-Sam law was illegal, and contrary to nature, and to the law, and to the Bible—"For the Scripture saith, Thou shalt not muzzle the ox that treadeth out the corn. And the labourer is worthy of his hire" (1 Timothy 5.18). In the law, Culpable contended, the Son-of-Sam law infringed upon first-amendment rights of free speech. Had it existed in the past, Culpable, cued by Calista, thundered, it would have prevented many great works of literature written in jail, like Henry David Thoreau's "Civil Disobedience," or Martin Luther King's "Letter from Birmingham Jail." Calista had discovered that some writers had actually found the pokey to stimulate their imaginations. Boethius wrote his *Consolation of Philosophy* in a Roman slammer, Jean Genet scribbled on bits of toilet paper in the dungeons of the Château d'If. Fyodor Dostoyevsky, whose art thrived on incarceration, would have stayed mute in the czar's prisons had the Son-of-Sam law been in force in Romanov Petersburg. And Eldridge Cleaver's classic *Soul on Ice* had come straight from the lockup. Calling on these ancient and venerable precedents, Culpable climbed to the heights of his rhetoric: "So sacred is the author's relationship to the products of his imagination, his art, that the Son-of-Sam legislation is not only arbitrary but abominable to the laws of God and man." All his idealism was in vain, however. Ginger took the train back up the river after the trial, and there was a nasty scene on the courthouse steps between Pegasus and Forked-Tongue, in the course of which Calista Joad lost her temper and a heel kicking the drunken Savage down the steps when he tried to tell her how mean his mother, Lillian Hellman, had been, refusing to acknowledge him or to provide any support beyond meager payments to the indigent freelance copy editors to whom she had farmed him out as an infant.

With the raise she got for her work on the case, even though her firm lost, Calista was able to move out of Nano's flat, after a big row about the necessity of poverty to true art, having found a penthouse on Sutton Place she could share with Dimitri Parnassus, the graying golden Greek who was the senior partner in PP&C. It was even rumored around the office that PP&C was going to make her an affiliate, and in time a partner, specializing in art law. But not just yet. Her working days were filled with sketching out a "moral rights of artists" bill, commissioned by Senator O'Hoopla, which would put the full force of law behind certain natural rights long and unconstitutionally denied to artists. Genuine artists would be certified by the government and their value to society recognized by providing those so certified with subsidized housing, income tax remission, and frequent fellowships. No "site-specific art" could be moved and no changes could be made in any painting or art object without the approval of the artist who created it. Royalties would be paid to the author each time a book was checked out of a library, and the creators of any artifact would receive half of the increase in value each time the work was sold. Nano, for example, to judge by his physique, might well be descended from Henri de Toulouse-Lautrec, and could be in line for a percentage of the millions of dollars of compounded increase in values that the French dwarf's paintings of gin mills, cancans, and prostitutes had accumulated since the end of the nineteenth century. Since Nano and Toulouse-Lautrec were both physically challenged, there might well be an additional "bias penalty." But then, just as she was beginning to write up a draft of the "moral rights of artists" legislation, the whole romantic-modern art world based on the creative genius of the artist and the hard, gemlike flame of the art work came apart.

An avant-garde French critic, the Ivy University professor of deconstruction Pierre de Hors, filled an entire Sunday magazine of *The New York Smirk* with a "Manifesto for a Democratic Art," declaring that painting, literature, theater, classical music, and dance were not the true arts of democratic America in the twenty-first century but the moribund remnants of an old authoritarian, bourgeois, capitalist, materialistic art that expressed the values of the exploiters, not the people.

> The real artistic energy of modern democracy is to be found in what the obsolete fine arts scorn as "pop art" or "Post-Y2K art." Postmodernism and deconstuction provide the true aesthetic theory of democratic art. They break down the artificial barriers between the arts and other human activities; they assume a diminished sense of reality; they recognize absence in presence, and presence in absence; they politicize art at its roots by deconstructing the difference between artist and audience, master and slave. Technology, not the old-fashioned Asiatic handwork

> of a cottage-art industry, is the dominant mode of production of true democratic art. Photography, movies, television, comic books, amplified rock music, theme parks, advertising, graffiti, and computer games, these satisfy far better than the old authoritarian fine arts the prime democratic value of "the Many." Everybody can go to the movies, everyone can understand and appreciate them, and with cameras getting cheaper and cheaper, more and more people can make their own movies and act in them. The same with rock and country music, and with photography. Everyone can play. The truest democratic arts are the participatory, "interactive" arts. In the old fine arts, the artist was an autocrat, standing back like God and paring his fingernails, as James Joyce put it, while the audience groveled before him—always HIM, never HER—and tried to understand his carefully concealed meanings.

Disturbed, but thoughtful, Calista put down the mag and, tapping her teeth with her pencil, took a yellow legal pad and began to make big notes:

> This de Hors stuff about democratic art is serious
>
> If it takes
>
> PP&C is going to have to think about art and law in a very different way if the old firm is going to surf the wave of new democratic art
>
> De Hors is scheduled to give a lecture at the New School
>
> CJ had better be there, along with all the rest of the art crowd

De Hors was as challenging in person as in his writing. A bit paunchy, but with head thrown back, eyes closed, intoning words that seemed to come from far away, delivered with only the greatest pain, he resembled a biblical prophet:

"Look, my dears, [big sigh] let's begin with the basic fact. Art is what we say it is, not some objective reality to be found in nature. It's not even a social constant like religion or the family. When Fifi La Pelt dances naked except for her chocolate syrup, that's Performance Art, though the Ballet Russe doesn't want to have anything to do with it. Sergei Knockoff puts New York on the map with his site-specific *Wall of Hope* down the middle of Broadway, and when the other guy, what's-his-name, pisses on crucifixes, that's Political Art showing the triumph of the individual's vitality over religious institutions, death, and suffering. When Mad Dog Supertwine thinks about hurling handfuls of paint in a wild rage at a canvas, that's Conceptual Art, or when a chimp daubs colors on a canvas, that's Gonzo Art, or sometimes what is called Natural Art. And all of these are types of the art of democracy, Post-Y2K art."

At this point there was a disturbance in the back of the audience where the ushers were wrestling down a dwarf. Calista knew it, Nano was up to his old tricks. She tried to get to the aisle to stop him, but no one would move their feet, so she watched helplessly as the dwarf, wiry, though small, escaped the ushers' clutches somehow and raced to the platform, where he seized the microphone from a bemused de Hors and shouted:

"OK, OK, OK, so Art is historical, not a Platonic absolute, but it does have a history, and true art is the best work that has appeared during that history. And the best work is that which allows a people and a time to understand themselves and value their way of life for what it is. That is art. Michelangelo and Shakespeare define a much more interesting and useful conception of art than do Electrobang and a chimpanzee."

The audience shuffled their feet nervously, and there were a few audible remarks: "What is this shit, Shakespeare? Michelangelo? This guy will be telling us next that truth is beauty."

Knowing that he had only seconds before the cops got him, Nano raced on. "Because a concept is socially constructed we are not free to define it in any way that we want, we are limited by its history. What has been called true art in the Western world has been work—paintings, statuary, architecture, literature, photographs, and you name it—that is distinguished by the skill with which it is created and by the insights it offers into life."

There were boos and hisses now, a genuine New York raspberry here and there. "Sit down and shut up, Shorty. Let's hear what the professor has got to say."

But Nano was undeterred. "Something meaningful to say, and a powerful style to say it in, that is true art. Can we simply turn our backs on Homer and Titian to call copies of Campbell Soup cans, or a pile of bricks arranged in some random way, Art?"

By this point the New School security had arrived. They grabbed the dwarf from behind in a chokehold and dragged him roughly, his heels bouncing, off the stage.

Pierre de Hors was used to this kind of outbreak at his lectures, in fact he rather counted on it, and he had been standing looking at his opponent contemptuously. "I know that idiot," he said in a conversational tone to the audience, "he is an old-fashioned artist, and a new-fashioned revanchist troublemaker, who tries to paint like old has-beens like Edward Hopper and Winslow Homer. 'High Art,' [snort] that's the trouble, there isn't any such thing as 'High Art' any longer, it literally is history, and all the out-of-date aesthetic furniture that went with it, the creative imagination, genius, composition, aesthetics, structure, symbolism, and so on. There is only art, the things that the people choose to admire and call art, and a pile of bricks or a plastic bedpan fits the bill as well as (or better than) Michelangelo or Shakespeare.

"When this is understood everyone in democratic America can become an artist. He and she need only *mettre en abyme* the old tyrannous high culture, declaring the product of their hands and mind, Art. And does it make any difference what the artist makes? Not a bit, a pair of handcuffs or putti, *The Nightwatch* or a big red canvas with five yellow stripes on it. *Art is anything made by anybody that we choose to call Art* [this in a loud, conspiratorial whisper], and what we call art now is interactive techno-art, the art of the people, by the people, and for the people." De Hors took a drink of water from the glass on the podium, hand steady as a rock, and smiled at the audience as he began putting his papers in his red ostrich-skin briefcase.

The audience sat in stunned silence. How foolish Calista had been, she thought, to believe in the old aristocratic high art. But she was still uncertain about the how this "neo-nouveau art which is not Art," this "Post-Y2K technological art of democracy," this "*mettre en abyme* art" was going to relate to the law. She sat pondering in the empty auditorium for a time: *If everyone is an artist, and every made thing is at least potentially a work of art, it is hard to see how the artist can claim any special status and how his work can be treated in any different way from other artifacts. In fact, if true art is now Post-Y2K, then it might just be that art can exist outside the courts. What kind of tort can be committed against objects that become art whenever anyone says they are art, and cease to be art whenever someone else says they are just junk, not art. Art which has no creators who can be wronged, which does not exist except as an idea, which is everything and nothing? Neo-nouveau, Post-Y2K art is going to be difficult, impossible really, to pin down long enough to give it the substance required in a court of law dealing in real property and sensible torts. The new art—technological, interactive, nonrepresentational—might be impossible even to copyright. This is a whole different ball game.*

Before anything else, though, she had to try to straighten Nano out. She found him on Fifth Avenue trying to conceal a rip in his pants, and they went to a bar where they argued for hours about the nature of real art and the need for the courts in defining it.

But whatever doubts Nano might have, folk creativity exploded in a wave of a new techno-democratic-interactive Post-Y2K art. It was a time of high unemployment, and since little capital and very little special skill were needed to set up a Post-Y2K artist's studio, hordes of young men and women became instant artists. In the rent-controlled lofts of lower Manhattan bearded young destitutes began airbrushing heroic Day-Glo pictures of *Senator Whitewater Entering New York in Triumph on the Brooklyn Bridge.* In the abandoned meat lockers along the East River the sound of chainsaws was heard from morning till night carving huge logs into images of American folk totems, Rudolph the Red-Nosed Reindeer, Godzilla, and Mickey Mouse. Arco-acetylene torches turned the night to day in empty parking garages where the sculptors of the people welded car fenders, washing machines, manhole covers, urinals, and old steam engines together to create bold images of the future.

The cutting edge of the new art, however, was the interactive electronic arts in which the hegemony of the artist and the fixity of the aesthetic object vanished like dew in the summer sun of virtuality. Electronic art forms tended away from the minimalist and toward the complex in computer games like the immensely popular "Goniff," in which the player became the artist remaking his/her identity by a series of virtual existential choices. Variations on this game were developed for different professions. There was Business Goniff, for example, in which the player could end up either a Bill Gates or a homeless bum, depending on his choices. Then there was Military Goniff, which was taken up and used at the War College to test the ability of senior officers to make the right career moves. There were also digital event scenes, emerging worlds, and other applications of digital, quantum, or biological phenomena. Very popular with the cognoscenti were "Cybertown" and "Virtual Living," which had many imitators such as "Flesh Games," "The New Age of Analog: NanoTech," "Ergodic/Cyborg Literature,"

"Phreaker Mystories," "Faith in Chaos," "Biotech and Meatspace," "Representational Avatars and the Flesh That Loves Them," and, what was felt by some to be the summit of electronic production of neo-nouveau art, "The Arrival of the Post Human."

Filmmakers such as the Media Studies Working Group produced Y2K films like *Bang Bang, Shoot Shoot!* and their *Pictures of a Generation on Hold* in the postdigital filmic mode made history. These films were described as "employing new approaches to quantum and biotechnological topoi from a plurality of discourses interfaced with a variety of circulatory systems such as semiotics, psychoanalytics, feminisms, hermeneutics, and other approaches that transform, disrupt, and otherwise distort established theoretical syntaxes." A Lacanian revolution in film, with pictures such as *Eyes Wide Shut*, *eXistenZ*, *Fight Club*, and *Holy Smoke*, took audiences to the limits of what is bearable, to ways of being with a constitutive lack, encounters with an impossible jouissance, and a journey along the death drive. Y2K experiments in filmic art were legitimated by the appearance of new aesthetic theories like "Memetics (Memes)" and "Hyper-Rhetorics of Computer Games."

But, like all things, the new, new art had its backside as well as its front. In quite a short time it appeared that while everyone who wanted to be one was an artist, turning out art by the carload, neither the profession nor the product was any longer really very interesting, even to the artist, insofar as he/she/it was any longer ontologically certifiable. When the audience was transformed into the artist, there was, disappointingly, no longer a distinct audience to admire the work of the artist. Nor did the audience always make a satisfying artist. When people got on stage in the interactive psychodramas that had taken over the legitimate theater, they tended to say little more than ". . . duh." A few days of playing "Super-Goniff," and the identities constructed in that game began to have a tedious sameness: a muscular young man, the abducted son of a king, raped every woman he wanted and blew away his putative pop and mom and anybody else who told him to get home early. Indeed, soon there were only a few standard Goniff plots, almost all involving huge amounts of sex and violence.

Live TV shows were exciting enough at first when a hunk was placed on a desert island with ten beautiful girls and told he would win a million dollars if he was not seduced by any of them. But the end was inevitable, and in the meantime there was a lot of sleeping and eating, and boredom soon set in. A guy on a pillar, like Saint Simeon Stylites of old, was only a guy on a pillar, and the audience ratings soon dropped to zero. Deafening rap lyrics like "fuck, fuck, fuck, kill, kill, kill," did not satisfy in the manner that had long been claimed for an open-ended art. Besides, amplification at the megawatt level by so many musical groups was threatening to crash the power grid of the entire country.

The Post-Y2K art bubble was about to burst. Never had there been more art. Everyone was making art, night and day, but no one was at all interested in it. In fact it had become about the most boring thing on the face of the earth. Post-Y2Kism and democratic art had arrived at the point of self-extinction. They were actually looking into the abyss posited by the deconstructive philosophers who had opened the way for the new art. No one knew what art was anymore, and works existed, if at all, so evanescently as to make even temporary identification impossible. You couldn't tell an artist from any other person walking the streets. One day people looked around and there wasn't any art, nor were there any artists. Once in a while someone might ask where those things we used to call "art" had gone, but not often, and when they did, other people just looked at them blankly.

The chainsaws were broken and the light of the arco-acetylene torches was low. No longer did the photographer set up his camera in front of the Empire State Building and run it continuously for twenty-four hours. Millions of backs were still hunched over computer games, but they were no longer artists creating a virtual reality, they were just nudnicks and goniffs without full-time jobs.

Five

The Politics Gene

"All doctors and technicians on Team Happenstance! Type 3 plus Emergency, F3A! Happenstance, Emergency, eighteen-hundred hours, F3A." The hospital loudspeakers' shrieks and blurred vowels were barely intelligible over the backup beepers on the electric carts, the constant ringing of unanswered telephones, the noise of the dozens of pagers, but the members of the Happenstance team—the two surgeons, the internist, the grief counselor, the anesthetist, the ethicist, the pre- and post-traumatic stress experts, the medical insurance actuary, the lawyers (one for defense against suits, one for suing), and the acupuncturist (by law, "alternative medicine" had now to be represented on every treatment team)—began assembling from various parts of the hospital.

"The Happenstance case has taken a very bad turn, and the most radical action would seem to be called for."

"Yes, I feared the worst. It hasn't been looking

well for some time, but I had hoped we might avoid an emergency if we left, so to speak, no stone unturned."

"Yes, but no matter all we do, things often, in fact always, take a turn for the worse before we're done. If Americans did not think they could live forever without any distress or pain, it would not be necessary to practice medicine so aggressively. A lot of people are beginning to think that immortality is just a matter of time and money."

"Ah so, but let me remind you that the series of 104 corresponding brass needles in the buttocks and the shoulders has not yet been used on Happenstance, nor has the slow but constant contraction of the testicles with copper wire, though this has had most gratifying results for centuries in inland China."

"For whom? The patient or the quack? Ha, ha!"

"Now, now, in a time of crisis we must remember that we are a team and that everything depends on our pulling together." Ellsworth Joad felt that his associate's certificate in medical ethics, acquired at Lone Tree State University after the breakup of his family, required him to remind other team members of the American ethical imperative of community spirit, even when the members of the team, as he knew too well, loathed one another almost as much as they did the patient, and his family, and his medical insurer.

Doctor Slops scarcely heard him. "Well, talk all you want, shilly-shally about forever, but we must face facts. The reality is, and there is no getting around it, that old Happenstance's medical insurance is about to run out and that, rich as he once was, he hasn't enough money to pay for another enema, once it does."

"Yes. It is a shame, and just when we seemed to be really getting a hold on the problem. We feed him through a tube in his nose, pump air into him through a tube down his throat, stimulate his phagocytes, have him hooked up to a dialysis machine that drains and cleans his blood every four hours, test and supplement his bodily fluids hourly, control his liver with the new computer, and restart his heart with the catatonic palpitator every time it stops. And just to be sure where we are, we run him through the MRI any time there's an opening in his schedule. The patient seemed to be getting better, though strangely enough when he could talk for a minute the other day he said something like, 'Please, let me die,' but he couldn't have said that, with all the miracles of modern medicine that have been made available to him. Still, facts are facts, and we have a major emergency on our hands."

Ellsworth felt it was appropriate to speak up again and remind his colleagues that all this medical treatment, necessary as it was, was still hard on an old man and perhaps they should ease off a little, give him a day to collect himself. "Remember," he said, "that the first duty of a physician is 'to cause no harm.' "

"And what about a doctor's sworn responsibility to treat the disease rather than the patient?"

"But will his family sue if we stop treating him at this point? Perhaps our learned friend, Counselor Tort, can advise us on this matter."

"Not until I know whether there is enough insurance left to cover my five-hundred-dollar billable-hour fee."

"Doctor Joad, to the conference room for a plenary meeting of the Medicalization Committee. Doctor Joad . . ." The loudspeaker kept on shrieking as Ellsworth broke away from Team Happenstance and made his way down the corridor to the elevator and up to the penthouse where the Special Committee on Medicalization met plenipotentiarily to discuss the future of the healing arts. He wasn't really a doctor, but everybody around here wore a white or green coat, carried a stethoscope, and was called doctor, so he simply followed suit, and one day he had been appointed staff ethicist to the crack Medicalization Committee. He had come to its attention as a result of an article he had published in *The New England Journal of Casuistry* that attracted a lot of notice. In fact, it had won him the Casuist of the Month award, which usually went to a Jesuit, but Fr. O'Banshee's essay arguing that you need not keep bargains made with the devil had been thought to endanger the sanctity of contracts.

Having taken a course in school, Ellsworth was particularly sensitive to children's rights, and particularly the denial of digital freedom on television and on computers to children. He had tried once to argue with Pa Joad about his right to stay up late and watch a program on the living dead, and had gotten a hand to the chops for his staunch assertion of his rights. Nowadays the problem had escalated technologically, and parents were installing v-chips and blocking software that would deny access by children without the necessary code to specific areas programmed in by parents. This outrage had become particularly critical in relation to the flood of ads on TV and on computers, which some misguided parents claimed were corrupting their children, turning them into mindless materialists and consumer zombies. "The Joad Maneuver," as Ellsworth's strategy became known, showed that "culture and technology are particularly important to the young, and that therefore their rights in this area of social activity should be even better protected than those of adults, who claim absolute freedom on the World Wide Web. Surely the kids are entitled to the same rights and freedoms in the areas of their special interest that are being fought for so bravely in theirs by women, blacks, gays, the disabled, illegal aliens, convicted felons, and other oppressed groups! Television and the Internet are the mediums of the child, and argal not to be denied in any part by sinister politicians like William Bennett, Pat Buchanan, and Amos Brightgrin, who are hyping the dangers of TV and the World Wide Web for their own political purposes."

"Reasoning like this opens the door to the future," said the citation that accompanied the ten-thousand-dollar prize, also won by Ellsworth's essay, offered by the American Nuts and Screws Corporation for the best defense of the viewing rights of responsible Americans, "and ensures that our cutting-edge technology does not turn into a 'net nanny,' keeping the kids safe from knowing what the real world is all about."

The Medicalization Committee was a small group meeting here at the Little Sisters of Misery Hospital but also part of a national organization charged with considering how the discovery of new diseases could be most beneficial. Ellsworth felt honored to be in this group and contributed what he could, though the discussion was often beyond his depth.

Today there was excitement in the air, for NERDGO (the New Research and Development Group), a spinoff of the Special Committee on Medicalization, was going to make one of its rare reports. NERDGO, a theory-driven group of scientists, was funded by the National Institute for Rotary Motion (NIRM) which had been recently set up by Congress, always interested in circularity, and charged with the mission of coming up with new medical understanding in the area of rotary motion.

When Ellsworth arrived, a trifle late and breathless, NERDGO director Dr. Angelo Circulari, who had for some years quietly been doing groundbreaking work on rotary motion, was already laying out his task force's discoveries. They had, apparently, arrived at a breakthrough general principle that rotary action, despite centrifugal forces, is always more efficient than reciprocal movement. As Dr. Circulari explained, "In the world of machines almost all energy is now generated and delivered by rotary motion, the turbine rather than the walking beam, the centrifugal rather than the vacuum pump, but in the biological world many of the most critical functions continue to work on a reciprocal basis, the heartbeat of systole and diastole for a critical example. Such vital functions as sexual intercourse also still move reciprocally, the old 'in and out,' so to speak. NERDGO, however, has devised ways to 'rotarize' various human functions, as it were, and massive sums of research money have been spent in its state-of-the-art laboratories to conduct experiments for converting age-old human reciprocal activity to far more efficient rotary motion. The implications for new kinds of rotary medicine are dazzling."

Ellsworth raised his hand and got a reluctant recognition from Dr. Circulari, who was anxious to describe some of his new machinery.

"Well, do you think it is right, or even safe, to fiddle with nature in any way that seems to promise efficiency? After all, even if we no longer believe that God made the world, we can believe that over the years nature has developed satisfactory and useful ways of doing things."

The medicos began to look at Ellsworth with strong dislike, and without even a simple yes or no, Circulari moved ponderously on toward his point.

"In the matter of sexuality, for example, a human male has been placed face down on a large plastic plate, his rigid penis projecting through a hole in the center of the plate, and inserted into the vagina of a female strapped motionless to a platform below. When the upper plate carrying the male is then turned at 360 rpm, ejaculation, and hypothetical impregnation, are achieved with only a mean twenty and two-thirds turns, plus or minus a factor of three. The energy involved per ejaculation thus amounts to no more than 200 foot pounds, whereas orgasm by the usual biological means requires an average expenditure of 217.5 foot pounds."

Circulari now turned on his pencil laser and focused the beam on his graphs. "With approximately six billion people in the world, three billion of each sex, roughly two billion couples will engage in sexual congress three times a week on average. Use of the Rotary Orgasmic Device (ROD) will therefore save 17.5 × 2 billion, or 35 billion foot-pounds of energy, more or less, every other day, enough to build the Pyramid of Cheops or dig the Panama Canal once a week. Enormous amounts of useful work can thus be done every day if humans give up their traditional intercourse mode (TIM) and install in every house or, lacking that, in centralized rental locations, one of our ROD machines."

But Dr. Circulari had to confess, ruefully, that while empirically successful, the ROD experiment had failed to meet its target dates for sociological reasons. Put bluntly, "People have not taken to ROD, and it has become impossible to locate any more volunteers. Offering large amounts of money had no effect, for some reason. Even Bob Dole wasn't having any of it. No company seemed interested in manufacturing and marketing ROD." NERDGO had patented ROD, but depressed by the lack of interest, the research team had turned to other uses of rotary motion like compact, user-friendly kitchen centrifuges for extruding all the waste materials from frozen food and repackaging it as fertilizer, thus at once aiding agriculture and relieving the growing pressure on sewage treatment plants.

Despite the failure of ROD to find its niche in the world market, there was a polite round of applause for Dr. Circulari and for NERDGO. He bowed and took a seat. The chairman of the Medicalization Committee, Dr. Arnold Surdstein, thanked Circulari and NERDGO for bringing the senior committee up to speed on rotary motion and then turned to report on some of the exciting recent work of the Medicalization Committee itself.

As is well known, he began, the history of mankind is essentially a history of disease. "In Paleolithic times, almost every bodily state was thought to be perfectly natural and inevitable. Broken bones were an obvious medical condition, of course, even the biggest dummy could see that there was something abnormal when part of your leg was sticking out of your skin and you couldn't walk. But gradually the early doctors like Hippocrates and Asclepius began to realize that certain conditions that occurred frequently, if not regularly, were far from natural, were in fact sufficient departures from the healthy norm to be properly called diseases, which required treatment and care from expert medical men like themselves. Diagnosing chills and fevers as sickness was a big challenge, for example, because primitive people were either hot or cold all the time. Bringing madness into the fold of disease was one of the biggest steps forward of all time, for there were loonies all over the place who continued to insist that they were just as sane, sometimes saner, than the rest of us. Indeed, it would be fair to say that the battle to medicalize madness has to this day not been entirely won, as our esteemed honorary member, Dr. Toussaint Transférans, knows only too well."

Transférans rose, flashed his brilliant smile around the room, and imitated drumming with his hands, while chanting,

> Never suppressss the instinct-u-al,
> Anal, Oral, and Geen-ee-tal.

The group laughed appreciatively, and after Transférans resumed his seat, Surdstein went on to make his point, "Freudian psychoanalysis went a long way toward solving this problem by showing that the true medical situation is exactly the opposite of what the patient says it is. If someone says, for example, 'There is nothing wrong with me just because I like to shoot stray cats, doesn't everybody?' the analyst can now cut through the defense in a flash and show that saying you are not nuts is a sure sign that you are nuts, and that the patient is actually asking the analyst for help." There was a titter from the empiricists, who were in the majority.

"With advances like these, medical progress has pressed relentlessly onward, for human knowledge always seeks the heights, and today we live in the Biocultural Age, in which it has become possible for the first time to glimpse the possibility that *everything* people do is a sickness of some sort, requiring treatment from an expert, from a fully trained and licensed doctor of medicine. Even some of the most common things, a passive *membrum virile,* for example, an age-old problem, long thought to be sadly in the course of nature, has been discovered to be a disease with a name, 'erectile dysfunction,' an acronym,

ED, and a cure, Viagra™, available, of course, only with a doctor's prescription.

"The master insight of bioculturalism, that life *is* a disease, like so many of the great medical discoveries of the past, is difficult to date exactly, for we find the idea spotted here and there throughout history. Friedrich Nietzsche, the German philosopher, for example, in the late nineteenth century described man as 'the sick animal.' But for me, the perfect expression of bioculturalism came years earlier, when the hunchbacked, tiny English poet Alexander Pope spoke with extraordinary insight of 'this long disease, my life.' Life itself as a virus, or a genetic malfunction, what genius that poor man had to be able to see that not just his own twisted form but all human shapes and actions are forms not of health but of disease and as such demand medical intervention, analysis, remedies, and insurance administered by properly trained, qualified, and professionally licensed personnel. All, of course, without any intrusion by the government in the sacred patient-doctor relationship.

"We have, particularly in modern times, made great strides in identifying more and more human activities as diseases and creating the necessary protocols to deal with them. The schoolchild offers a prime example of just how far medicalization can go in capturing an entire stage of life. It used to be that kids went on their way and no one paid much attention to them or their problems. They were sick from time to time, but sickness was considered just a bump in a rather uneventful period of life. Young girls who did not eat very much were, for example, said to be dieting because they wanted to be fashionably thin or 'off their feed,' but now they have diseases, *Anorexia* and *Bulimia*. Very active children were once simply thought to be restless and fidgety, behavior problems, but with time patient researchers discovered that they suffered from the disease of *Hyperactivity,* and that with the administration of several doses of a new drug, Ritalin™, they could be reduced to a torpid and manageable state. Children as young as two are now on regular doses of various tranquilizers. Other children were inattentive without anyone thinking very much about it, other than remarking that they were bored with school and perhaps giving them an occasional pay-attention cuff. But now medical science has discovered that they suffer from and need special care for the disease of *Attention Deficit Disorder.* If you are slow to learn to read, it is not stupidity or a lack of diligence but another disease, diagnosed now as *Dyslexia,* in which you see letters upside down or reversed.

"And on and on. Infancy has been a particularly fruitful locus of medicalization, and now the placid baby, cooing and sucking on the bottle, is not only battling diaper rash and colic but is struggling through life's greatest battle, which Dr. Transférans has so tunefully—Ha, ha!—described, in a desperate attempt to progress from the anal to the oral to the genital stage. Layers of unhappiness are being sedimented in the infant's Id in the form of repressed primal scenes and unresolved Oedipus complexes. Denied all the things it really wants, the increasingly neurotic infant restlessly seeks out disguised, inadequate, and harmful symbolic gratifications.

"The success of medicalization, where every twinge is arthritic and rheumatoid, every cough is asthmatic," Surdstein continued, "has been demonstrated in a way that modern statistics make strikingly clear. A recent study of major diseases, chronic and traumatic, has shown that every American has at least four and five-sixteenths potentially fatal diseases, not just nuisances but life-threatening diseases. I won't go into the details, but a few examples will make the matter clear. Five out of six women will get breast cancer, 35 percent of the population will die of AIDS, 60 percent of living human beings will die of heart disease or stroke, 90 percent of minority children have asthma, two out of three people need emergency psychiatric treatment, millions are poisoned by lead paint and radon gas in their cellars, sickle-cell anemia is rife in the Afro-American population. Add them all up, as you can from items in your daily newspaper, and you will discover that 300 million Americans are not enough to, how shall I put it, 'staff all these diseases.' Every person has, in fact, as I have said, to have four and five-sixteenths fatal medical problems, plus a lot of minor ones, to bear his or her share of the medical responsibility. And meanwhile disease grows everywhere, literally grows on bushes, in fact. All small animals are now potentially *Rabid,* every bush conceals a *Lyme Disease* tick, every bird carries the new and mysterious *West Nile Virus.*

"Now this is progress, of that there is no doubt, and as people become more terrified of the many diseases they are subject to, they flood into the hospitals, emergency rooms, doctors' offices, HMOs, and clinics demanding more and better treatment. They cry out for more nurses and paramedics and measure ambulance response times in seconds. The medical costs of the country and the GDP are on a collision course."

Doctor Malpractice was on his feet immediately. "This may sound like real success, my fellow physicians, but it has a dark side. The clamor of the people for some relief from the growing costs of medical treatment of all these diseases, and the wonder drugs produced at great expense by our pharmaceutical companies to treat them, have, unfortunately, most unfortunately, brought the government more and more into medicine. By now there is almost no medical matter that the Congress has not legislated, always in a way that interferes with the physician's sacred relationship with the patient."

Doctor Synapse, the noted brain surgeon, was on his feet by now, too, shaking his fist. "This monstrous governmental interference has been particularly scandalous in the refusal of Medicare and Medicaid to pay for some of the more experimental but quality-of-life-enhancing new defensive technologies and procedures. There has been, by way of one small example, the stonewall refusal to subsidize transplants of the head and brain, or even to pay for cryogenic freezing and storage of sick patients until a cure for their diseases is discovered in the future. There have even been nasty arguments about paying for cloning women and harsh, unsympathetic words about male pregnancy."

By then the chairman was red of face and loud of voice. The subject of politicians—"God, how I hate the bastards"—always raised his blood pressure to 201/96. But he gathered himself together and recaptured the momentum to bring out the surprise he had been working toward all along. "Politics and politicians, it has become clear, have emerged as the primary impediments to the total medicalization of human life and to the sacred patient-doctor relationship that nurtures it, but relief may well be at hand. Recently the completion of the mapping of the human genome has for the first time revealed the full extent of human sickness as written in the broken DNA of various mutant genes. Doctor Karl Catheter—stand up, Dr. Catheter. [Catheter bobs up and down again, skinny, with thick glasses and long hair, a stethoscope tucked in the pocket of his white coat] Doctor Catheter and I have been privileged, working as a team, to do some of the segmenting of the genes in chromosome 21, the strange chromosome that sometime contains three chromosomes rather than the usual two, a condition that leads to idiocy in families like the infamous Jukes and Kallikaks. In the course of mapping this chromosome we discovered a gene that in normal people has something to do with community spirit and helping others but that has a virulent mutant form that correlates with political activity. It appears by no means in large sections of the population, but it is a fairly frequent mutant. Catheter and I have named it the WJC gene, after that most total of all American political animals, the former president, William Jefferson Clinton, from Arkansas. [polite applause and murmurs of admiration]

"Man is a political animal, it has often been said, but modern science has now at last found that politics is a genetic disease. It may sound strange at first, but consider for a moment the maze of laws with which the politicians have surrounded us; the taxes on everything we do, own, or purchase; our lives endangered by the foreign wars of politicians anxious to divert attention from their own bizarre behavior; yes, it is not difficult to see that politicians are all as sick as Lazarus and mad as hatters. You need only to look at their behavior: their wagging fingers in your face and their rictal smiles; their ceaseless feuding over abortion while millions starve in an overpopulated world; their wrangling over gun control while schoolchildren murder one another; their willingness to spend trillions on arms but nothing on education; those gigantic, insatiable egos, yes, what could really be more obvious than that politics is a dangerous disease?" [looks of wild surmise all around the auditorium]

"It is a wonder that we medical scientists did not tumble to it earlier. The politicians have been signaling their sickness for years, no doubt unknowingly appealing to doctors for help. Richard Nixon telling the people after Watergate, 'Your president is not a crook.' John Kennedy planning with the CIA to get the Mafia to poison Castro's beard! LBJ sitting on the can while *reasoning* with senators and judges, Clinton talking on the phone to power brokers while being fellated by a Valley Girl, Nancy Reagan consulting her astrologer and telling her husband's chief of staff to mark on his calendar the auspicious days for action by the world's most powerful man. No, it shouldn't be hard at all, once you look closely, to see that politics is sickness. The American politicians have been acting it out for years. And the illness of our pols is mild compared to the political pathologies of other less happy lands of gulag and concentration camp, where tyrants like Hitler, Stalin, and Mao slaughtered their own people, where from Beirut to Belfast, from Sri Lanka to Jerusalem, freedom fighters reduce their lands to misery in the name of some empty principle which will have been forgotten by the time the last survivors throttle one another with emaciated hands. But still, our pols are bad enough to be diagnosed as sicko by any reasonable standards, though it may not be easy to convince them that they are and give them the treatment they so desperately require. This, I think we can say, is the most important mission the medical profession has ever undertaken. The fate of the nation rests on our success."

Surdstein grinned wickedly and paused to let it all sink in. But his peers knew that the politicians were not going to admit they were sick enough to vote funds to discover an antipolitics pill or set up prekindergarten courses to suppress political instincts. Chairman Surdstein was not at all fazed by these concerns. His sharp, penetrating voice restored hope in an instant as he reminded the medicos that as the medical sciences had advanced, so the social sciences had been put on a firm scientific basis. Not only was there a science of genetics these days, there was also a science of persuading people to believe the things they needed to know for their own good. "Let anyone who doubts that behavior modification works look at advertising," he said, "for an ironclad verification. Would the hard-headed, practical captains of industry and finance pour billions of dollars into advertising if it did not produce miraculous results? How else do you get poor ghetto kids to pay hundreds of dollars for the newest kind of athletic sneakers that they hope will make them champion basketball players? How do you get dentists to buy huge, four-wheel-drive sports utility vehicles designed to cross the Yukon to drive only on superhighways?

"Scientific motivational research wrought these and many other miracles, and it can medicalize politics as well and put our diseased politicians, and our suffering country, on the road to full recovery. We are so fortunate as to have here today one of the leaders in this science of motivation engineering, C. Stanley Moosebugger, and he will now sketch out where we go from here. Moose!"

The inevitable tripod appeared with a tablet of large sheets of paper, the first with bold blue letters, "POLITICS, THE KILLER DISEASE." Moosebugger took off his blazer and snapped his red, white, and blue suspenders a couple of times, shot his cuffs, and looked confidently around, a mild upward turn of lip indicating contempt for anyone who did not understand that anything in the human head, even sex or motherhood, can be manipulated in any way desired. For him human beings were as malleable as Silly Putty, small machines with hot buttons to make them do and say whatever you want them to say and do. He ripped off the first page with a big flourish, pinned it on the wall, and revealed a new sheet inscribed with big red letters, "THE POLITICS GENE."

"We will begin," Moosebugger said in a low, firm voice, sounding much like the minister in your church of early childhood, "with Dr. Surdstein here, announcing to the press and TV [CSM rips off another sheet and reveals, "THE WJC GENE"] what his research team has discovered in the human genome, on which he has been working all his life. He will tell them that there is on chromosome 21—a pretty odd old chromosome anyway, with links to mental abnormality—a smidgin of DNA, WJC, twisted up like a piece of old, rusty barbed wire. It would be premature for the wizard to say that this deformed gene causes political activity, but it looks very promising. So promising that he is asking some of our leading pols, like old Salamander Gingrich, and Senator Naomi Whitewater, Senator O'Hoopla, too, or even maybe President of the United States Byway, to provide him, in the interests of science, with a swab of their spit—that's the right place, the mouth, all right, to find the political gene—[laughter] so he can check out whether their DNA shows this mutation he has found on the sample genetic material.

"Everyone will have a good laugh, 'those crazy scientists,' and then after a wait for the idea to germinate, we will inform some smart investigative reporter, like Buzz Mordant on the Nebbish Network, that the White House [another sheet appears, "WHITE HOUSE KNEW"] has known for years that our politicians are sick, but it has buried a top-secret report on the matter deeper than the bottom of perdition."

"Just a doggone minute, Mister Moosebugger!!" Ellsworth Joad, who had been furiously at work on his calculator trying to transform Dr. Circulari's ROD decimal statistics to thirteens, was on his feet, shouting at the speaker. "It sounds to me as if you are trying to pull the wool over the eyes of the public. This is a reputable medical institution, and Dr. Surdstein is one of the world's great scientists, long-listed for the Nobel Prize. We can't be associated with an outright swindle like you're planning to pull off. The politicians may be sick, that sounds like a good medical hypothesis, ethically sound, too, but I never heard of any government study of a political disease, and I don't think anybody else here has either." Looking around him defiantly, Ellsworth sat down, confident that he had fulfilled his duty as the resident ethicist.

Everybody else looked at the floor, but Surdstein glowered at his ethicist—there would be a payback, and soon—and Moosebugger threw back his head and laughed uproariously.

"You're right, Mr. Ethicist, and I for one am glad that you are here to remind all of us about our responsibilities to truth and honesty, things we are sometimes likely to forget, being human, but isn't that just what we are doing? Right now we don't know if there is a file or not, but there well might be, and we can find out by getting the press to use the Freedom of Information Act of 1999, or whenever it was, to demand the file."

"But what if the White House says they don't have and never had such a file?"

"They won't do that. Their database is in such a mess, they haven't been able to find anything for years, so they won't be sure if they have it or not, but they can't admit that though, and so they will stonewall it, insisting that release of the study will adversely affect national security. Then everybody will know for sure that they have it and that our suspicions were right all along. As the Sweet Swan of Avon put it, 'This is the way that we of reach and bias by indirections find directions out.'" Ellsworth sat with his mouth open but said nothing.

"Meanwhile the media will be in a frenzy demanding that the truth be made known to the nation and constructing all kinds of scenarios in which a nation governed by genetic monsters is capable of doing anything. Public indignation, strikes, student sit-ins will bring the government to a standstill. A national organization will grow up, something like 'Citizens for Open Genes' (COG) [CSM is now ripping off one sheet after another and throwing them into the exuberant gathering], a weekly magazine will be published, huge national rallies will be held, talk-show discussions, you name it; and in the end the politicians will roll over and have to admit that they are sick and need to consult the doctors about everything they do."

As Moosebugger finished, there was a stunned silence in the auditorium, then murmurs of admiration, even from Ellsworth, and a few calls, "Moosebugger for president!" Finally, wild applause and talking in small groups that lasted for half an hour before Surdstein gaveled the meeting to order.

"Well, folks, we have a plan of action, and a brilliant one. I will make my announcement about the WJC gene to the press tomorrow. After that all systems are 'go,' and it remains only to instrument the rest of the plan. For that we need some man of impeccable reputation and the highest moral standards to set in motion the machinery so brilliantly worked out by CSM, and for this critical work we are so fortunate as to have among our membership a man of sterling reputation, if somewhat limited experience, the young medical ethicist, Dr. Ellsworth Joad, whom you have already heard on this matter. The Joad family has long served the nation, traveling down many a dusty road toward progress, and now one of its members will once more render signal service to America. Godspeed, Dr. Joad!!!" The Medicalization Committee roared its agreement.

Ellsworth was still a bit confused about what he had heard, but before he left for Washington he thought he would just stop in for a moment to see how old Happenstance, once so rich and powerful as to be known as "The Capitalist Tool," was doing now that all the tubes and machines that his insurance would no longer pay for had been removed. Ellsworth had in the past read to the old man at his request out of books like the Bible and Shakespeare many times, and he thought that they might have perhaps established a little understanding for one another through the maze of catheters and wires.

Happenstance was lying in his bed in his empty room, his eyes closed, his hands folded on his breast. Ellsworth touched his forehead lightly, and the old man opened his eyes, looked straight at him for a moment, and motioned for him to sit on the bedside chair.

"Little Ellsworth, although you are part of the medical team that has tormented me for so long and emptied the remnants of my estate, built up selling the sensationally popular cheese spread, "The Better Mousetrap," and mostly lost trying to corner gold, of its last penny; and though you practice the most idiotic of all the expertises the modern world has contrived—ethicist, ha, ha—I think I can see in your face a trace of good-natured humanity still, and I would like before I die to leave in your nearly empty head a few very simple ideas, from whence they may sometime tumble out by accident. I don't know why I should. Why not just die quietly and let the world go on its mad way, as it will anyway? But vanity is never quite extinguished, and I would like to leave in at least one mind, even so simple a one as yours, the shadows of what it once was to be a human being. Pay attention now.

"I am an old man, 'four score and upwards,' as King Lear said, and I can barely remember what my mother's face looked like or hear my father's voice. My wife is dead, my children are now of an age where they have forgotten me, and I am lost in time. But this is the human condition. We live alone for a brief instant on a planet that is torn apart, heaved up, plunged down, and ripped open again by earthquake, volcano, hurricane, fire, flood, and drought. Our world and our lives are only a flicker in an infinity of time and space in which billions of suns shine with unimaginable brilliance and vast galaxies wheel majestically about one another, but only dim rays of starlight reach us eons after they first shone. And yet in this brief illumination we think that we are able to understand the vastness in which we live, and with our puny minds remake all being to our desires. In the pursuit of some half-formed illusions we torment one another and ourselves with desperate strivings. Millions are murdered in the name of some fitful dream. Our bodies are as limited as our minds, and our brains mock us with the illusion of absolute knowledge.

"And though as a result we live lives of wrenching anxiety, we have it always in our natures to live simply and happily in the world given us. Limited as we are, we fit into our world, and we need only to live in it without forever seeking to rearrange it. We are born, the world nurtures us, we find glancing fellowship and procreate. We enjoy the benefits of language and invent simple devices that feed and protect us. And then in time, we wear out, and death comes as a long-awaited visitor."

With the word "visitor" Happenstance waved his hand lightly, as in welcome to some visitant who had just silently entered the room, sank back on his pillow with a smile on his face, and left this world behind. Ellsworth was shocked, even a little frightened. He was not familiar with death, it seemed unnatural to him, but above all he wondered: *How can a man die in the despair that Happenstance has just revealed? To be willing to die just because you thought your time had come? Or just because you had worn out? No, there must be more to it than that. Of course, all his medical support had been removed when his insurance ran out, so that must have been it, without medical insurance and full medical support, life was not worth living.* With his confidence restored, Ellsworth stumbled into the corridor and on into the beckoning future where politics was waiting to be medicalized.

The press conference to announce the discovery of the politics gene—it had already been elevated from a hypothesis to a fact by dint of repetition—was to be held at the National

Institute for Rotary Motion, which stood to gain some much-needed media exposure and increased name recognition by being the site of the announcement.

Ellsworth did his best, but he was new to the game, and there were not many reporters at the news conference. Doctor Surdstein was okay, but he had brought Dr. Catheter along, and he stumbled around a good deal and wasn't able to explain the politics gene very well. Ellsworth thought maybe the good doctor didn't understand it, but that couldn't be, Catheter was a Nobel Prize recipient, just like Elie Wiesel.

That night Ellsworth, who, having no expense account, was living at one of the La Rue chain of motels, out on the Beltway, got out his laptop and sent Buzz Mordant the most consequential e-mail the investigative reporter would ever receive:

> discovery announced at nirm by drs. karl catheter, nobelwinner, and dr. arnold surdstein, long-listed for the nobel, that all politicians are sick. have genetic disease from broken gene, WJC, named after president william jefferson clinton, master politician, on chromosome 21, the crazy chromosome. government has information from earlier study, but has concealed file. chameleon at whitehouse will deny any knowledge of report. signed, a friend of truth.

Mordant got too many tips of this kind to be overwhelmed by it, but still he mentioned in his prizewinning *Bodybag News* the next day on Channel 666, just by way of a passing joke, that science had in its research on the human genome project discovered that there was an aberrant gene, the Herbert Hoover gene, that might correlate with political activity. He then forgot the matter, but it caught the attention of an editor at *The New York Smirk* who was looking for a way to harass conservative politicians, and on the next day there was a small front-page article, by the stringer Cindy Colorado, just out of Harvard, below the fold, but still on the front page, saying that NIRM was asking, in the name of science, for a saliva sample from a number of the leading politicians in Washington. The article continued on an inside page that ours is an open government and that the politicians, including President Byway, will surely be glad to supply the needed specimens so the country can get an idea of just how life-threatening the political gene is and how widely it affects Washington.

Politicians pay attention to the papers almost as carefully as they do to polls, and the article, clipped by staff and put on their bosses' desks, caused congressional stomachs to clutch up just a bit tighter. Everyone had always told them, even when they were little kids, that there was something odd about the way they were obsessed with smiling, promising, talking, and running things, so maybe it *was* genetic. *But surely it's not a disease? Perhaps it's only a trait,* they told themselves.

There were, of course, the usual showoffs. Senator Henry Proudfoot gave his saliva sample in front of the cameras while running his standard ten miles a day before dawn. Congresswoman Heavy Thinker went to a free clinic where she gave a little speech about how building the new Indian gambling casinos that Congress was now considering would pay for needed gene testing on the reservations. Senator Codswallop O'Hoopla flew up to Philadelphia and staged a full public medical exam in Independence Hall. Other senators were not so sure. The main problem was that there really were some rather unpleasant biological traits loose, mostly in the House, but some in the Senate as well, that the politicians didn't want their constituents to know about. A full-scale public disclosure of what politicians had in their genomes could be troublesome.

Across the country the media began demanding the release of the government's gene-study files under the Freedom of Information Act of 1999. Old Boris Chameleon, the turned KGB operative, over at the White House disinformation office swore that they didn't have the files, never had had. Fredson Ananias and the FBI vowed to find the scientists who had put together the report. REPORT? It now had, as Moosebugger had foreseen, a life of its own, and within days grassroots organizations like Citizens for Open Genes (COG) held a "Million Genomes Town Meeting" on the Washington Mall to force the government to release a full report on the political gene and a list of those who had it.

Only ten thousand genomes actually showed up, but media pressure began to tell, and the Democratic Party chair leaked that the political gene was to be found in 78.3 percent of Republicans, while only a handful of Democrats suffered from it. The Republicans denied it and immediately introduced a bill that would require all schoolchildren to brush their teeth in school at the start of the day, while reciting the Pledge of Allegiance. Senator Brightgrin, the new Senate leader, was furious and determined to get to the bottom of all this political gene business by setting up a special blue-ribbon committee, with himself as chair, to examine the question. Doctor Surdstein, of course, now the head of the AMA, would be included, and the famous Dr. Fallopian.

"That's good, we need a Jew."

"He's Armenian."

"Well, no one will know the difference."

"We will need a religious leader, of course, and no one is so well suited as the Right Reverend C. Beecher Retrofit, the honcho of Religion USA. Some trouble about him being multisexed, but what the hell, these days anything 'multi' is good, he had better serve as chair. Women are needed, certainly. How about Senator Whitewater, the former FLOTUS? It's true, people were still upset even after she explained that her fur coat was made from two pandas that had died of natural causes in the National Zoo, not poisoned by the CIA, as the media charged. But, hey, this is Washington, and nobody's perfect. I hear she just got a twelve-million-dollar advance for her new book, *Betrayed in the Oval Orifice,* promising to reveal the full Monica. My legislative assistant, Ellen Barratri, can be the committee counsel. The main thing is to proceed scientifically, no politics in this matter so vitally affecting the health of America. We want, in fact, for this committee to be perceived, as it will be, as an investigative arm of NIRM."

Among other members of the panel the name of Ellsworth Joad somehow appeared as a compromise between a left-wing and a right-wing ethicist. With many fanfares the committee was charged with making clear to the American people the full facts about the politics gene. No time was lost in getting started. The first step was to have the CIA surreptitiously open the tombs of some of the great politicians of the twentieth century and collect hair samples to test their DNA: Josef Stalin, "Baby Doc" Duvalier, the Ayatollah, Mao Tse-tung, Pol Pot, Richard Nixon, Bill Clinton, and others who had shown real political savvy. A few of the CIA agents were caught, but the other samples were sent to the FBI testing lab. Then the lab's computer broke down and there was a scandal about their testing methods, so months passed and still the results were not ready. While waiting for Science to speak, Hollywood stars were called in to testify before the committee on what they knew about DNA and the politics gene. Not much, it turned out. Charlton Heston thought every American had a right to all the DNA he or she wanted, and Julia Roberts thought it was okay as long as they were in love. Filling in at the tag end of a long day, the saintly Reverend Jim Casy said that DNA demonstrated that God had made the world, not some crazy scientific theory of evolution.

Publicity-wise, the committee didn't get on the matter a bit too soon. By now all the newspeople were after it. Barbara WaWa, Diane Sawyer, Cokie Roberts, and Sam Donaldson, his wig as firmly four-square as ever, all interviewed Dr. Surdstein or Dr. Karl Catheter, "Why are you so sure that the pols are humanoid mutants of some kind?" Rosie O'Donnell fumbled badly and got into a long, mumbling discussion with Dr. Circulari about left and right spin on DNA molecules in some kind of acid. By then *The New York Smirk* had run one of its famous balanced editorials saying that while this is probably all a Republican plot to elect Rudy Giuliani, who was running for the U.S. Senate once again, if his health would allow it, that in the interests of the country its politicians owe us a full airing of the condition of their DNA. The National Organization of Outraged Women found medical people who testified that the mutant political gene is to be found on the male sex "y" chromosome and is therefore not to be found in women. NOOW issued a press release asserting that a gender-free, unbiased study of the genome would establish "the barbaric way in which phallic hegemony has inscribed itself on the body of the female." By now COG, empowered by the Million Genomes Town Meeting, was publishing a magazine, with tie-ins to hotels, theme parks, airlines, car rental agencies, T-shirts, and on and on.

Politics was well on its way to being medicalized, and the politics gene had a reality of its own. But the skeptical Senator Brightgrin was grimly determined to reveal to the American public that partisan politics underlay the entire WJC gene business.

"How do you scientists know for sure whether the political gene is there or not?" The question stumped the witness, Dr. A. du Pois of the Southwestern Louisiana Bayou Genetic Laboratory, a heavyset biologist, but only for a moment. He nearly blurted out that he had read about it in the newspaper but stopped himself in time, and replied, "Well, son, the human gene pool is a mighty big place, and deep too, and there are lots and lots of things swimming around in it, hyar and thar. I wouldn't be surprised if you could find an ol' gator in it, or a cottonmouth moccasin, whump! if you dip your net in the right place. Or, you might jus' find a politics gene [with a big wink], if you get me?"

And so the discussion went on day after day, reported by big black headlines in the papers and excited voices on the evening TV news. Doctor Surdstein would say in an interview that there was also a mutation on chromosome 19 that looked mighty peculiar and might in time turn out to determine certain particular kinds of political action, like gerrymandering or poll taxes. Doctor Slops would swear there was nothing to be found on 19, but there were some mighty odd twists on 13, and that he had found these same mutations in a rare sample of the hair of Fidel Castro's beard that had been obtained years ago by the CIA and locked away in the director's safe.

"But do all American politicians' genes have these twists and turns?" the committee counsel, Ellen Barratri, asked, with some exasperation in her voice after long days of getting nowhere with similar direct questions.

"Well, who knows for sure. And who is to say who is a politician and who is not. Elected officials? Well, many of them are not really very *good* politicians. If you read the famous Dr. Pierre de Hors, professor of deconstruction at Ivy University, he would have us believe that no two things are ever really like one another, and that all classes and categories are cultural myths, and, by golly, there is something to what he says when you come right down to cases and try, for example, to establish who is and who is not a politician."

By now it was becoming clear to the Retrofit Committee that the only way of really getting to the bottom of this was an actual examination of the DNA of all practicing politicians, whoever they might be, and a comparison of their genetic makeup with a sample of the rest of the population. This was going to take a long time and cost a lot of money, and even then, as de Hors was quick to point out in his weekly column on the op-ed page of *The New York Smirk,* the results might not be entirely certain. The Republicans favored doing the survey by statistical methods, but the Democrats wanted an actual count on the grounds that the statistical approach would underrepresent the illegal aliens, the homeless, and the single mothers.

Matters came to a head when the famous Lemming College Poll reported that 87 percent of Americans thought politicians *were* sick and that the problem was certainly chronic and might very well be genetic. At this point the dam broke, and the politicians, who live and die by the polls, began slipping into their doctors' offices to be tested. Standard medical procedures did the rest. No responsible doctor was going to tell a complaining politician that he or she was not suffering from something, and deep spinal taps showed sure enough in every case that the politicians were sick people.

Said one distinguished medico on a Sunday-morning national talk show: "It is easy to tell they are sick just by looking at them when they come into the office, nervous, jittery, unable to look you in the eye, concealing their symptoms, talking incessantly about the wonderful things they are going to do for the poor, the handicapped, the migrants, the jobless, the homeless, the illiterate, and on and on. Serious? Yes. Fatal? Possibly not, for them. I think we may have caught it in time if we can persuade the pols to have a CAT scan and an MRI once a week, give up alcohol and fatty foods, reduce cholesterol intake, provide universal health insurance with prescription payment, stop smoking Castro Coronas, and avoid legislation that interferes with the sacred doctor-patient relationship."

In the end the Retrofit Committee, which by now met only occasionally to talk in a desultory fashion, was unable to come to any conclusion about whether politics was a genetic or a social disease. But a report of some kind had to be written, and Ellsworth Joad, as the committee ethicist, was thought to be the most likely person to take the fall for what was bound to be a disaster. So he was designated to write something that would satisfy the public, which was by now sick of the whole business. Ellsworth had little or no idea how to proceed, but worked away diligently; he had never written very well, often got letters backwards and upside down, and he was totally confused by all the conflicting views on genetics he had heard in recent months. Then he remembered that he was an ethicist and, rather pleased with himself, pointed out that "whatever the facts, it is important for everyone to do the right thing."

Brightgrin took one look at the draft—"Who is that idiot?"—and saw sure trouble in the making. It looked as if the medical profession might really at long last have the politicians by the balls. But then he and Speaker Culpable got together over a long weekend and, with the aid of Ellen Barratri and some of their staff, put together a few ideas that they tried out here and there. On a day when only the Right Reverend C. Beecher Retrofit and Dr. Fallopian, both of whom understood compromise, were present, they floated their version of the report of the committee.

It preambled that any threat to the politics of the country constituted a defcon one emergency requiring immediate congressional action. The WJC gene therefore required that a genetic emergency should be instantly declared, and should be followed immediately with a declaration of war on disease. All doctors, regardless of age, would be immediately drafted into the army and sent to the nearest hospital, all of which became military reservations under federal control by the same bill. Pay scales would be the same for the drafted doctors as for army officers. Universal medical insurance against damaged political genes would be generously funded. Manufacturers of drugs and other medical materials were to be declared essential defense industries, their operations and prices controlled by a new agency for the prosecution of the war on genetic disease.

President Byway made noises about not signing the law declaring war on disease, but he came around when a rider was added in conference requiring that all election funds that formerly came from the medical doctors, hospitals, and drug companies be made up by federal monies. Another rider funded a new Step 1, GS-1 ethicist, in the Surgeon-General's office, at $17,520 per year, to which General Slops immediately appointed Ellsworth Joad.

Six

Klutz-Brightgrin H.R. 1984—
The John Quincy Thud On-Line Biography of Great Americans

The new Congress was riding high. Gone were the bad old days when the nation believed that all political activities were a disease caused by some kind of mutant gene. Flushed with its recovery, Congress swept on, under the leadership of Senate Majority Leader Amos Brightgrin (D–Calif.) and the Speaker of the House, the Honorable Elmore Culpable (D–N.Y.), to a series of legislative triumphs safeguarding civil rights for all citizens. Freedom of religion was guaranteed by a statute prohibiting the display in any public place of religious symbols such as crosses, turbans, or yarmulkes that might offend members of other religions. Freedom of expression was reinforced by a constitutional amendment guaranteeing corporate and individual donors their right to give as much money anonymously to the political party or candidate of their choice as they wished. The right to bear arms made sense only after every man, woman, and child was required to be armed with at least five weapons, including a mandatory assault rifle for recreational use.

Success sometimes eluded the Congress, but only rarely. The death sentence for any person convicted of a bias crime against another person on the basis of creed, color, sex, origin, etc., was defeated by filibuster, while capital punishment for minors who smoked cigarettes was returned to the Senate Judiciary Committee by a close vote.

Education had already been thoroughly politicized over the years, with some remarkable results, but recently, at the prodding of Save the Children, children's rights had at last been established in law, and a program to see that they received free legal representation without notifying their parents had been funded after intense lobbying led by the rebarbative Max Imus. Parents had already been sent to jail in some states for slapping or spanking their offspring.

But, still, enough was not somehow sufficient. On the Hill, dissatisfaction was in the air. The pols felt somehow unfulfilled, as if some unknown goal eluded them. "The eye is not satisfied with seeing, nor the ear with hearing," as the Right Reverend Doctor C. Beecher Retrofit, the new Senate chaplain, very sensitively put it, quoting scripture, of course. One day in the members' lounge there were audible complaints that the people were always bellyaching about taxes and laws that intruded in their lives, like the recent criminal penalties for not wearing crash helmets in their homes, because they didn't understand politics. "What people don't seem to understand," Amos Brightgrin remarked, "is that in a big country like this with over 400 million people, each one of them wanting different things and ready to fight for their own interests, politics has to be deal making, if you don't want civil war. And the politicians have to be the deal makers. Some people say we're just crooks, and sometimes it may look like that, but the truth of the matter is that we are the kind of people who know you have to give something to get something. We're REALISTS, and all the rest of the people are just dreamers who think that they are in the right and that their side ought always to prevail."

"What people don't understand is that our business is not doing good but doing politics," roared the ferocious congressman Thurible Yell (R–Miss.), the sponsor of the Stars-and-Bars law, putting down his paper. "We're here to do our proper business, just like any other American business, to make our particular product, politics. And a damned good product it is, too, the best in the world. We let the people keep far more of our money than they deserve.

"The founding fathers didn't intend for us to sit up here on our butts. We are a legislature, and what's a legislature that doesn't make laws? In the old days you used to hear people say that no man's life or property was safe so long as the legislature was in session, but not anymore. People laugh at us nowadays and say openly that we are a bunch of incompetent bums who can't even impeach a president, let alone pass a bill of attainder."

"Now, now, now, no need to get all lathered up, this is an old problem." Congressman Solon Klutz (D–S.Dak.) was the oldest and savviest member of the Congress. He had served thirty terms in the House and was over the proverbial four score and ten years of age. The years had been good to him. His weight had passed the four-hundred-pound mark, but he moved around spryly, breaking a chair here and there, grunting only now and then with effort to be the first to squirm through the door of the congressional dining room when it opened, to get a bowl of the specialty of the house, the navy bean soup he loved.

"Our guv'ment has been getting more and more powerful through the years. There seems to be no limit to what a democratic guv'ment can do. Kings and dictators just mess around worrying about revolutions, but democratic legislatures have real clout. Hurricanes flatten billions of dollars' worth of property, and the Congress simply replaces the loss by saying, 'Let there be hurricane insurance to encourage rebuilding on the floodplains and the ocean beaches.' Great rivers are damned, mighty forests laid low, interstate roads 'sweep unerringly through the rifled hearts of mountains and under the torrent's bed.'"

"Hear, hear," came from all sides as the pols in the room gathered around, drawn once more by the Klutzian rhetoric, to pour themselves an afternoon bourbon and branchwater and listen to their peerless senior explain the intricacies of their special expertise, guv'ment.

"The many levels of American guv'ment," Klutz swept on like one of his unerring turnpikes, "federal, state, county, town, neighborhood, school, and sewer district, have been passing laws for several hundred years now, and, it is true, have made vast strides in establishing the basic rights of guv'ment in a democracy.

"Millions of dangerous sociopaths are now incarcerated in prison or on parole, and in time every perpetrator will be locked up as more and more laws are passed that make more things a crime. The FBI, even under the firm hand of its superbly trained new director, Boris Chameleon, may have a little trouble catching them all—agents *have* been shooting one another pretty frequently lately—but the local police forces, which as a result of federal law-and-order subsidies now number in the millions, can be counted on to run the perps down for every crime against democratic freedom, an expired inspection sticker, or not wearing a crash helmet."

Except for a few radicals who always dragged their feet, everyone sitting around murmured approval. Klutz cleared his throat, spat in his handkerchief, and looked intently at what was there. Brightgrin picked up the baton without missing a step. "How right you are, Solon, old friend; but despite our enormous and growing power some areas still escape us, parts of America, to put it another way, where guv'ment has not yet established basic democratic freedoms. We can go on passing laws until a man won't be able to piss without consulting a lawyer, but I can't help wondering if there isn't a better way to establish complete freedom while preserving intact the capitalist system, the mighty economic engine that powers the free world?"

"How about lowering taxes? The people are always complaining about how complicated the tax system is and how confiscatory the rates are. Maybe we should give them a break for once. We might begin by dropping the emergency 10 percent wartime levy on telephone bills passed in 1942, it's been running for nearly a hundred years, and maybe the emergency is over."

The speaker was the one socialist in the Congress, the sardonic Ethan Allen from the Green Mountains of Vermont, who was always putting forward some kind of radical populist idea. He was immensely unpopular with most of the legislators, who thought of him as an unclubbable crypto-communist. But Brightgrin knew just how to handle him.

"Ethan, you are a good fellow, always thinking of the people, and God knows we've been trying to lower taxes since 2001 and George W., but it's a complicated business and we don't want to endanger the prekindergarten program or dismantle Social Security. Besides, I think you may be missing the consensus here by just a bit. What we want is not to withdraw guv'ment from some parts of life but to move guv'ment into areas of national life that are not yet fully democratized, so to speak. Only, and I know I speak here for the entire Congress, when we have a completely open society will we have a truly democratic society." [quiet applause for another of the leader's little gems. "Someone should take his mots down and publish them."]

Klutz came in fully up to speed. "You know, Amos, I have been thinking along these lines myself for some time and trying out various possibilities with the members of my National Information Committee. One of the ideas that keeps floating to the top is doing something about the case of poor old Winfield Joad that has been in all the papers and on the TV lately. An outrage, an absolute outrage."

Pa Joad had gone down to Sears and Roebuck one day, determined to buy an air conditioner to make life bearable in the heat of a full-scale global-warming summer. His assisted-care living center didn't allow private air conditioners, but in the present heat wave they winked at little infringements of the rules. Pa had his Social Security check, but it was only enough for the down payment, and he had to buy the air conditioner on time, which meant filling out a lot of papers to establish his credit rating. The salesman was real helpful, and the girl in the credit office couldn't have been nicer, and in a few days the service people were there and cut a big hole in the wall, put in a new heavy-duty service line, and even provided a drain to the main sewer. Pa hadn't really intended to get involved in anything this big, but they gave him a handheld vacuum cleaner as a premium, and the air conditioner purred away and kept him so nice and cool that some of his neighbors took to gathering in his room to play checkers.

Then one day Pa had a "courtesy call" from the Sears main credit office telling him that a check of his credit rating had revealed that he had none and that therefore the full balance of the cost of the air conditioner, $456.93, was due immediately, plus interest, and credit check and installation charges of $1,105.39. "How do you propose to pay?" Pa didn't have the slightest idea how to pay. He had no savings, living from month to month on his Social Security, so he told them that they would just have to come and reclaim the air conditioner. But the deinstallation charges were even bigger than the installation charges, especially when you considered what would be involved in filling the hole in the brick wall and tearing out the service connections.

The credit manager, whose voice was getting icier as the courtesy calls went on, suggested that Pa call several numbers and get them to check and make sure that they had his credit information correct in their computers. A call that took several hours of punching "star 3" or "pound 5," or something, *God knows what,* finally produced the information that because he had not in the last seven years borrowed any money or bought anything on time, he had failed to establish a credit rating, and argal had no credit. But his file did contain a couple of garnishees. The Brightgrin National Bank, on whose mortgage he had defaulted when he lost his house in Have It All Valley, had a lien on any money other than Social Security, which was protected by law, that he might earn. The other lien was even more troubling. American Nuts and Screws had filed a class action suit against all former shareholders in Liquidity Pumps, Inc., who had failed to meet an agreement to recompense American Nuts and Screws for any losses incurred by the drop in the value of Liquidity Pumps stock owned by their retirement fund.

At this Pa blew up at the young man in the credit agency, who was really being quite sympathetic: "God almighty, man, I never owned a share of stock in my life, how can I owe these bandits a penny?"

"You may not have been aware of it, Mr. Joad, but in the year of our Lord, 2000, your retirement fund at A-One Rockets invested very heavily in Liquidity Pumps, a risky business venture, and the major stockholder of A-One Rockets, American Nuts and Screws, agreed to the transaction only if it was fully protected against any drop in the value of Liquidity Pumps. When Liquidity Pumps went belly-up, people with a stake in the pension fund, including yourself, were declared LP stockholders of record and owed American Nuts a lot of money, which they, very generously, have never pressed the A-One Rockets workers to pay. But they did get a lien on every worker with a stake in the pension fund, and to protect themselves they had a notice of the liens attached to each of their credit ratings, if they had one. I don't know what could be fairer than that."

Pa Joad had been fuming and could contain himself no longer. "Jesus H. Christ, you young pipsqueak, American Nuts robbed me and all the other workers of our retirement savings for thirty years of hard work, and now they want to get paid again for what they already stole from us? American business is being run these days like carnival confidence games."

But the stove didn't explode until the next day, which brought a call from a law firm Pa had never heard of, Squeeze & Grind, saying that it had bought his debt from Sears and threatening to have the sheriff sell him out unless he paid all he owed, plus interest and penalties for failure to pay, within ten days. Pa was stunned—*how the hell did I ever get into this mess, and how will I ever get out?*—and things weren't made any easier by the management of the assisted-care living center, which began to make nasty noises about the hole the Sears folks had left in the wall of the building, and the service lines that were causing trouble in their own systems.

Pa was nearly crazy with worry, but there was no sense in talking to Ma, who had long ago disappeared into Alzheimer's. The kids were all God knows where and weren't doing well enough to help him out. Might as well be dead.

He watched the television news with a listless eye that evening, unmoved by the day's usual disasters. So what if the police had fired forty-one slugs into a Tbongo immigrant who waved his wallet at them? *He should have my troubles.* The Popsicle Rapist had been caught after violating twenty-three nonconsenting women with a Good Humor. *Nuts, so what? kid stuff.* The 666 News Team program *Here's the Lowdown* had forced an automobile paint shop to repaint a car after its first paint job had washed off in the rain. *Stupid, why go to those gyppos in the first place, hey, wait a minute, if the 666 Team can get money out of a crook like that, maybe they can help me deal with the swindlers who have got their hooks into me. Won't hurt to call them anyway, I sure don't want another lawyer.*

"Mr. Winfield Joad? My name is Taffy Spreadeagle and I am here in response to your call asking for help from the WNIT Channel 666 Team *Here's the Lowdown.* We are aware that in this modern world many injustices take place for which there is no legal remedy. I feel this situation particularly because

I am a Native American myself, and my people, who lived in what used to be called Indian Territory but is now called Oklahoma, were driven out of their lands, guaranteed to them by solemn treaty with the United States of America, early in the twentieth century to make room for a lot of rednecked cotton farmers and oil-well drillers who raped the land."

Pa decided to practice a little taciturnity for once and meekly said only, "Yes, we old Americans have to stick together."

Taffy was as good as her word, and the evening news ended with an attack report:

> [camera closes in on old Joad, sweating heavily and very forlorn, looking at yellowed photo book]
>
> [segueing, nursing home, close-up of hole in wall where air conditioner had once been]
>
> [shift to cool, clean offices of Squeeze & Grind, where a female spokesperson, beautifully made-up and perfectly coiffed, is explaining that her firm has a spotless record in defending the rights of the poor]
>
> [cut to a close-up of a Liquidity Pumps bond stamped "worthless"]
>
> [shot of American Nuts and Screws skyscraper, all in black glass, no right angles or plumb-line perpendiculars anywhere, doors blocked by mounted police]
>
> [Taffy Spreadeagle in war paint and headdress, tom-toms in background]
>
> "Time to go on the warpath again in name of justice and decency. One more of America's tired old citizens who have worked all their lives for our country and want just to fade away in peace has been devastated by big business, big government,

> and big lawyers. Once more the paleface has come with forked tongue to rob one of the people of their Manitou-given heritage. But the braves of the Channel 666 WNIT tribe will not let it happen. You have Chief Spreadeagle's word on it." She then briefly tells the tale of old Joad's disasters.
>
> [fade out with Taffy Spreadeagle's blood-curdling war cry—wa, waa, waaa, wa—as she goes into a war dance around the studio chopping the air with her tomahawk]

Nothing in America could stand against this kind of full-court-media-press, and the next day Sears had delivered a truck load of air-conditioners to the nursing home. Squeeze & Grind had moved its offices and had retained the dean of American public relations experts, C. Stanley Moosebugger. The CEO of American Nuts had gone off on an inspection trip of factories in China, where the company was making a line of new-age "revolutionary kits," everything needed to transform teenagers into Che Guevara or Eldridge Cleaver. But this was not the end of the matter, by any means. The case had made quite a splash in Congress, which was prepared to act in some bold manner to insure that the sinister hidden forces that had destroyed Winfield Joad would no longer blight America's Fruited Plain.

The discussion on the floor was heated.

"It is good, exceedingly good, that we should speak here about the importance of protecting the privacy of all citizens. If those parasites on the roots of American life, the credit-rating agencies, had not been able to keep a file on poor old Joad and report that he wasn't creditworthy because he had never gone into debt, he would be sitting in his home being gratified, like the Lord in Eden Garden in the cool of the evening, by air circulated through that mechanical contrivance he bought from Sears and Roebuck. The privacy of Americans is being invaded and their souls sucked out by the information industry, in which the guv'ment is in the foremost rank."

It was the only member of the Anarchist Party of America in the Congress, Senator Lockin Load, armed to the teeth as usual in exercise of his second-amendment rights, voted into office by a number of primitive communities in the mountains of Idaho.

"The last census took three weeks on average to fill out and asked not only trivia but things that no one since Hitler and Stalin and Mao have asked their citizens. Race, color, creed, sex, income, parents' race, grandparents' race, arrival in this country, religion, political party, diseases, treatments, prognosis, income, taxes, you name it, everything supposed to be private matters to Americans, and it was all there in the census of the United States, which is supposed to be just for enumerating the people. But now it is in the government computers and available to any business that wants a list of suckers who are likely to buy their particular brand of snake oil."

Lockin Load was not a favorite in the Congress, any more than Ethan Allen, and he had no clout whatsoever. He was a preacher, in addition to being U.S. senator, and the spirit moved him to get up and speak out from time to time on moral issues that the other members would just as soon leave unmentioned. This was one of those occasions, and though his color had gotten dangerously high he went on:

"You Pharisees laugh and scorn the ways of the Lord, but real Amurricans, like real Christians, have always reserved a part of themselves, their inmost beings, as it were, safe from the noses of Paul Prys and Inquisitors like yourselves, who want to number and count them, like Herod of old, in order to enslave and use them. I know, God knows that I know, that you argue that it is all done in the name of efficiency and the necessary collection of information, and you tie federal monies to it so that the greedy and the grasping will line up to be shorn of their secret selves, but in truth, as your social scientists, those abominations stinking of sulfur from their infernal database, have often, and for once truly, said, 'Information is power.' And power is what you want, but let's turn our backs on this demonic temptation to know all and rule all, and stamp under the feet of righteousness all credit-rating and other personal information databases."

This was the kind of thing the majority leader was at his best dealing with, and smooth Brightgrin already had his manicured fingers on Lockin Load's shoulder, carefully avoiding the crossed ammunition belts and dangling hand grenades. "Old friend, Lockin Load, no one admires your defense of liberty more than I do, and no one guards freedom more zealously than the Democratic Party, of which I have the honor to be the majority leader in the Senate of the United States. But I think you have this particular issue by the wrong handle. A democratic society is an open society, not a society in which each individual guards a little cache of dirty secrets. We are a proud people whose pride it is to be known to all the world for what we are, and what better way to do this than to make available to all the world all information about ourselves, just as good friends do in the quiet neighborhoods of our peaceful and prosperous cities. But being openly yourself is not so easy as it once was on maple-shaded streets and drowsy town squares. Ours is a technological age, I say it without fear of reproval, and openness now requires the help of technology. What we need therefore is not to prohibit publishing information about each of us, but just the opposite, a national database, on the lines of the Internet, which the guv'ment also had the prescience to start, in which every citizen is listed and information on him or her can be input interactively. What I have in mind is not some dinky little credit-rating system but a really big database that includes every detail from birth to death about each of our citizens. Then, truly, Lockin Load, my friend, we will have a true because an open democracy, and good men like Winfield Joad can walk without fear into Sears and Roebuck because the full truth about them and their model lives will be available for all to see. What sunshine laws did long ago to open up political cabals, the new Sunshine Identity Law setting up a national personal database will do for the dark and dangerous inner recesses of private life."

"That's it," said the admiring legislators, "The ID Sunshine Law, what genius that man Brightgrin has, no wonder he was such a success in banking before coming to the Senate. If anyone has, that man has found the bottom line of guv'ment: full and open information on every citizen." Only Lockin Load shrugged his shoulders, with some effort, considering the weight that was on them, and thought, *Thank God for all the forts we have built up in the mountains. Better buy some more machine guns and ammunition.*

The chairman of the House of Representatives National Information Committee, the Honorable Solon Klutz, introduced the National ID Database Law, Klutz-Brightgrin H.R. 1984, in his committee, where, after a bit of preliminary sparring they got down to hearings. Pa Joad was called as a witness, and his son, Ellsworth, took his lunch hour from the National Ethics Office and met him in a touching scene.

"I can't figure out what an 'etheecist' is. Sounds like a good job, but I can't make out what you do besides tell the politicians that whatever they do is right."

"It's complicated, Pa. Before my time they never even thought about whether something was right or wrong, but now it always gets brought up, and sometimes I have to come over to the Hill and explain the Ten Commandments, and the Categorical Imperative, and pragmatism, and such things, so they can go ahead and do what they want to do."

"Well, I hope they will get those bloodsuckers off me. I can't put up with those duns and those lawyers much longer."

Joad was only the first of many witnesses. There was the usual parade of movie stars who unanimously regarded the database as good publicity and couldn't see why anyone would object to it.

The committee had half an idea that instead of creating an entirely new database, they could link the many existing smaller ones to create an instant composite of any given individual. Social Security numbers, there was no question, would be the keys in the entire system, since every citizen had one, but it was decided only after a bitter fight that they would not also be required on automobile license plates. When Ethan Allen sarcastically suggested that they should be tattooed on everyone's forehead at birth, there was not even a grin. This was serious business.

The genetic biologists convinced most of the members that the ability to identify the genome of an individual was so advanced that in another few years DNA would replace Social Security Numbers as the absolute key to identification. "Nature's ID tag," they called it, "rather than society's," and it was easy to see that while you could fiddle with Social Security numbers, DNA was unique and with you for life. But genome technology had been set back by congressional refusal to fund any further work on the genome after the WJC politics gene scandal. Further doubts arose when the American Genome Patent Protection Society pointed out that every gene in the human genome had been patented by one group or another and thus a license and payment would be required if they were to be included in the database.

"You mean to say that the genes in this body of mine," said an irritated Chairman Klutz, pointing to his four-hundred-plus pounds, "belong to you and not to me? How come I have a full set of my own? [sarcastically] Are they on loan from the rightful owners, the American Genome Patent Protection Society?"

"That's about right, legally, Mr. Chairman, but I don't think you need to worry, they probably won't be called in. Too big a job. [much laughter] Besides, hasn't it been assumed from the beginning that the federal government, as always, will be exempt from its own legislation?"

"Well, I should hope so. How else could we get the members to vote for all these laws?"

"But copies in a database, we're talking a different ballgame."

Representatives of the existing major personal databases appeared one after another to praise the committee's work and to assure their cooperation. Social Security, of course. Form 1040 income reports, a trifle touchy, but without the IRS, critical information would be lacking. Military service records, already on disk and a gold mine of info like insubordination that provides a warning of asocial behavior later in life. The various law enforcement agencies were already cooperating through the FBI computers and would be very pleased to expand their systems to join the national database. "The days are past," said Boris Chameleon, speaking for the FBI and the National Law Officers' Union, "when seatbelt scofflaws, delinquent traffic ticket holders, and drivers with expired inspection stickers should walk the streets with bold impunity." Medical records were more dispersed, and therefore not so easy to collect, especially since all the doctors and medical personnel were still on active military service in the war against disease. But the AMA, hoping to get the medical draft ended, was happy to testify that having everyone's medical records on open file would boost the national health. "Suppose you were hit by a truck when you were out of town and needed emergency treatment?"

"Mr. Chairman, will handicaps like blindness or communicable diseases like AIDS be recorded?"

"I think we can safely leave that to the House to debate when the bill reaches the floor, and perhaps to the courts in later years when they hammer out the details."

Birth—and death?—marriages and children, sex and parents, everything right down to the color of the eyes was already available in the vital statistics records maintained by every state.

By and large big business was for the database since it made the net worth, investments, insurance, and work and credit history of every prospective employee freely available. "Go to the computer, punch in a Social Security number, and you can tell in an instant whether you are dealing with an honest person worthy of credit or employment, or with some kind of crypto-deadbeat," said the representative of Hip and Hop, a leading personal debt analysis research center.

The media were, as usual, not helpful, however, and the headlines of the gutter press screamed provocatively, "Check up on your friends on NDB!" Who would have access to the database was, however, still up in the air. Everyone or just certain authorized officials? Would the database, be interactive? That is, could you open your own identity report and make changes in it, or could you append queries or explanations to, say, an arson investigation? Could you add to the file of others if you knew things that were not recorded?

Klutz-Brightgrin H.R. 1984 in barebones form came out of committee and began to work its way through debate on the House floor. As it did so, it began to collect the barnacles that attach themselves to any legislation passing through congressional waters, particularly a bill like this one that was sure to go all the way. Congressman Thurible Yell (R–S.C.) known as "Rebel" Yell because of his fiery devotion to the Old South, got a rider attached that required notice of whether an individual believed that the Confederate flag should be flown publicly. *The Yell amendment may cause trouble later, but it can disappear in some of the many late-night conversations and rewrites that we will now begin to hold.* Kendra McFacile (Green Party, Oreg.) wanted some language that would require that all the dams in the Snake and Columbia Rivers be torn out so the salmon could swim upstream, unimpeded, and restore their ancient fishing grounds to the Indians of the Northwest. This was okay with the other congressional members from that region so long as the lost electricity and irrigation water use were replaced from some other source to prevent any increase in costs to their constituents.

"Will this database have a place for the victims of abortion and other fetuses who have been murdered in their own mothers' wombs?" The raspy voice was that of Representative "Rebel" Yell. "You know it will not," he went on, "the workers in these human abattoirs, the abortion mills, will get their guv-'ment checks, as usual, and unborn murdered human beings will die in anonymity. Let it be understood that this bill will never pass this House unless it is amended to require recording those abortion victims' names so long as I can stand tall in the saddle and ride to the sound of the guns."

There was a highway here, a canal there, an exemption from the bill for members of labor unions, who would have their own database. A rider was added by unrecorded voice vote that provided for cutting off payments to the United Nations because there were communist countries in the General Assembly.

Outside the Beltway there remained a surprising amount of negativity. It was clearly time for a major blitz on the media, and Klutz, backed up by Speaker Culpable and other party notables, called a press conference at which he explained "Sunshine" to the country. "Sunshine" had been chosen by C. S. Moosebugger, the PR genius, as the positive-spin icon for this law. At the press conference, in the background, you could hear a country-and-western band playing, "You are my Sunshine, my only Sunshine. Please don't take my Sunshine away." Photo lights flashed, there was a forest of microphones, and the cameras ground away.

"You fellas are prob'ly going to wonder," Klutz began, "just why your guv'ment never before hit on the idea of a national database for every living American. God knows [hand over heart to indicate no irreverence] the people of this great land deserve, after so many years of toil and labor, after so much pain and sacrifice, to enjoy full recognition of all the greatness that grows so tall on our Fruited Plain. For many years the guv'ment has taken hard-earned money out of the hands of the American worker, but now at long last it is time to pay the people back, to give rather than to take. The widow and the orphan [Solon Klutz did not quickly discard older political locutions, or constituencies, or the new], the single mother and the drought-stricken farmer, the victims of breast cancer and obesity, the physically challenged and the multitude of life's victims, will all, in the Sunshine National Database, all, at last march arm in arm together, *together,* be it noted, into the promised land, into the vast utopia foreseen by the wisdom of our Founding Fathers, God bless them all, where no one, not even the most unfortunate citizen, will any longer be lost in anonymity."

Speaker Culpable, who when aroused was himself likely to fall into the time-tested political rhetoric of the stump and soapbox, understood that an overextended Klutz might well be counterproductive, and grasping the congressman tightly by the elbow, he thanked him and said that he thought that it was time to let the gentlemen and ladies of the Fourth Estate ask any questions that might have occurred to those sharp-witted guardians of our freedom.

"Will everybody be on the database, I mean everybody?"

"Yes, every living American citizen, from the infant just born to the golden-ager breathing his honorable last, and after death he and she will be transferred to the Great Americans of Yesteryear Memorial Database."

"How much information will there be on each person? Will their 1040s be made public? Their medical records? Past arrests? Credit ratings?"

"Well, the details haven't been worked out just yet, and some of them may have to be left to the courts. The House is considering sending to the Senate a stripped-down plan that will record only the basics, like Social Security numbers and vital statistics such as sex, marital status, birthmarks, etc. Then, as time passes and the national interests require one thing or another, like communicable diseases, for example, [an audible gasp] they can be added as needed."

"Mr. Speaker, can you possibly mean AIDS by 'communicable diseases'?"

Culpable saw the danger immediately and recovered gracefully. "No, no, by no means, I was actually I was thinking of West Nile Virus and other life-threatening diseases, Typhoid Mary and that sort of thing, that can be transmitted from a carrier to another unsuspecting citizen. Diseases, that is, for which isolation and quarantine have traditionally been required by strict medical standards. Only when we get all these things out in the open at last will we end the War on Disease that we are already committed to. No more will discord mar the peace of the nation, no more will the lame, the halt, and the blind—I mean the victims of handicap, of course—have to compete on a level playing field with more fortunate folks.

By now the press corps was beginning to look a bit puzzled about just what was really going on here, but they really couldn't believe it, so they continued baying down the scent. "Does that mean, Mr. Speaker, that everyone will have equal access to the National Identity Database? That it will be available on the World Wide Web to everyone who has a modem and a telephone line?"

"That's pretty much it, boys, pure Sunshine. Of course there will have to be a few restrictions, we don't want the Mafia, ha, ha, locating their victims this way, or the burglar, or any enemy of the United States finding out where Star Wars is headquartered."

"Mr. Speaker, have you and your cronies, excuse me, colleagues, considered what is going to happen when everyone's secrets are available online? This society, or any society, works only so long as people know only a limited amount, and that carefully censored, about one another."

"Well, Buzz [this was Buzz Mordant, the famous investigative reporter for the Nebbish Network], I think you boys in the media have a jaundiced view of this sort of thing. You spend your lives uncovering all the things that the sickos in our society try to hide, so you think that secrecy is what everyone wants. But most real Americans can hardly wait to tell you anything you want to know about themselves. Just look at the talk shows on TV, my God, those people will *say* anything, but we also have scientific polls showing conclusively that secrecy is the last thing Americans really want. Open up all the closets, put all the skeletons on view, and the Fruited Plain will bloom as never before."

"But just suppose that some political biggie, like yourself, just suppose, had been arrested as a juvenile for indecent behavior, flashing in the park, say; would knowing that help his constituents to judge him correctly?"

"Now, Buzz, ha, ha, you are just trying to get at me, that old charge was nolled, and besides, I'm sure you know that federal officials are exempt from all guv'ment legislation, as they are from Social Security."

Mordant shook his head in disbelief, but sat down and let another reporter have the floor.

"How much is this going to cost, and where will the money come from? The guv'ment, damn it, I mean *the government,* is going to set up the biggest computerized information agency the world has ever seen, but you haven't got any bucks to spend. The economy has collapsed again. The army is on strike for higher pay, the Capitol is falling down from disrepair, and we have just borrowed a hundred billion from the International Monetary Fund to keep from closing down the guv'ment, *government,* until the budget, which is two years overdue, is passed, where's the beef?"

"That's one of the beauties of Sunshine, it will pay for itself."

"Not the Social Security Trust Fund again?"

"No, no, we all know now that that was a mirage, but what could be more reasonable than to charge each individual for the number of bytes (counting spaces) his or her entry uses in the database? After all, to have this kind of information about yourself, and your good neighbors, made public is worth quite a lot of money to everyone involved. Or, an annual surcharge levied directly on your income tax might handle the costs very nicely. Now, boys and girls, excuse me, women, I know this will all sound pretty new and strange to you, but we have handouts available here, and the staff will stick around and provide you with explanations of any of the details you may find troublesome. Thanks for your help in all this, it is always a pleasure to meet and talk with the media. We know we can always count on you to inform the people exactly what is going on."

Some trouble came from the White House, where the lame-duck President Byway, protecting his party's traditional dependence on the votes of various marginal groups, threatened a veto unless the NDB identified all those who were living below the poverty level. "What about the victims deprived of computer skills, how could they take advantage of the database to find out the number of convictions their landlord had had for housing code violations? Will welfare records be available in the database, because if they are, given the American prejudice against the poor, the broad safety net that has been put in place under American society to assure the dignity of all persons since the days of the New Deal and the Great Society will be threatened." The White House release went on, "If the president is going to sign the Sunshine bill, the law will have to forget welfare information. In this same regard, immigration records should also be treated as sensitive, particularly of illegal aliens." The committee rewrote the bill to exclude information about welfare, immigration status, and food stamps.

But the concerns of the media and of the White House were as nothing to the fury that was rising in the streets. The pols were astounded by the vehemence with which various groups expressed themselves. Huge numbers poured into the capital and blocked traffic for miles around the Mall. Ma Joad came on a busload of protestors all the way from California and, helped by Ellsworth, carried a big sign, "WHEN DO WE WANT IT? NEVER," and seemed rejuvenated by the experience. Pa shuffled along somewhere in the crowds as well, though he and Ma never met, trying with difficulty to hold up a tattered banner, "HOW DO YOU SPELL RAPE, CREDIT-CARD USURY."

But the real pressure came, of course, from the big single-issue, tax-exempt, activist groups like the Man-Boy Love Sodality, the Lesbo-American Relief Brigade, the Victims of the American Injustice System, the Compassionate Society of American Debtors, and on and on. Everybody in America, it seemed, had a secret that they would die to protect and an organization to help them conceal it. Their signs told their anger. "WE HAVE PAID OUR DEBT TO SOCIETY, DON'T CRUCIFY US ON THE NDB." "TWO SEXES? DON'T BE SILLY."

Culpable and Klutz, having discovered the hard way that it was a waste of time to try to control the flood of changes and amendments that now attached themselves to the bill in response to the protests and the flood of mail, decided to leave all the thorny issues to time, the courts, and the Senate, banking on those more deliberate bodies to put it in shape. If Brightgrin failed, or made an even bigger mess out of it, then things could always be straightened out in late-night meetings of the conference committee. So with some quick adjustments, Klutz-Brightgrin H.R. 1984 came out of the House of Representatives providing for the establishment of a national personal identity database, "Sunshine," constructed around Social Security numbers "and any other pertinent information." There were, however, as always, a few details. The bill specified that NDB provide for listing nine different sexual preferences, include names given to unborn embryos, prohibit records of former conviction and imprisonment, make the statement of religion a felony, mandate information on whether an individual had ever been a socialist or communist, and list whether he or she was against the display of the Confederate battle flag.

It also contained barrels of pork for tearing down some dams and building others, new roads, canals, and a tunnel under the Rocky Mountains to provide easy access from the rest of the nation to the West Coast. Tucked away at the foot of a long paragraph of small type was a special provision compensating American Nuts and Screws for losses incurred in experimenting with refinancing its employees' pension fund. No one knew where the last item came from, but it was on the marked-up bill that passed the House 390 to 13.

While the House had been debating, the pundits and the investigative reporters had been busy. Talking Heads from the many institutes for public policy had explained the effects of Sunshine endlessly, and experts on demography, on entitlements, on the tax basis, and on ethics had quarreled sharply about the effects on the United States of all private information on individuals becoming public. Senator Lemuel Bulbous (R–N.C.) announced on a talk show that he had already moved a cot into his office and was preparing a filibuster if the bill contained one penny for art.

In the Senate, hearings on the bill were given to the Subcommittee on Political Manipulation and Resources. Brightgrin had begun taking Viagra™ to deal with his negative tumescence and was involved with its chair, the gorgeous senator recently appointed from Georgia, Pomona Hardstones, and he thought that their pillow talk would keep him abreast of developments. Unfortunately they were both so busy in the months to come that they never had the time to take off their pants. Pillow talk was apparently a luxury reserved for the unemployed, but they had nothing to talk about.

The committee members listened for months to special interests testifying on what should be included and excluded from the database. The ill and the handicapped wanted their medical records suppressed because prospective employers would never hire them and insurance companies would never insure them. It turned out that in certain states, child molestation in New Jersey, for example—"Why is it always New Jersey?"—the Supreme Court had already declared unconstitutional the notification of the community that a sexual predator was living among them. Hard Homo, the militant homoerotic pressure group, wanted information about marriage eliminated altogether, since its members were unjustly denied it, but they wanted inclusion of all civil unions. The Board of Analytical Psychiatrists pointed out that they had been trying unsuccessfully for many years to extract the suppressed secrets that were crippling their patients, whose bosses would fire every one of them if they learned that they had mental problems. The Association of Major Universities testified that they could not comply in providing transcripts because they had long ago ceased to record grades. Testimony was even heard from a crazy professor of deconstruction, Pierre de Hors, who claimed that the whole database was based on an illusion. There were no such things as persons, he said, only random agglutinations of biographical-type events.

Bankrupts and folks who had maxed out their credit cards got hysterical in trying to describe what would happen to them if everyone knew their financial history. There were deserters and peace activists to be heard from, TV executives and small farmers, teachers and students, producers and consumers, young and old, the atheistical and the godly.

America, it suddenly appeared, was a land of secrets which felt it could function only so long as those secrets remained unpublished. But one group's secrets were another group's necessary public information. As the testimony cascaded over the committee, so did the rancor of the citizens who wanted their secrets protected but wanted to know the secrets of others. In their anger the people broke up into a multitude of small and antagonistic groups. Factionalism had always been the de facto reality of democratic life, but now all pretenses of amity were abandoned and the streets were filled with huge crowds bearing hate placards—EUTHANASIA NOW or ALIENS WILL EAT FATTIES FIRST—exhorted to violence by loud bullhorns, challenged by the TV cameras and provocative reporters roving through the crowds asking inflammatory questions. "Do you intend to storm the Capitol today, or will you wait until tomorrow?" "Have you heard that the committee is listening to the golden-agers again?" "The disabled have just given a billion dollars in soft money to the Democratic Re-election Committee." Or, "Fair Play for Debtors has just gotten a 100 percent tax break on bankruptcy costs. What have you gotten?" Militant factions trained with the arms they had been forced to buy to realize their second-amendment rights, and were readying themselves to fight in the streets if they were not given what they considered fair treatment. Never had the people spoken more loudly or angrily or frequently or confusingly to their elected representatives.

The mobs fortunately did not get inside the Capitol building, where in the various offices, committee rooms, cloakrooms, and bathrooms the bill was licked into shape by a series of deals. Lobbyists for Microsoft and America Online wanted special breaks for computer users, who were the future of the country. Big tobacco was determined to get a tax subsidy for lost sales to minors. The pressure was so great that members were no longer speaking to one another, not even trading insults, so determined was each to load his/her favorite pork on destiny's wagon. The leaders were at their wits' end—not a far stretch—on how to deal with the Pandora's box they had opened.

The showdown came when a special group of House and Senate conferees met late in the evening at the end of the winter session.

"Byway has chickened out, he says he won't sign it, and neither will President-elect Thud."

"That's but a trifle here, we have the votes to override a veto. It's the people I'm worried about, the mood on the streets is ugly."

"Let's hear the FBI on this. Director Chameleon?"

"We have infiltrated every group of radical antidatabase crazies in the country, and our undercover agents report without exception that the whole nation is ready to blow if its secrets are made available on-line on a national identity database. I really don't believe that the silent majority of the American people objects to this realization of true openness, it is only the agitators and the commies and the Jews that are as usual stirring things up. We are all for it over at the bureau because it will make law enforcement so much more efficient that I think I can safely say that once Sunshine is up and running we will have 10 percent of the nation locked up in no time."

"Maybe that's what's exciting them."

Klutz had his heart wrapped up in this one. "I hope at the end of my sixty years of service to this great nation to leave a memorial to my work, a memorial that will make known to everyone all that is best about the American people. What more fitting monument to a life of service than Sunshine?"

It was Broadgrin's call, and he knew it.

"It is a great idea, but we can't do it head on. Too much rides on it. For the present at least, ours is, I am sorry to say, going to remain a nation of dirty little secrets. 'Consent' is the key term, my staff tells me. 'Consent'! Anything that we put in the database must be something that the people want put into it or don't care whether it is included or not. So we start with a voluntary questionnaire requiring all citizens to list their Social Security number, that's the key item, and then after that ask them to fill in a number of harmless categories like "major achievements," "life goals," "philosophy of life," "favorite TV shows," and so on. Maybe we can help out Crankshaft, who is being pressured by the automakers, by asking what people want in a car, and do the same for laxatives, toothpastes, breakfast cereals, and a few other throwaways. Maybe ask for a nice picture with boyfriend or grandchildren and a dog. We can call it an upgraded census. But along that line, I think we had better give the database an attractive new name, something like the national biography of an open America, or maybe still better [thinking quickly], THE JOHN QUINCY THUD ON-LINE BIOGRAPHY OF GREAT AMERICANS. That will for sure take care of any veto."

Mouths were hanging open with admiration all around the table. Their shining chief had done it again, and just when disaster seemed imminent. Klutz was enchanted, but he was also troubled.

"What good would a lot of unreadable junk like that do? We want really to know who votes for what and why they do it, and we will never find that out from descriptions of my summer vacation."

"Oh ye of little faith," the Senate leader sighed, "we can enter all this stuff in the database, it will take care of the unemployment problem permanently, but the Social Security number will allow us to link the individual to all the other useful preexisting databases, like criminal justice, credit rating, income tax, educational records, party affiliation, hospital records, charitable giving, etc., etc. No need to make a big thing out of it, 'Just Do It,' as the ad says. If, later on, the national interest requires other data, like communicable diseases, unlisted assets, or draft status, new legislation can handle the matter discreetly, one category at a time.

"All the amendments and riders will of course stand, no one knows or cares much about any of them except the sponsors and their friends, but we need their votes. It is particularly crucial, however, that the tunnel under the Rocky Mountains go forward on schedule. Without it the nation faces a transportation crisis in the near future."

All went as planned, and just before recessing the Congress turned its attention to a number of other issues that needed attention. There was always the budget, now three years overdue, but that was old stuff, and there were much more interesting regulations in prospect. The new "Tell and Tell and Tell" policy in the armed forces was an easy winner, as were the bills criminalizing all forms of prejudice, and the raising of the age of consensual sex to twenty-eight, or the fourth climacteric, to control illicit sex. There was a proposal to amalgamate all religions by law, but it had little support, while a constitutional amendment to prohibit all same-sex marriages sailed through. The "Ever-Normal Art Supply Act," Crankshaft-Curettage S. 1526, had bipartisan support, but the move to make the Lizzie Borden Brigade, sometimes known as "Forty Whacks Women," a part of the regular army failed by a narrow margin.

Completed questionnaires flooded in, pictures of grandchildren and puppy dogs filled caves in Nevada designed for atomic waste. Folks could hardly wait to achieve eternal fame by being registered in THE JOHN QUINCY THUD ON-LINE BIOGRAPHY OF GREAT AMERICANS. There were the usual whiners, of course, but Chameleon and the FBI seemed to have them in hand, and not many complaints were heard about even the high fees charged for the biographical entries.

The political season was enlivened socially by the divorce of Senator Brightgrin from his wife of thirty-nine years, La Belle Brightgrin, and his immediate remarriage in the White House to Senator Pomona Hardstones, given away by the newly inaugurated President Thud. The question of the propriety of two senators marrying one another was sent to the Surgeon-General's Office of Ethical Behavior, where it landed on the desk of the assistant ethicist Ellsworth Joad, who found that it violated no law of God, man, or nature.

Seven

Poshpenny v. Lone Tree State

Above, riding the currents of warm air, the vultures circled, scenting flesh far below. At the next level down, the private jets followed one another in a holding pattern waiting to land at Idi Amin International Airport. The planes contained the cream of the American bar, the personal injury lawyers, going to the lands of the Tongos and the Bongos, who had for some time been killing one another for what they considered the clear and sufficient reason that one group was Tongos and the other Bongos. Since the Tongos and the Bongos had very shallow pockets, in fact they had no pockets, their suffering had not earlier attracted the attention of American tort lawyers, who had been busy righting the outrages perpetrated on Americans victimized by the asbestos and tobacco companies, gun makers, hospitals, manufacturers of artificial breasts, and other malefactors. But now, recent ethnographic discoveries at Lone Tree State University had put matters in Tbongo in an entirely different light.

The anthropologist "Jungle Jim" Potsherd assisted as always by his native informant Jack Robinson, had published an article in his trade journal, *American Ethnophobe,* proving that there were no genetic or even many cultural differences between Tongo and Bongo. One tribe historically and linguistically, the Tbongo had been craftily split in two early in the twentieth century when the dominant colonial power was following the old adage "Divide and Rule." Somewhat later, when the imperialist states had withdrawn, and the country had been taken over by Big Banana Ltd., the company found it useful to reinforce the politically manufactured distinction between the Tongos and the Bongos to make them more economically efficient. The Tongos, the less numerous group, became managers, while the Bongos had become laborers.

Now, it had suddenly become obvious to the American bar that Big Banana Ltd., which had very deep pockets indeed, was legally responsible for having launched, in the vile search for profits, a murderous genocide. The race was now on to sign up as clients in a class-action suit against Big Banana any Tongos or Bongos—that is to say, everybody—who had suffered loss in the recent wars.

The first Learjet to land was the "Illusion Team," still rich and famous for using an ill-fitting glove, which was now their logo and painted on their plane, to get a not-guilty verdict for their client in a sensational murder trial. Hard behind them came the "King of Torts," with a few rust spots here and there on his plane, which blew out a tire on one of the pieces of ragged iron lying on the tarmac. Then, slipping neatly to the left and leveling out perfectly to avoid the junk on the runway, came the plane with the big white horse, Pegasus, Parnassus, Culpable, & Joad, which firm, languishing since "high art" disappeared into the democratic abyss of "total art," was looking for new sources of revenue. First out of the plane was Calista Joad-Parnassus, showing the savages the latest in civilized dress: stiletto heels and miniskirt, high-piled blond hair, pinstripe suit, and thin black crocodile-skin briefcase. Her nails were blood-red and three inches long, her mouth was crimson, and golden jewelry jangled from every vantage point.

At the entry to the corrugated iron shack that served as a terminal, just below the "Mazo Lite" sign and the broken neon letters that once had spelled out "Idi Amin, Lion of the Jungle," stood two armored cars, and in front of them several formally dressed gentlemen sitting under a banner that said "Central Africa Bar Association." A welcoming steel band was chanting an ancient native tune,

Bongo, Tongo, Bongo,
I don't want to leave Tbongo, no no, no no.

The Central African barristers explained very politely to Calista, whose legs they admired immensely, and to the King of Torts, and to the Illusion Team, that anyone who hoped to practice law in their country had to join the Central Africa Bar Association.

"And just how do we do that, Brother? Give us the forms."

"Unfortunately, we are out of forms at present, but that is of no matter since CABA is almost full at the moment. There is, in point of fact, only one opening, which will soon be filled by Counselor Joeaad, the blond lady with the long legs and deliciously small breasts—the mammary style of our own dear women has begun to weigh a bit heavily. If you, dear lady, will just get into the waiting taxi, the driver will take you at once to the Jungle Hideaway Resort, where the local chapter of the bar frequently meets. There you will be given a pleasant room, and an application for bar membership, and can join in the lively ceremony that will celebrate your election."

After Calista left, holding up her hands to signal the rest of her team that there was nothing else she could do just now, the other lawyers pressed closely around the representatives of the bar association.

"How long will it be necessary to wait for an opening?"

"Who can say? The great god Torque is good, and all the members of the bar are in tip-top health at the moment. But if you each leave five thousand U.S. dollars as a sign of intent we will notify you when an opening occurs and send you the necessary forms to be filled out in triplicate."

"Well, I guess we came a long way for nothing, so we might as well get back on the planes and go home."

"Yes, and if you go around the corner of the terminal you will find a desk where you can pay your five-thousand-dollar arrival and departure fees, per head."

"Outrage, robbery, We won't pay."

"Very well," the machine guns in the armored cars cocked noisily, "but you will find that without payment your planes will be impounded for landing without clearance."

In the end, with the help of a seedy Somerset-Maugham kind of missionary for Religion USA, who was hanging around asking anxiously about a long-delayed replacement, the lawyers paid with credit cards, gassed up, took off, and flew back across the ocean to where there were still plenty of pickings. Nearly everyone was by now suing someone or being sued by someone, and the courts were so jammed that it took many years for a case to come to trial. And years after that for the trial to be concluded because of long delays in picking the jurors, presenting and questioning evidence, calling and challenging witnesses, sequestering the jury, and waiting while their interminable bickerings and requests for rehearing evidence built toward a hung jury and a mistrial. Even if there was eventually a verdict, the judgment was immediately appealed to the next level of courts, and on and on until a judge was found who ruled in favor of the appeal. And then the entire process began all over again.

In this legal climate, Calista's brother, young Thompson Joad, had expected to flourish when he had graduated 426th in a class of nearly six hundred from Lone Tree State's noted law school, Non Sequitur Hall. Thompson had dreamed of a clerkship with a famous judge, and then of a big firm with leather furniture and six-figure starting salaries, but things had not turned out exactly as he expected, and instead he found himself working for Squeeze & Grind. Thompson was paid, piecework, without benefits, to write letters on his home computer to people whose bad debts the firm had bought at a heavy discount, threatening them with immediate legal action. He didn't have to shout at them over the phone or go around to their houses and threaten to break their legs with an aluminum baseball bat. That was the work, later on in the collection process, of a squad of heavies without legal training. But still, the job was depressing.

Templates for every situation were on the computer, but Thompson had to assemble the pieces into something that would scare the pants off a specific debtor. He was not very good at it, but after checking all his numbers—*those damned thirteens will haunt me forever*—on a decimal calculator, he tried his best to sound ferocious:

> Dear Crook,
>
> Ours is a country of laws, and one of the laws is that you have to pay your honest debts. You are now $3,874.86 in arrears in your payments on your green vinyl Lay-Z-Boy Lounger Chair, your Sleeptite mattress, and your Louis XIVth dining room suite. These goods have now been repossessed, but they were damaged and worthless, and you therefore still owe the entire balance remaining on the original purchase price, plus accumulated, compounded interest and penalties for late payment. While you delay paying, the penalty and interest charges on the balance due grow at 26 percent per month.
>
> We had thought we were dealing with an honest man, but now that we know that you really are a deadbeat, we intend to make sure that you pay

> what you rightly owe. You have until next Monday, July 17, to pay your debt in full, including any interest and penalties, or we will take the necessary action. This will involve the sheriff arresting you and taking any chattels you may still be seized of for sale at the next public auction, the proceeds to go to pay your honest debts.
>
> Let us hear from you at once that you want to prove that you are an honest and decent citizen of this great country of laws by sending us a check for $3,874.86 plus interest and penalties, for a total of $5,617.23.
>
> Thompson Joad, LL.D.
> Debt Recovery Officer
> Squeeze & Grind

Thompson was a softy, though, all the Joads were, coming as they did from the heart of the people, and knowing what hard times were. He was determined to find another way of making a living than harassing *some poor guy who worked for minimum wages and had gotten drunk and maxed out his credit card to buy a mattress, hoping to get rid of his backache, and an extruded simulated walnut dining suite, trying to keep his wife happy. Then his eye had lighted on the green vinyl Lay-Z-Boy Lounger, and he imagined long and easy evenings with a can of cold beer in his hand, his feet up, the recliner back, watching a football or baseball game on TV.*

Thompson wrote his sister Calista, who was a partner in a big New York law firm, and she got him a job in the California branch PPC&J was just opening. But then Calista disappeared in darkest Africa, and the firm had only given him a desk in the office with the receptionist-telephone operator, where he was instructed to deal with any of the walk-in cases off the street, which were always more of a nuisance than anything else. Thompson worried for a while about his sister, but she had always been a cat for landing on her feet, and so he moved happily into PP&C. "Joad" had already been scraped off the door and new stationery ordered. He hung his degree over his desk. On the wall beside it he also hung the framed wisdom old Professor Disputandum had given his jurisprudence class at Non Sequitur Hall:

> The law is what distinguishes civilization from barbarism, justice from brute strength. At the best its operations are a reasonable number of clear statutes, a few wise and impartial judges, competent juries of peers, reasonable administration, and a limited number of lawyers. Happy is the land with these benefits, vile and miserable the land where matters are otherwise.

Just how "otherwise" America was, Thompson learned when his first client walked in the door.

"Mr. Joad, [hand extended] my name is Peter Poshpenny, I'm an educated man, but I've never been able to earn up to my potential because those miserable bastards screwed me out of what is rightfully mine."

He was a slight youth, well dressed on the casual side, with a tendency to stutter, who sat, with some visible nervousness, in the wooden chair to which Thompson waved him, sighed, stroked his thin mustache, and began his story. "I was always a very forward little boy, an Eagle Scout—in a non-discriminating pack, of course—oodles of merit badges, wonderful what you can do rubbing two sticks together—good in school, and everyone said that I was sure to get ahead in the world. Dad didn't take to me very much, or to Mom either, and he dropped out somewhere along the way, was it in Sandusky? Or East Lansing? I can't remember. Well, anyway, I went to high school in Dubuque and graduated at the top of the class, and then won a national scholarship to Harvard University in

Cambridge, Massachusetts. I burned up the track at Harvard, winning all the awards, and was the pride of the Department of Somatic Studies. 'The Desiring Body in New England Fiction' was the title of my senior thesis, in which I explored the plethora of strategies used in the work of early American writers like Cotton Mather and Anne Bradstreet to realize the fullness of Eros. My purpose was to incite my readers to enter a world in which desire had at long last been dislodged from regulatory regimes, and, by God, I succeeded."

"Yes, I am sure you did. I think I may even have seen you quoted on the Internet, www dot corporeality dot edu. Wasn't there something about 'aggressivity in women promising equal opportunity for desiring bodies deeply gendered'?"

"That's it, that's it, but what a genius you must be to pick up and remember my little mot."

"Well, there was something memorable about those words, hard to forget. But this seems a success story, what grievance can you possibly have?"

"I'm coming to that, councilor, I am coming to that." Poshpenny paused and swallowed hard, then took out an inhaler and fired several bursts of spray into his nostrils.

"When I graduated from Harvard I was told that if I wanted to get a Ph.D. in somatic studies, I had to go to Lone Tree State University. Harvard was not advanced enough as yet to offer a doctorate in the subject. But the body department at Lone Tree was, however, on the cutting edge. There was, of course, no problem with admission, and I sailed, simply sailed, through the courses, until at the end of the second year I took my general exam, and they failed me. FAILED me. Do you understand? How with my abilities could I have possibly FAILED anything?"

"Well, lots of people fail exams all the time, you just go back and take them over again, and eventually you pass."

"I did take it over again, and they FAILED ME AGAIN. It was at that point that I realized that there was something badly wrong, very badly wrong, and that it was time for me to see a lawyer, as all my friends advised me, and here I am."

"I can see that you have a case, Mr. Poshpenny, and PP&C is always ready to serve personal-injury-wise in filing class-action suits for you and the many other victims of judgmental bias. But let us consider on what grounds shall we proceed? Was there someone on your exam committee who disliked you, or, better still, was there someone who was prejudiced against you, [hopefully] was this perhaps a hate crime?"

"What is there to be biased against in little me?" [a simper]

Thompson tried to think of some other devastating wrongs that might have been committed against young Poshpenny. "Were you perhaps the victim of some incapacitating disease, like dyslexia or attention deficit disorder, that caused you to need more time than they gave you to finish the exam, or were you later diagnosed as having an incapacitating disease that you did not know of at the time of the exam but that would have caused your brain to malfunction?"

"No, no, no, no, you don't see the point. You keep thinking in terms of *me*. But I am not the agent, I am the victim. If I failed the exam it was because I was poorly prepared for it. And who had the responsibility of preparing me? The Department of Somatic Studies at Lone Tree State University, to which I, or more accurately, my government Title Z scholarship, had paid many thousands of dollars to prepare me to pass the general exam."

All the lights went on at once inside Thompson's head. *How many people fail exams every year? Don't know, but surely millions. Why do they fail? They don't fail, the teachers and the schools, maybe even their parents, don't prepare them adequately for the exams. Who pays the teachers and runs the schools that do such a miserable job? John Q. Taxpayer is the ultimately responsible party, and he has very deep pockets, the deepest. A class action suit could represent every misfit and every dummy in the country, any-*

one who ever failed an exam, the client of clients. I think I will be moving out of Long Beach to Bel Air very soon.

"Well, Mr. Poshpenny, you have a case, failurewise, no doubt of that. It is an outrage that a responsible university should have taken your money to prepare you for an exam and then failed you. You will need to provide me with admission documents, catalogs, letters of recommendation, transcript, and other material relating to your course of study, but I don't think that any court in the land will fail to see the blinding injustice of your case. If an institution of higher education takes your money to teach you something and then doesn't teach it to you, it is patently they who are culpable, not you."

After Peter Poshpenny left with a promise to return with the documents, Thompson could hardly wait to get to see the senior man in the office, Emmit Rattenkrieg, and he pestered his secretary until he finally got five minutes to tell him what he had found, on his first day at work.

"The idea sounds maybe a little too up-to-date, even postmodern, but when you stop to think about it, it's as old as education? Don't we hear every day that the teachers and the taxpayers of this great country are at fault for the miserable showing in the reading and math tests of our primary and secondary school students. It is a terrible thing to say, but maybe we shouldn't be surprised that a few students every year take the law into their own hands out of frustration and shoot a few teachers, as well as other students who blunder into their line of fire? Everyone believes, to come to the bottom line, and talks as if the teachers and their institutions failed the students, not the other way around. Only in the law is failure the responsibility of the failee, and we can change that, yes sir, change it once and for all."

Pegasus, Parnassus, & Culpable recognized real legal moxie when they saw it, and they at once offered Thompson an associateship in the California office and a role on the team that would try the Poshpenny case, which boomed in remarkable ways from the start. Poshpenny himself soon had an agent, and a flood of book offers, advertisements, movie rights, and tie-ins with hotels, cruise lines, gasoline companies, and Wal-Mart. America instantly took to its heart this young man, Peter Poshpenny, who had at last asserted what the people had always known: they weren't stupid, just badly educated. And now someone was going to tell those smart alecks who had failed them that it was the failers' fault, not the failees', and that their sneers were going to cost them big bucks. Everyone wanted in on the act, for everyone had failed something at one time or another.

The case was a natural that generated endless other legal issues. "If you failed a doctor's examination could you sue him for his failure to keep you healthy?" Reluctantly, it was decided that the doctor was not legally, though morally he might well be, responsible for your illness. "Maybe, but possibly we ought to wait a bit before going to a full-court press and claiming that anything unwanted that happened to a victim is the legal fault of the agent."

There was no trouble getting *Poshpenny v. Lone Tree State University* on the court docket as a class-action suit, even though other petitioners had waited for years to find a place. This case involved the whole country and raised issues that went to the very heart of democracy. Since democracy can only work with an intelligent electorate, the intelligence of the people might well be said to be THE democratic question. And *Poshpenny* focused that question in the hard, clear light of a court of law. "Are people naturally stupid, or is innate intelligence perverted by malevolent forces?"

Pressure to preside over the case was enormous. Judge Dextrous was a leading contender, but he had been turning too many wife beaters loose lately and taking home some of the shady ladies who appeared before him. Judge Momus? No one could have been more suited for this heavy responsibility. As everyone said, "if there is anybody in this country who understands stupidity, it surely is Momus." But the long shadow of *Retrofit v. Puss* would follow Momus to his grave. So it had to be Nolo, broad of face and narrow of mind. A pillar of the law for many years, he could sleep through any trial, no matter what its subject—he had once slept through a detailed description of the putative rape of Ginger Clitterhouse by her lover, a thuggish deacon in Cathedral USA—and still managed to look gravely concerned. He had forgotten his law years ago but had replaced it with a set of standard gestures for dealing with all occasions up to and including capital punishment.

Lone Tree State was confident that Poshpenny's own ignorance had defeated him in his effort to get a higher degree. But, still nervous about the tendency of modern juries to sympathize with soi-disant victims and recommend huge punitive damages, Lone Tree State had hired the best defense counsel available. "Only the best and the brightest lawyers will do for this sensitive case," the vice-chancellor told the university counsel, Rex Firewall. "And that means, no matter what the cost, despite our annual budget deficit, we have to go for the very best people with a real respect for and understanding of the law, who have been around for a long time and represent the responsible portion of society. We owe it to higher education and to the country as well as to Lone Tree State. If the idea gets loose that failure in an exam is the fault of the examiners, not the examinee, it will shake the nation to its very foundations."

"That's dead right, J.R.," Firewall replied, "and we can count on, as we have many times before, the firm of Retrograde, Replevin, & Persiflage. Old Judge Retrograde won't hire anyone except the very best legal talent. His partners are all over six feet tall, hatchet of face and jut of jaw, club of tie and glen of plaid. The firm's chief trial lawyer is a savvy Pole named Ignace Slinkowycz who now goes by the name of I. Harrison Slinker III."

"Slinker doesn't sound like such a trustworthy name to me, maybe Slinkowycz's English language infrastructure is a bit shaky; but I have absolute trust in you Rex, and you had better not slip up on this. Too much is riding on it."

The opposing team that PP&C put together was a mixed bag. Thompson Joad had to be included despite his lack of experience because he had found the case, but the leader of the team was the brilliant Emmit Rattenkrieg. It also included the feared Fiona MacAdder, known for her rapier skills in cross examination. There was a jury specialist, Letitia Graphite, a DNA expert, Ed Zygote, and the public relations wizard, C. Stanley Moosebugger. There was also a rape counselor, Linda Statutory, just in case it turned out that it might be possible to claim that PP had not only been violated, he had been raped.

To ensure the triumph of reason and justice, Moose had already kicked off a big-time public relations campaign. Poshpenny had appeared on television with Jay Leno and gotten into a fight with Geraldo, had interviews with Mike Wallace and Barbara WaWa, who persuaded him to stand on his head, and was the subject of a skillfully managed set of daily news releases that portrayed him as an all-American boy. Quick and clever as a youth, yes, but no egghead; rather a true representative of the best in American manhood. "To treat him as ignorant and stupid, even to suggest that he was the victim of his own laziness and ineptitude," *The New York Smirk* pronounced in an editorial, "is not only ridiculous, it is un-American, for it is in effect to say that Americans are stupid, when everyone knows that our democratic political system works because of our intelligence. If any American fails an exam of any kind it is a crime against society committed by those charged officially with getting that individual ready for the exam."

Long days and nights went into trying to develop the right legal strategy for the plaintiff, something that realized the full potential of the law, something new but not radical, something that the courtroom had not seen before. The lawyers took turns quizzing one another in extended rehearsals.

"How do you demonstrate that somebody is smart and that their failures are the responsibility of someone else?"

"You tell them the answers, put them in the witness box, and let them answer some hard questions correctly. You call in their grade school teacher, you get the Harvard registrar to certify that PP took a number of courses, and you grill his graduate school profs to find out what they did *not* teach him."

"Good thinking, Thompson, but it will put the jury to sleep. You might as well call his mother, who is, by the way, anxious to help out, to testify that Peter was a model child, smart as a whip."

The strategy problem remained very troublesome until Rattenkrieg made a breakthrough late one hot day in the conference room, his feet on the huge table, picking his nose surreptitiously, looking out the big picture window at the ocean.

"Ours is a scientific age and nothing is believed unless it is scientifically proven. We can put PP on the stand to testify, and he can sound like Einstein, but no one will really believe he is smart unless we can somehow make it scientifically real to the jury. What is the central point of our case, Thompson?"

"Why, E.R., it's all there in the folder, the faculty of the somatics department at Lone Tree State didn't prepare PP well enough to pass the general exam they set for him for the Ph.D. We have to find some way to show that PP is really very smart, that his teachers were remiss in their duty, and that failing his exam could not possibly be his fault."

"Well, maybe, but my courtroom sense tells me that the real legal issue is somewhere else and that we had better find that somewhere if we want to win the case. Moose, you're a man with a real feel for the pulse of America, what do you see at the heart of the case?"

"Waal, I'm not an educated man, E.R., but it seems to me that when you look hard at any issue it is always really about something a little off to one side of what it seems to be about. Why is it that we never talk about the things that really matter to us but always about something else? Maybe it's because we're ashamed of what we really think, but damned if I know."

Rattenkrieg, too, was inclined to philosophize a little in the warmth of the late afternoon sun shining through the big window. "You're right, Moose, people aren't really so bad. They don't amount to much, and nobody could say today that Americans live a noble life, but they wouldn't really be so awful if they didn't always try to pretend they are better than they are. La Rochefoucauld may have said, 'Hypocrisy is the tribute that vice pays to virtue,' but in truth it's hypocrisy that makes horses' asses out of all of us."

"Yeah, anyway, we're always concealing something. That's the way it is. Nobody, including the jury, is really going to care about whether the professors prepared old PP for his exam. How can you really tell anyway? What they are actually going to care about is that they are sick and tired of being laughed at and called stupid by a bunch of professors and other smartass experts when they know that they really have a lot more good sense than any of those pretentious bastards. So, they'll be inclined to be on young Poshpenny's side, since one way or another, if Letitia chooses the jury well, and who can doubt she will, they have all been failed in exams all their lives by intellectual snobs."

Letitia looked superior, but said nothing, and Moose plunged on.

"But there are problems. Poshpenny happens to be a first-class pain in the ass, a phony, who probably never cracked a book or worked hard at anything, even if he did graduate from Harvard. In person he will put the jury off, so what you had better do is try the profs. Keep PP out of it. Try the profs and you will win hands down."

"Babe," Rattenkrieg, much relieved, looked at Thompson, "you know your way around these local schools, so why don't you go over to the Ronald Reagan Research Center for the Study of Higher Cognition. Find out just what kind of resources they have that might help us demonstrate scientifically to the court and the jury the point that Moose has just so brilliantly made, that intellectuals are the real enemy of democracy and its people."

Ronald Reagan was just a taxi ride away, and the cognitors were anxious to help. "You name it, the Program of Post-Digital Cognitive Studies, POPS, has got it," said Dr. Buster Lamprey, Ph.D., delighted with the media exposure that the case of the century could give him and his still somewhat marginal subject. "We are the most advanced cognitors in the world, and we can produce nifty visuals that will instantly inscribe in the jury's memory chips any view of intelligence you think will be helpful to your client. But it does sound as if my basic course, 'BRAINSTORM, INTELLIGENCE IN AMERICA, POPS 10,' fits your case like a hand in a glove."

Thompson was appalled. "Look, Lamprey, this is big-time stuff, the fate of American democracy is riding on it, an intro course doesn't fit the bill."

"Well, wait till you see it. The message that the course inscribes is that in American culture, intelligence is highly suspect. First I give them a couple of old films like *The Manchurian Candidate* and *The Million-Dollar Brain*, and a few other sci-fi films where evil scientists and mad professors capture and dumb down patriot hunks and blondes with big tits. Then I show them some of what Americans really like, a sort of easygoing, nonchalant goofiness. Homer Simpson on TV, you know, or Lennie in *Of Mice and Men*. These, they are soon sensing, are the true geniuses of democracy: warm feelings, getting right to the heart of the matter, their visions unobscured by fancy educated ideas or complicated ways of thinking. Then I knock them out with the finale, the idiot savant, *Forrest Gump,* a crazy smarter than any of those bastards who think they know so much."

"Sounds," Thompson chanced, "like you have something against the academic establishment. But forget that. You use an awful lot of movies, don't you? Are they really very scientific? Wouldn't it be better to have some charts and graphs, some statistics, some surveys of the '*g*' factor, and some summaries of the Stanford-Binet standard intelligence tests? Maybe even some genetics? What about reading and math scores on the SATs and the GREs?"

"Where were you, Buddy, when the shit hit the fan? Visuals—movies, computers, TV—screens are where Americans get their real believable information today. You don't get the truth out of printed materials; you get it on a screen. Music has it, too, like those great folk rock songs I use as background, "You Never Told Me What I Need to Hear," or the old country favorite, "I Was Just Your Playtoy for a Time." But we can give you anything you want, like I said, man. There is some fine statistical work being done in POPS on the frequency of antiintellectual views in pop culture, 91 percent, and some really heavy studies of whether television corrupts intellect or morals first. But if you really want my advice, *and you look like you need it,* I would hire us to put together for you a classy little multimedia *son et lumière* that would knock the jury's socks off.

"This boy of yours don't have any repulsive social habits or anything like that does he? He does? Then maybe some clips from *Elephant Man.* We need something with a bit more pizzazz than what I've given you, but you get the idea. Let us have specs of what you want and we'll prepare a sample package."

Thompson was fully persuaded. Nothing like this had ever been done before in an American court of law. The O. J. Simpson case was judicial kindergarten compared to the scenario Lamprey was creating. Never had advanced technological know-how and postmodernism been brought together to focus their laser beams so powerfully on knowledge, truth, and justice.

Back at the firm they were not so convinced: "Movies?" But Thompson, whose mind had been totally blown by Lamprey, argued that here was an opportunity to make legal history, and for only a million bucks—the first time a price had been mentioned—with the chance of cashing in on billions when Lone Tree and the state of California had to pony up for the financial losses and the mental anguish they had caused thousands of students whom they had failed to prepare well enough to pass the exams they set for them.

"OK, OK, it was your case in the first place, and we'll let you hang yourself if this doesn't work. Now, let's talk about the strategy for jury selection."

This ritual, which had once been a minor part of the courtroom drama, had now taken center stage, and here in *Poshpenny v. Lone Tree State* it was absolutely critical. But it was also particularly ticklish here, as Letitia Graphite explained to MacAdder, Rattenkrieg, Thompson, Moose, and the rest of Team Poshpenny. "All Americans think that they are smart, but some of them really are considerably smarter than others. And these tend to be the people who pass exams and think that if Poshpenny were really intelligent he would have passed his exam no matter how poor his preparation." *KEEP THESE SMART FOLKS OFF THE JURY,* Graphite wrote in block letters on the blackboard. "On the other hand," she went on, "it follows that those who think they are smart but really are not so smart will tend to fail exams and they will think that Poshpenny has been shafted, just like they have been times innumerable. This will not be the first trial in which the jury was selected for its unacknowledged stupidity."

The actual courtroom jury selection was going to be Fiona's work, and she was concerned that it is always difficult actually to tell who is smart and who is dumb. Obviously rocket scientists and brain surgeons were out, right away, while building custodians and beauty science specialists would inevitably be challenged by the defense but welcome to the prosecution. Beyond these obvious cases, though, intelligence is incredibly complex. Educational level might look promising, but there were college graduates who couldn't tie their shoelaces, and there were high-school dropouts who were astute investment bankers. "Maybe the best rule of thumb for measuring intelligence is that the smart don't think they are smart, while the dumb think they are smart as hell."

This was Graphite expounding her lore. "You can't ask for IQs since most of the panel will not have scored very high on the test, and besides the very mention of a standardized test that measures intelligence will probably result in a mistrial on the basis of being discriminatory and elitist."

It began to look as if it would be impossible to tell who was smart and who was dumb with any certainty, "which is," someone remarked, "the real point of the case." As the lawyers argued fiercely among themselves about who was smart and who was stupid, all their prejudices came out. Some really thought that women were dumber than men, but MacAdder and Linda Statutory laughed this out of court, so to speak. Others considered all blacks to be dumb, but you couldn't put together a jury these days without black members. Jokes were told about how many Polish electricians it took to change a lightbulb, and someone told the old joke about whether Romanians or Hungarians were smarter? "Both will sell you their mother, but only the Romanians will deliver." In the end they just had to go to court and take their chances that MacAdder, with Graphite coaching her, was smart enough to select the dummies.

Cameras were present in the courtroom from the start, Judge Nolo would not sit at the bench without them, and every major news agency in the world was represented. Jury selection went slowly, and the pool began to dry up as one arbitrary challenge after another was issued. Finally, knowing they had to get on with it, both sides were reduced to simply operating on their prejudices, which they called "intuitions," and the jury for *Poshpenny v. Lone Tree State* ended up looking pretty much like other American juries. A couple of housewives, a plumber, a black insurance salesman, an unemployed house painter, a Turkish masseuse, a secretary, a bindle maker, a retired government employee, a schoolteacher, a political activist, and a telephone repairman. The foreman was the government employee, Imre Antonescu.

"All be upstanding. Honorable Judge Anthony Nolo, Special Circuit Court of California, case of Poshpenny versus Lone Tree State University."

Nolo sat down, banged his gavel a few times, smiled at the cameras for several moments, and leaned back to hear the case.

Slinker and the lawyers for Lone Tree State did pretty much what was expected. They offered statistics showing that 92 percent of the Ph.D. candidates in the Lone Tree State Department of Somatic Studies did pass their general exams, and argued that those numbers proved that the department was providing reasonable preparation for its students. They introduced the professors who had set PP's exam, and each of them told stories about simple questions that Poshpenny had failed to answer satisfactorily. For example, "What difficulties do members of the Sapphic Sisterhood have in embracing stereotypes?" Or, "How will third-wave feminism sexualize the body politic?" Poshpenny had apparently floundered badly on these and other basic matters. Teachers in his various courses testified that he had often seemed to be preoccupied in class, even reading the newspaper at times, and had evinced confusion about such essentials of somatic study as "The shadow that the body throws over the rubric of romantic love."

The jury began showing open sympathy for the complainant. *This Harvard kid must be smart enough to know that these questions don't make any sense.* But the Retrograde, Replevin, & Persiflage lawyers were tone-deaf to what was happening, and they wheeled in some more experts on intelligence, people who had spent their lives studying opinion-formation, misinformation, the creative imagination, the scientific attitude, intelligence-gathering, and mystification. All these experts had examined PP and agreed that there were gaps in his cognitive abilities that you could drive a truck through. In short, as one of them, a cognitional economist who was an expert on knowledge, thought, and creativity as forms of capital, summed it up, "The complainant is running a structural and worsening intellectual deficit." All these experts agreed, however, that his professors could have gotten Poshpenny, dumb as he was, through his exam if he had paid attention to what they tried to teach him in the classroom.

By the time these experts had finished, people were asleep as far away as Watts, and there were some in the jury who appeared to be in something like terminal deep sleep. They staggered out of the building to revive in the bright sunshine of Southern California. Whether they could ever be forced back into the *Poshpenny v. Lone Tree State* courtroom was a question the bailiff had to ask himself, but after a long weekend they reluctantly straggled back into their seats.

They were in for a surprise. Emmit Rattenkrieg approached the bench and asked Judge Nolo's permission to offer a somewhat unusual argument for the plaintiff. One that would absolutely prove without question that Peter Poshpenny, and with him all American youths, were not stupid, only ill-prepared by their teachers, the intellectual professors of this country, for the exams they failed in such disastrous numbers. Nolo grunted something that was taken for assent, the blinds were lowered on the windows, a silver screen appeared on the sidewall, and a projector whirred.

[Camera closes in on crackling wires, bubbling test tubes, and huge electrical switches. Thunder and lightning.] Doctor Victor FRANKENSTEIN, in long white scientist's coat, at work in his laboratory, pulls switches that send huge jolts of electricity across a sputtering arc into a MONSTER strapped to the operating table. [Close-up of monster's tormented face, remarkably resembling PP.] Monster stumbles to his feet, ripping off restraints, and clumps across the floor toward window. Mumbles "Love," "Goodness," "Beauty," to the flowers in the windowbox. Clumsily tries to pick them but rips them out by the roots and offers them to the BRIDE OF FRANKENSTEIN, who is removing her clothing nearby in preparation for a bath. He smiles awkwardly at her and she at him. [Fade] [Cut to Dr. Frankenstein stepping into a lecture room.] "Artificial intelligence is of the greatest interest to ve cognition scientists, for in the first crude thoughts at the machine level ve can see the fundamental structure of human thought itself revealed." [Monster's arm reaches out from background to seize Frankenstein, but he calmly zaps it to a heap of quivering subjection by firing a hundred thousand volts into its circuits.] "You zee, there are no terrors in the universe for science, but ve have to be cruel to mold the intelligence of ordinary machines and men to our vill, ach! *will.* Ours is the power, not theirs, and we can make them pass or fail various tests we set for them as it suits our purposes." [Dr. Frankenstein fades away into mist with awful laughter.]

[Pan quickly to Glorious Technicolor scenes from *The Mind Snatchers from Outer Space.*] [Medium crane shot of icky little green things getting out of a spaceship and wiggling into the bodies of the professors of an American college, where they take over their personalities and eat their brains, à la Hannibal Lecter.] [Cut to Dean Meerschaum summoning Dean Bunson Burner.]

"Burner, what is wrong with our professors? They look more like aliens than usual, though I must admit they act more purposefully. I think I even saw one of them in the library, ha, ha!"

"Dean Meerschaum, we are the victims of a dastardly plot from outer space to control our students by having alien professors destroy their intelligence."

"I thought our professors were already doing that. Just kidding! Yes, you're right, and I think it may already be happening. Students are appearing on campus before noon, shaven and with their hair cut, and they appear to be reading books and on their way to the classrooms. The co-eds' skirts have gone, alas, from mini to maxi."

"Unless an antidote is found quickly, these alien professors will dumb down all our students, and they will all fail their exams, and American's colleges will have to close their gates. With our colleges shut down we will soon lose our good old American know-how, and it will be easy for *The Mind Snatchers from Outer Space* to take over Planet Earth."

"Objection, objection, objection!" Harrison Slinker III was on his feet and shouting. "What have these schlock movies got to do with the intelligence of Peter Poshpenny and his inability to pass exams set by the distinguished faculty of Lone Tree State University? We have [putting his face right into Thompson's face] had enough of your theatrics and histrionics, and it is time that you produced some solid evidence or admitted that you have no case and let the esteemed judge and the honorable jury go their ways."

"Objection, smobjection," Thompson riposted smoothly, "by now the dangers of the teacher-student relationship have begun to become vividly clear to the ladies and gentlemen of the jury, through the powers of the creative imagination combined symbiotically with the art of the cinema. In *Frankenstein* and *Mind Snatchers* we see in mythic terms the ways in which our native intelligence has everywhere throughout time been threatened by evil forces that try to portray it as weak and ineffective simply because it is not highly abstract or academic in its primary and secondary cognitive activities."

The jury was wide-awake by now, even the judge. They had never seen or heard anything like this, and they were beginning to realize for sure that PP had been the victim of the same predatory intellectualism and protracted school experience that had blighted their own lives. Their suspicions were reinforced by the sounds of nature blasting free from artificial limits in the electrorockabilly music of Elvis and His Stones That Gather No Moss—"I Can't Take It Anymore, Teacher." Strobe lights flashed off and on, and here and there around the courtroom appeared clips from *Henry, Portrait of a Serial Killer,*

I.Q., Quiz Show, Mars Attacks! David and Lisa, High School, Welcome Back, Kotter, and a multitude of other films and TV shows that have shown the American people how dangerous and unnatural any kind of rationality and formal education are. All the clips showed intellectual hegemony closely linked to gender, social class, and racial domination patterns.

By now the courtroom was in a hubbub, and reporters were racing out to phone their editors stories about how American jurisprudence was being turned upside down and how movies were for the first time being introduced as evidence to show that there was a deep plot to make young Americans stupid, a plot in which the schools, intellectuals, and professions are complicit.

But the big finale, the super-weenie, was still to come. Awesome strains of "The Lost Chord," haggard face of Sherlock Holmes, played by Basil Rathbone, the sick-genius detective, appears on the screen. Baker Street is wreathed in fog, and on the corner Professor Moriarty is stabbing two or three nursemaids, just for the hell of it. Inside, Dr. Watson sleeps on, Holmes gives himself a shot of heroin, and takes up his violin. To scratchy, out-of-tune sounds, the fog closes out this bleak exposure of sicko, indoor intellectualism.

The scene brightens, the sky turns blue, the sun shines once again in Southern California, and the happy sound of "Rock Around the Clock" is heard in the distance. Scantily clad inline skaters dip down and glide effortlessly by the palm trees on one skate. On a bench by the edge of the sea everyone is gathering around and shaking hands with Dustin Hoffman as RAIN MAN, a mental case smarter than any of those bastards who think they know so much. He smiles enigmatically, calculates instantly in his head the number of drops of water in all the oceans, writes the sum as a factor of thirteen on his slate, shows it to everyone, and joins hands with his multitude of happy friends.

The headlines were in thirty-six-point bold type,

JUSTICE TRIUMPHS

POSHPENNY VINDICATED

AMERICANS NOT DUMB
ONLY BADLY EDUCATED

The years dragged on with one appeal after another, and not a dime found its way either to Poshpenny, who had become the master of ceremonies of the reality TV program *Bet Your Life for a Billion,* or to the coffers of the old firm. *Poshpenny v. Lone Tree State* became an albatross around the neck of Pegasus, Parnassus & Culpable, and in a fit of annoyance one day the partners decided to outsource the case. The only offer they could get was from a firm that specialized in collecting bad debts, Squeeze & Grind, of two cents on the dollar, payable on settlement. It was an outrage, probably unethical, too, but they were desperate to be rid of *Poshpenny v. Lone Tree,* and the deal was quietly consummated. Since Thompson Joad had for years been the only lawyer working on *Poshpenny*, he went with the files.

EIGHT
A Long Way Up the Arroyo

"Talk to me, you never talk to me, we never discuss anything, that's what's wrong with our marriage."

"I didn't know anything was wrong with our marriage. We talk all the time, we never stop talking about our marriage, how can you possibly say we never talk about our marriage?"

"Well, yes, but we never talk about what is important."

"Like what?"

"Like sex, Earle, like how you always look at other women, but never look at me, like why we never have sex anymore."

"Of course we have sex, we had sex last Sunday afternoon when we locked the bedroom door and the children fought outside."

"Well, you may call that sex, and I suppose *you* enjoyed yourself, men always do, but it didn't do much for me. I could tell from the grim, tense way you looked that you were working hard and thinking, *How can I satisfy the old bitch?* [a few tears]

And why do you always insist on going to meetings and conferences alone, like the one next week on the sex of a democratic people? You probably meet students there, and these days they will do anything."

"I have work to do at those conferences, I have to meet and talk to people to find out what is going on and to keep my career moving. You don't want me to stay an assistant counselor in Gender and Sexuality Services all our lives do you? There's a tenure-track professorship in deconstruction, my old subject, going at Ivy University, and I mean to knock the socks off Professor Pierre de Hors, the head of the department, who will be at the conference, and get the job."

Earle had started years before on a part-time basis at Lone Tree State in the deconstruction department but had been let go the next year when enrollments fell and then got a temporary administrative position dealing with placements in remedial courses. An irate parent and powerful alumnus, Mr. Ralph Dungan, had demanded that Earle be fired for the way he had handled his son's case. The administration had thrown him to the wolves, but they tried to soften the blow by finding him a place in Gender and Sexuality Services, advising undergraduates to wear condoms, get abortions, treat their herpes, and take tests for AIDS.

His work had brought Earle over the years to a belief that the view expressed in his handbook, *One Way or Another,* 44th ed., of the official handbook of the American Sex Counseling Society, was right: all sexual activities, from crushing aluminum beer cans to bestiality, are normal. Sex in any form is the essential human act. He had come to this understanding, sitting in his office one hot afternoon, green with jealousy, while a student told him in graphic detail about simultaneous sex with his professor and three other undergraduates, two female and one male. *The world really is totally hypocritical about sex, and in fact everybody screws as many people as possible all the time. If they don't screw somebody else they screw themselves, and in an amazing variety of positions.* Earle had thought of writing a postmodernist book about the amazing variety of sexual activities practiced by the students, but somehow he never got around to it. The coming congress on "The Sex of a Democratic People," however, provided a forum where he could at least make his view known to the world that deconstruction provides a perfect philosophical background for postmodern sex.

"Well, why not take me along, then? I would like to hear some of the papers, too. Remember that I went to college, for a time anyway, and I know something about these things, at least I once did."

"Drusilla, how can we afford a baby-sitter? Besides you know you wouldn't have a good time, wouldn't know anybody, would be bored with the talks, and would end up, damn it, sitting in our room crying and blaming me."

He felt guilty, though, partly because he did have something, innocent of course, planned for the conference, but mostly because he felt responsible to some degree that things hadn't gone the way for Drusilla that they had planned when they met ten years ago and were going to become collaborators in research and publication that would set the world free of outworn sexual beliefs and customs. When Earle arrived at Lone Tree State, Drusilla was one of his decon students who followed him everywhere. She used to come to his office and spend long hours talking with him about her senior thesis, "Reception/Rejection of Trans-Sexuals by Society." He hadn't had much interest in the subject, or known much about it, but he had a lot of interest in her short skirt and the unrestrained breasts under her T-shirt.

Inevitably, he put his hand under the skirt one day while she was standing beside him, leaning on his desk, his heart pounding for fear that she would say something like, "That wasn't what I meant at all," and report him to the harassment officer, Judith Holofernes, who ran the local testosterone bashing program. It was she who had had the brilliant idea, instantly funded by the MacArthur Foundation, of appointing two people in each dorm, one male and one female, to look for any sexist attitudes and report all instances of gender bias. But Drusilla had squirmed with pleasure, and they had found their way to the delights of love amid the piles of ungraded blue exam books on his cluttered desk.

Earle had never appealed very much to women, but Drusilla's casually and frequently bestowed favors began to make him think quite well of himself. He liked being seen with her at college functions and even took her, rather daringly, to a few departmental parties. She gave him the reputation of a rogue male, screwing one of his most attractive students, and he began to wear bow ties. Given her radical views on everything, he was surprised when she indicated that she thought they ought to get married, but he didn't really know any reason why not, and her nakedness still excited him beyond control. The heavy breasts, the jet-black brush, the curve of hips out from the small waist, and the pert buttocks, too much.

But after they married, things had become more difficult. There were somehow, despite contraception, two children. Her teeth had gone bad after she breast-fed the first child, which she insisted was the only natural way, and a complicated tubal pregnancy left her washed out. She drank and smoked heavily to forget her troubles, and after dealing with numerous family emergencies that caused her to neglect her assignments, she had been forced to drop the on-line extension work that she had hoped would lead to completion of her degree.

A life that had begun promisingly was now wrecked on the shoals of female biology and cultural realities. She blamed men for what had happened to her, and, under the nom de plume Drusilla Fury, wrote retaliatory novels with titles like *Jackie the Gripper,* in which a ravishing beauty squeezed her lovers to death using her extraordinary lower-body strength. *Jane Breaks It Off in Dick* described graphically the fun a faithless wife could have with a wimpish husband. *Queen of the Phallic Women* opened in the jungle with lesbian transvestites drinking deep from male skulls, moved on to explicit descriptions of drugs and primitive orgies deep in the bush, and ended with the sacrifice of all the men who refused to take over household chores. Her books seemed to arouse interest, but she never made much in royalties. Three-Holer Press had an option on *The Nuptial Bed,* a collection of Drusilla's short stories, but her agent was haggling over the movie rights.

The flight hadn't gone well, not well at all, as Earle knew it wouldn't. After being canceled once, it had been delayed by a bomb threat, the weather was stifling, and Drusilla had one of her extraordinarily heavy periods—a spin-off of the tubal pregnancy—accompanied by the usual miserable migraine and a deep, deep depression. The Scaroon Ritz, where the meetings were being held—had refused the family credit card, which Drusilla had maxed out to pay the children's orthodontist and the Suzuki violin lessons, and they had been able to scrape together only enough cash to get into the Ruptured Buccaneer Economy Motel, one of the La Rue chain, downtown. When Drusilla called home to check on things, the older child screamed that she hated the baby-sitter, who didn't speak much English, and was going to run away, and that they would be sorry that they had gone to the old conference rather than to Disneyland as they had promised. Earle's stomach was churning by now, though he had drunk nearly a bottle of Maalox, and he was already an hour late meeting Chancie Illwill in the bar of the Scaroon.

It had been the purest chance that his old flame, working now as a consultant on gender bias in computers in Silicon Valley, had sent him an e-mail saying that she had noticed that he was going to speak at the sex congress, and that she was too, on "women, the obscured producers of critical dialogues about cyberspace," and why didn't they meet, have a drink, and talk about old times? He knew he shouldn't, but what after all was wrong with having a drink with her and reminiscing about some of the fun things they had once done?

To stay here now, with the shades drawn and an occasional eruption of sobbing from the rough shape on the bed covered with the spread, was not going to accomplish anything except more misery, and so he fled to the quiet darkness of the lobby bar at the Scaroon. Chancie was not there, of course, she was an impatient girl, but the silence and a glass of white wine restored Earle before he wandered into the lobby to see if he knew anyone and to get a sense of how things were going.

The Sex of a Democratic People was the really big sex conference of the year. Sponsored by the National Association for Democratic Sex and hosted this year by the Manatee Institute of Social Technology, it was designed, he read in the brochure he picked up,

> to explore the various terrains in which sex might become intelligible. It will consider libidinal investments across visual and discursive practices, corporeal enactments, and virtual identifications. These provisional locations, which imply a constitutive and reflexive negativity of absences, will involve repulsions, failures, and banalities.
>
> After welcoming remarks by Dr. Karl Fallopian, Krafft-Ebing Professor of Sexological Studies at Manatee, the conference will open with a tour of workshops in which interested persons will be assisted by experts in the construction of a wide variety of sexual identities. At the Sex Kingdom Science Fair, the large device known as ROD (Rotary Orgasmic Device), said to offer a more efficient way to arrive at orgasm, developed under the auspices of the

> National Institute of Rotary Motion (NIRM), will be demonstrated, using volunteers from the audience, before the public for the first time. Pedophilia, sadomasochism, lesbianism, homoeroticism, foot and other fetishes, coprophilia, gang rape and defenses against it—all will have their special booths. Vibrators, penis enhancement devices, and other mechanical applications will also be demonstrated.
>
> Fans, photographers, writers, filmmakers, students, theorists, professors, and sexual culture activists from all over the world will be here, and some of the best-known experts on the full spectrum of sexuality will be speaking.

Earle noted with satisfaction that in the center of the lobby a large sign advertised that the plenary address would be given at the official association banquet the following noon by Doctor Earle Joad, of Gender and Sexuality Services at Lone Tree State University, speaking on "Sex: Duty or Desire?"

He looked at his watch, realized that it was time for Professor Fallopian to open the congress, and made his way in the icy air-conditioned atmosphere of the hotel to the Seventh Veil Room on the mezzanine, where the conference would begin. There was only a scattering of people in the auditorium. *Most of the conference participants will be in their rooms experimenting on one another,* Earle thought, *trying out some new sexual position rather than listening to papers. But appearances have to be kept up, and if the universities are going to continue paying for their faculties to attend conferences, somebody has to listen to these dreadful speeches. Probably the only people here are those who are more interested in professional networking than in screwing. Some choice.*

Fallopian, a brisk little man in a blazer of many colors, rapped for order and began in a high-pitched, insistent voice: "Welcome, fellow sex scientists, to the conference on the sex of a democratic people, under the auspices of the National Association for Democratic Sex, and sponsored by Manatee Institute of Social Technology, dedicated this year to Dr. Alfred Kinsey, who broke much of the ground we will be plowing in this conference. I won't take much of your time, but let me briefly tell you that in the papers and sessions to come you will be listening to people who have made sex their lifetime study, hoping to throw light on this darkest and most tangled of human activities. The very title of the papers gives a sense of what I mean by 'tangled.' Take, for example, Dr. Annette Kolloidol's intriguing paper on 'Oral Sex: Edith Wharton's Dinner Tables as a Locus of Struggle and Seduction.' Who would ever have thought that this novelist's lavish dinner parties are really symbolic representations of violent sexual conflict? We will also hear Dr. Hypatia Faux-Rose use multicultural parameters to zero in on 'Sapphic Spectatorship: The Erotics of Looking.' Hot diggety!! How about that? [strained and brief laughter] All of these papers and many others you will find stimulating, and none of you can afford to miss our plenary speaker at the official association banquet, Dr. Earle Joad, talking on a subject that goes right to the heart of our enterprise, 'Sex: Duty or Desire?'

"But I don't want to keep you any longer from the garden of delights that lies before you, so with hearty voice and best wishes from Old Manatee Tech, I bid you welcome to this conference, and Good Cheer."

Glancing at his program, Earle had difficulty picking out a paper he wanted to hear. Should he go to "Sexual Preferences of Gender, Race, Class, Age, and Ethnicity"? Or "Do Most Drag Kings Perform Straight Masculinity?"? "Misogyny or Femme Phobia?" was sure to be enlightening. Finally, though, he was unable to resist the straight-from-the-shoulderness of "Is There a Different Category of Gender Fucking?" But just as he was about to walk into the Glowing Embers Room to learn the answer to this heavy question, he caught sight of Chancie, who smiled and waved her program for him to join her.

"I'm sorry that I missed you. I waited for a while and then came up here thinking that I would probably see you in the crowd."

"Well, you see you were right. Here I am and I've been just dying to see you again, after so long. My God, but you look wonderful, in fact you are even more beautiful than you were at Ivy. You are thinner, it becomes you, and, if you don't mind, your breasts are even bigger than ever."

"Don't get too forward. [playfully] After all you're an old married man by now, a father I hear, and a sex counselor at Lone Tree State University, and, a little bird told me, the leading candidate for the empty chair in anomie, or is it deconstruction, at Ivy."

"Either, or both. It's true, I'm getting old. I tell you frankly that I want that job at Ivy, I'm sick of telling people all day long to wear condoms no matter what they do, even when they masturbate. But there are complications, and unless I really bring my paper off, I am going to lose out to Meece Abeem, who is Pierre de Hors's latest catamite. De Hors has never really liked me, you will remember, since he was on a discipline committee at Ivy that tried me, for, of all things, plagiarism."

"Look, there's nothing really interesting going on this hour. Why don't we go up to your room and talk, catch up on things?"

"Can't do, I'm not staying in this hotel."

"Okay, my room then."

"Okay."

Earle knew he shouldn't, really shouldn't, but it literally was impossible for him to say "No." He knew she was going to fuck him, he could feel it in the heavy warm weight in his loins; he knew, too, she was just showing that she could do whatever she wanted with him. But all his caution weighed nothing against Chancie's bouncing short red hair, her jiggling breasts, the long bare white legs in the scandalously short miniskirt, the flash of white panties underneath. Her eyes glistened with life as she posed in front of him in the "insolent twat mode," hand on her cocked-out hip, her skirt swirling wickedly as she turned toward the elevator. *It is ridiculous,* Earle thought, *there is in men no resistance, logical or moral, whatsoever, to women when they offer their sexual favors.* He couldn't think of his family and his marriage, his profession or his career. He couldn't remember that he really didn't like Chancie Illwill very much.

"Oh God, Honey, how I missed you. Nobody knows just the right spots like you do. Your cock's still the biggest ever, hard as a rock, oh yeah, yeaah, yeaaah."

"Where do you want me to put it, baby, where does it feel best?"

"Everywhere, all the places, put it wherever you want to, oh my God, I'm coming already, I shouldn't come so soon, do you want it in my mouth?"

"God, yes, do you still come for hours on end when you get really going? You'd better stop now, if I come it will be all over, at least for a while."

"Guys really are limited, but why don't you go ahead, we don't want to miss the next round of papers."

And there in the king-size bed, the faint smell of institutional disinfectant in the air, curtains drawn, the occasional dim hum of the elevator, the reality of sex, warm, sloppy wet, hard and soft, illicit and unfamiliar, as much a taking as a giving, was acted out still one more time. *Beast with two backs, yes, ludicrous, deceptive, certainly, but exciting beyond belief, perhaps the one really exciting thing in the long boredom of modern existence.*

She smiled wickedly at him in the mirror, drawing in her cheeks, while putting on her face, still naked except for her high heels and glasses, still wearing her heavy jewelry and watch, a barbarian princess laden with pirate gold, and he could only grin, totally undone.

The paper they listened to, not really caring much what it was, sitting side by side on the folding chairs, a slight sexual odor still hanging about them, had a suggestive title, "The Whispered

Watchword: How to Read the Sex Code in Girls' Series Literature." It tried to show that girl detectives such as Nancy Drew, Cherry Ames, and Trixie Belden were secretly in love with their fathers and how their quests brought them step by step to the phallocratic bed and symbolic coition. An interesting idea, fantastic enough to satisfy postmodern truth standards, with some good three-cushion interpretations; but incest had really had its day by now and no longer aroused much interest.

"Shall we meet for drinks and dinner?"

"Look, I really can't, I have to meet someone."

"Your wife's with you, I knew it. I was a fool to think we could pick up where we left off, you were just having fun with me."

"No, no, no, anything but, I mean, yes, she is with me, and I have to go back and talk to her. She's close to suicidal, threatens it in fact when she has her period and thinks I am going to leave her. Look, I love you so much I will do anything, I can't leave you ever again, but go along with me for just a time while I calm her down and pull myself together enough to deliver my paper. It's the big moment in my professional life. If it goes well, maybe we can work something out so that we can always be together."

"You think Ivy University might have a job for me, too? I don't know how long Silicon Valley is going to pay me to tell them that women find computers too masculine, too systematic, too logical."

"Well, no one has said anything, of course, but these days if they really want you, professor-and-friend packages are pretty standard. Now give me a nice deep kiss, and I'll see you in the morning. We can have breakfast after the first round of papers."

The return to the Ruptured Buccaneer was not as bad as he feared. Drusilla had slept some, gotten rid of her headache, and was somewhat conciliatory.

"There's no sense spoiling the trip, let's go and have a nice drink and a good meal—I got some cash from an ATM with an old card—after I call chez Joad and make sure that the kids are okay. The storm has probably passed by now, but until I talk to them I can't help but worry."

Things were better at home, at least there was no longer any danger of anyone running away, and the human tendency to make the best of things, particularly with the help of a little alcohol, took over in the bar. But she wanted a third martini, and when Earle tried to stop her, knowing from long experience the fatal effects of the third one, her voice began to rise. The bartender went to the other end of the bar and began busily polishing glasses.

"Why are you always such a spoilsport? Why can't we ever have a little fun, like other people? My friends, and your friends, too, told me to be careful of you, that you really didn't know how to enjoy yourself, how you were really down on women, always thinking of your fucking work and your career. Even your mother told me she didn't like you. I *want* another drink!"

Earle was tempted to remind her of disastrous evenings when she had had a third drink. The fatal corkscrew at the Toussaint Transférans's anniversary party, the black panties flung, in imitation of her heroine Zelda Fitzgerald, on the dinner table at Dean Heavy Thinker's. *Maybe there was something to that paper about sex at Edith Wharton's dinner tables.* But he held his memory and his tongue in check, knowing they would only cause more trouble. They went off sullenly, after another drink, to eat a joyless meal at an overpriced restaurant with terrible food and worse service. They fenced during the meal, using indirections to find directions out—"Honey, I think your mother tying you to the crib must have something to do with your attitude about women, don't you? Which ankle was it?"—and talking about how the house needed new plumbing and a new roof, and whether his raise this year would be 2 percent or 3. After a couple of hours tormenting each other with small talk and paying a check they could ill afford, they retreated silently and glumly to the old Buccaneer. She took off her clothes, but instead of putting on her nightgown, she stretched out naked on her back on the bed and winked at him, partly to invite him, partly because she knew it would annoy him. Her long, bare, white body seemed to have no sex whatsoever, the breasts had slid to the side, the pubis was concealed in shadow, just a long, bare, white tube, and Earle went to sleep clinging to his side of the bed.

He left while she was still asleep, hoping to find a quiet place over at the Scaroon Ritz to work over his paper one last time. Chancie was in the breakfast room, however, and suggested that he work in her room. He did, and they did, fending off the maid service several times, until it was time to go to the annual association banquet and his plenary address.

Air conditioning at full blast, the room cold as a tomb, the scientists of sexology assembled for their annual banquet in the vast New Cosmos Room of the hotel. Small groups sat together at round tables. Here and there a solitary couple dined alone at a table for twelve, no one wanting to make conversation with strangers. The waiters bustled about in their starchy green jackets, the limp salad was brought out, and then the rubbery chicken and the acidic white wine. At the head table the officers of the National Association for Democratic Sex gossiped with one another until Fallopian tinkled a glass with a knife. The white noise in the room gradually died away, and the outgoing president, Simeon Lasher, de Sade Professor of Sexology at Lemming College, rose to say farewell and remark on the great successes that democratic sex had had during the last year. He touched briefly on the increase in the number of abortions, referred to the cloned human beings, the drop in the birthrate below replacement level, the "tell and tell and tell" policy on homoeroticism in the military, and the spike in the number of single mothers. The only failure, he noted, was in the stubborn resistance of the nuclear family to disappear altogether. Some people, for reasons he could not understand, still insisted on getting married and having children. He then introduced his successor, the former first vice-president, who automatically succeeded him, the noted expert on sexual paybacks, Judy Holofernes, single mother of three. Earle knew her well from Lone Tree State and tried to avoid eye contact. The crowd roared its approval of this first citizen of the new era of democratic sexuality, and she in turn waved vigorously to them, pumping her arm from time to time. When she revealed that she had just been diagnosed HIV positive, the crowd screamed, there were whistles and shouts from all over the room of "Right on," and "Don't take it lying down, Honey," and "Sock it to 'em, Judy!" When the room at last quieted, the new president made a few inflammatory remarks about conventional sexuality and then introduced the plenary speaker of the occasion, "Professor Earle Joad, whom [thin smile and thinner laugh] we all know well from Lone Tree State University, who will talk to us about 'Sex: Duty or Fun?'"

"Men like to fuck, women can take it or leave it alone, and therein lies the central human tragedy." Earle had tried for a dynamite beginning to his paper. Actually "fuck" was the most clichéd word at this conference, but no amount of heavy wear seemed to quite kill it dead. There were hisses, as he knew there would be, from the half-drunk female sexologists about the room, cheers from some of the completely drunk males. Earle grinned good-naturedly and bored on with his analysis of the democratic revolution in sexual attitudes in America.

"As you all know, both as scientists and as human beings, the conventional wisdom gets it at least partly right when it tells us that society's primary sexual institution, marriage, which is supposed to solve the sexual problem, only intensifies it. While seeming to satisfy masculine desire, it in fact frustrates male sexuality by limiting him, or trying to limit him, to one woman. [raucous jeers from the male portion of the audience] In the end he either escapes, with all the problems that causes, or sinks into what Shakespeare called 'a dull, stale, tired bed.' The consequences of this repression of instinct are the usual depression, intensification of suppressed libido, and development of perverse outlets."

Earle thought that he had their attention now, *But what is that group off in the corner still talking trying to do, wreck my speech? And that guy with the red necktie, reading a book, the bastard.*

"The marriage bed at the same time stokes the fears the woman originally has of brutal penetration and rape. Her fragile sexuality retreats when her favors are taken by the husband as a male right rather than freely given. Sex becomes an invasion of personal liberty to the married female, however it may be disguised, and her libido shrinks to near disappearance. The latest scientific surveys show that 65 percent of married women, even with clitoral stimulation, which is unfortunately seldom given, still never, *never,* experience orgasm."

I'll bet some smart asshole asks where I got my figures. I should have said 62.3 percent to make it sound more scientific. Did I actually see the figure somewhere, or did I make it up? Well, the question period will resolve that matter. My mouth is getting a bit dry, maybe a glass of water. No, my hand will tremble.

"Society covers up the well-known but deeply denied fact that marriage is the hearse of sexual pleasure for both sexes through male frustration and female despair. But then sexual pleasure was not its purpose in the first place. That is only the bait. Marriage is an authoritarian social institution designed to curb the dangerous priapic energies of the male and limit him to one woman, while pretending to satisfy his lust, while at the same time providing women with the stable arrangement and the protection they need to rear children and survive in a world of dominant males. [Judy Holofernes pumps her arm several times, and the crowd roars] Marriage thus provides what society wants, order and procreation, but it exacts a heavy price from both men and women to accomplish its end. Never was there a better illustration that our genes use us to further their immortality, not the other way round."

There were signs of restlessness already in the audience, and a few of the thirstier souls sitting near the doors began to edge out. *Maybe I've gone too far, ought to draw back a bit, raise a few objections to my thesis, and settle them. Say something good about marriage? No, better to stick to the prepared text, if I leave it I may lose the thread of the argument.*

"The effects of this kind of authoritarian marital sexuality extend far beyond marriage itself. Marriage recognizes only two sexes, and those who practice anything other than the standard heterosexual kind of sex, using what we now jokingly but tellingly call 'the missionary position,' are declared perverts, their practices criminalized, and their lives put in jeopardy. The impotent, the indifferent, and the unattractive—and they are legion—are largely left out of the sex game. Marriage itself, which Lord Byron aptly called 'that moral centaur, man and wife,' [titters] becomes a hierarchical political institution in which men exercise tyranny over the family, in which the two participants are cast in adversarial roles on every issue from disciplining the children to spending money. In the end each becomes the other's jailer, and bitterness and boredom are alleviated only by recurrent and vicious quarrels."

At this point there was a strangled cry of rage from the back of the room, and Earle realized for the first time that Drusilla was in the audience. She was crying and furious, and as she stormed out of the room she flung a Parthian dart backwards, for all to hear, "If this is what you think of marriage, you bastard, then you can just go fuck yourself." There was embarrassed silence in the room for a moment or two, and then someone laughed, and then the whole audience broke into laughter and cheers. Who for? It was hard to say. Earle realized that he had without thinking very much about it sacrificed his marriage on the altar of his career. But, really, Drusilla was a drag, anyway, and he could see Chancie smiling, sitting in the first row with her skirt hiked up nearly to her waist. And so, after a grin and a sip of water, he plunged on. "Marriage is the ancien régime of sexual relationships, totally out of step with democratic instincts, which require liberty, equality, and fraternity, instincts that must be free to pursue happiness.

"Democratic sex," he rolled on, "did not break out of the closet in 1776 or 1789 but only in late twentieth-century America. The great escape began with the understanding after long centuries of repression that sexual practices, attitudes, and identities are culturally defined, not hardwired in biology, and therefore can be changed at will. Instead of the ancient binary division between male and female, America began to perceive that sexual identity lies along a vast continuum from the infrafeminine to the ultramasculine, with every niche occupied and active. To a democratic people, anxious to exercise their freedom to choose in all areas of life, especially one so central as the sexual, it became obvious that humanity is at liberty not only to occupy a number of preexisting sexual roles but to *bricoler* the sexual arsenal—fetishism, voyeurism, exhibitionism, commodification, autoeroticism, psychosexual dramas, symbiotic freedoms and restraints, celibacy and promiscuity, flirtation, digitalization, and on and on into infinity—any kind and any mix of sexual identities and activities that appealed to people." *Now, really sock it to them, I have been talking for too long, better give them the full treatment before they disappear on me.*

"With this breakthrough, everything was, so to speak, up for grabs. Men dressed like women, and women like men—as do the splendid transvestite motorcycle clubs that are here among us this afternoon—homoeroticism became a third major sexual role and lesbianism a fourth. Age-old fundamental sexual attitudes were transformed in a short space of time."

From the number of cellular telephones ringing among the audience, Earle knew his time was up, so he hurried a bit. A tactical mistake, it later appeared. "At the same time, the new freedom in sexual practice was reinforced by a technology that made biology as malleable as culture. Birth-control pills and abortion separated sex and unwanted pregnancy for good. Surgeons could and did perform sex-change operations, and penile and mammary enlargement or contraction became commonplace, all paid for by new health maintenance organizations, Medicaid, and Medicare. Artificial insemination and Petri-dish conception freed philoprogenitive women from the awkwardness of intercourse, and with the arrival of the ability to clone, the female became capable of being both father and mother to offspring who are her exact duplicates. We have broken the biological chains that bound us for so long to ancient patterns of sexual behavior, particularly marriage, and the future holds endless new possibilities for the human sexual will, not instinct or custom any longer, but will."

By now people were getting up and leaving the room without any attempt to be quiet, and those who remained were talking freely among themselves. Earle skipped a couple of pages of his text and sped on to his conclusion.

"The benefits of this sexual revolution are already all around us. The divorce rate continues to climb to over 52 percent of all new marriages, the number of single-parent families has increased geometrically, same-sex unions are commonplace, homosexuality is free to speak its name wherever it wants, pornography is available on every newsstand, and the World Wide Web—that most potent instrument of freedom of all kinds—is awash with sexual discussion groups and sites that cater to every taste. I think it no exaggeration to say that in sex, as in so many other areas of American life, people are now free to do what they want to do." *Christ, by now half of them are out of here, no one is even pretending any longer, they're just leaving.*

"Since sex is so basic to human life, we have to expect that deep changes in its cultural and biological patterns will churn up society at large. And we are passing through a disturbing time, but we can rejoice in the brave new sexual world where desire rather than duty rules, and know with certainty that the old superstitions of male and female, of marriage and procreation, are being left in the darkness of the ancient past. Thank you, good people, for your patience." *You pigs!*

The audience probably more or less agreed in general with what Earle had had to say, but it was familiar, and he was not a good speaker, and he had gone on far too long. There were also factions among the converted, and a number of hostile questions were soon heard. Pierre de Hors was the first on his feet, as Earle had known he would be.

"Professor Joad, perhaps, as a one-time student of deconstruction, you know that an emerging body of thought-provoking research has been exploring the intersections of feminist theories and the vectors of the new sexuality. This research, as you may also know, has paid particular attention to exploring sexualities from cross-cultural informatics in an effort to challenge Western definitions of sexuality, identity, and feminism. I would instance particularly Gashini Suttee, author of the highly acclaimed book *Homosexuality and Lesbianism: The Answer to India's Population Problem.* But the cross-cultural approach has opened up every niche of sexual theory: activism-fantasy—nationalism and sexual identities—postcolonial gender and sexuality—space, place, and sexuality—queer sexualities—sexuality and religion—sexuality, commodities, and capitalism—virtual sex—to name only a few areas that you have not touched on in your very helpful lecture. My question is, 'How do you see these various discoveries intersecting with deconstruction?' Please deal with these important questions in order."

Earle knew that he had to try to respond to this load of buckshot, and he knew that he shouldn't offend de Hors. But he had always been a smart-ass, and buoyed by having the lecture over, he grew reckless and used the old speaker's trick of a savage riposte, followed by rephrasing the question to suit the speaker's interests.

"I can tell from your pronunciation that you are not a native speaker of English, Professor de Hors, but I think that what you are asking is whether there are enough mysteries left for anyone to want any longer to have sex with anyone or anything, and to this I reply with a ringing 'Yes.' Sex is here to stay despite efforts to eliminate it by conservative moralists and overintellectualized pedants."

Chancie wiggled a bit and clapped her hands, though no one else did, but Earle realized with a sinking feeling that in the heat of the moment he had killed any chance that he might ever have had for the job at Ivy, which was probably not much anyway.

A long silence ensued until there were a few other questions here and there of the kind that people dredge up in an attempt to be polite.

"How does your view of sex relate to the Women's Needlecraft as Resistance program and its treatment of the textile arts in terms of their empowering, subversive, or political elements? Will you also consider in your answer the use of needlework as a trope in fiction/poetry/drama?"

After Earle had sweated through this one, there was another about postmodern animal rights and vegetarian identities. Then came a real stumper from the Edith Wharton sex-at-the-table woman.

"In addition to the prominence of the oral personality and oral sexuality in Edith Wharton's work, sexuality is conveyed by connections between culinary and other kinds of taste, gourmandism and sexual appetite, abstemiousness and control, food loathings, cravings, and eating disorders. Do you see any way that a responsible critic cannot conclude that all this emphasis on eating indicates an infantile sense of unsatisfied, insatiable oral longing in the author as well as the characters?"

Earle could do no more than respond with a limp "No," which seemed to quite satisfy the questioner, who smarmed at those around her and sat down contentedly.

At this point Dr. Fallopian took pity on Earle and rose to say that he thought the speaker had spent enough time on the podium and that everyone should give him a big round of applause for his helpful treatment of this obviously important subject. "If there are further questions I am sure the speaker will be happy to discuss them in the hall later or at the New Sex cash bar opening at five o'clock in this room."

There was a smattering of applause as Earle hastily gathered his papers, grabbed Chancie by the wrist, and fled the room for a dark bar where they could decide what to do. The die was cast. Meece Abime would get the post at Ivy, while he, Earle, would languish in Lone Tree State with Drusilla for the rest of his life running no-sex-without-condoms campaigns. That is, if she would have him back after what he had said publicly about marriage. *She probably will,* he thought without joy. His usual response to stress like this was a torsion in the small gut that reduced him to a whining penitent, sure that his entire life was a mistake, begging forgiveness from anyone he could find to ask. The feeling was already there, but, though he usually didn't drink spirits during the day, he dulled it with two vodka martinis. After the second he had worked up considerable bravado about his marriage and his job.

"I'm not going back there and put up with Drusilla's moods and the rank discrimination of that Lesbo psychologist in charge of student counseling, who is very down on me. I'm going to quit, and you and I will run away together, to Mexico perhaps. I hear it's cheap and pleasant there and no one will bother us. I can write my dynamite research book, the sexual secrets of college students, which will turn the understanding of sex in our society completely around, at last without interruption, and you and I can make love every day and every night."

"But how will we live? You know I don't need much, I'm really a very plain girl, but we do need a roof over our head and some food on the table."

"Listen, I've been planning this for a long time. I can draw out all my retirement funds at Lone Tree State, and we can invest them in government bonds and live on the interest."

"Doesn't it require your wife's signature? I thought women now have vested rights in their husband's retirement plans."

"Yeah, but I can fake Drusilla's signature, and one of my friends is a notary who will validate the signature for me."

"Just how much do you have in the retirement fund?"

"Oh, about thirty-nine or forty thousand dollars."

"Let's see, government long bonds are paying 5 and 15/32 this week, so you would make less than twenty-four hundred a year, or two hundred a month. I don't see that buying a lot of tamales with an exchange rate of 9.673 pesos to the dollar."

"Oh, come on, Chancie, don't be so materialistic. We love each other, we have for years, and here is our opportunity for happiness. If we don't seize this moment our lives will dwindle away into a desert of sameness and at last dry up entirely. Chancie, you know how much I care, let's go back to your room again and talk this over like adults with the courage to face the real world and make real choices."

It was a long way up the arroyo. The sun beat down relentlessly, and the rutted path was hard to walk in while trying to avoid the goat shit. But there was the trailer. He wouldn't have come back so soon, but he had spent his last peso, and his credit had expired long ago at every cantina in town. He had sat around the plaza for a time wondering whether he could face Chancie so early in the day, before a few shots of tequila had warmed her heart just a bit, but decided that he had to get out of the sun. Approaching the trailer he could hear her scream with fury inside, and there was a loud crash followed by a lot of swearing in Spanish, and when he peeked under the trailer there was a red ostrich-skin cowboy boot sticking through a rusted-out hole in the floor.

They had gotten as far as Durango before a cylinder blew in her old Ford Excresence SUV. They stayed overnight in a cheap motel and got drunk on tequila. Earle was impotent and Chancie began crying early in the morning and complaining bitterly that he didn't *really* love her or else he would be able to make love to her. Later on, dead drunk and nearly hysterical, she said that she was afraid he would leave her and that he would have to marry her, otherwise she couldn't face her parents. The thought of toothy old Philemon and Baucis Illwill in their assisted-living condo sobered Earle up, but he quickly had another drink, swore he loved her, and passed out.

After selling the Ford Excresence for ten dollars for scrap, they took a bus, crammed with big suitcases and clucking chickens, on to the tough town of Santa Ynez con Cojones. Rents were cheap there, but on two hundred dollars a month they had to cut corners, and so they appropriated an old trailer up a steep dirt path, abandoned a long time ago by some American hippies who had planned to live a utopian existence smoking pot, screwing one another, and raising a few vegetables. One of them had been a painter, and the walls were covered with strange colorful paintings of cruel-looking Napoleonic soldiers shooting dogs. Earle thought the dogs looked like those in the drawings of an old humorist he had once read, James Thurber, though that didn't explain the soldiers. Chancie had never heard of Thurber, so she couldn't help out. The hippies had just disappeared one day, and the trailer sat there rusting away, until Earle and Chancie moved in.

One sunny day, they were all blazers, when they were both hung over and thirsty, they had had a big fight over who was going to town to fill the water jar at the fountain and carry it back. Matters went rapidly from bad to worse:

"Talk to me, you never talk to me, we never discuss anything, that's what's wrong with our relationship."

"I didn't know anything was wrong with our relationship. We talk all the time, we never stop talking about our relationship, how can you possibly say we never talk about our relationship?"

"Well, yes, but we never talk about what is important."

"Like what?"

"Like sex, Earle, like why you always look at the young boys and the little girls who hang around the cantina, but never look at me, like why we never have sex anymore."

"Of course we have sex, we had sex last Sunday morning when the cantina was closed during church."

"Well, you may call that sex, and I suppose *you* enjoyed yourself, men always do, but it didn't do much for me. I could tell from the grim, tense way you looked that you were just working hard and thinking, *How can I satisfy the old bitch?* [a few obligatory tears] Well, forget about it, Earle, I like the Mexicans better, anyway, they have bigger pricks."

Earle blacked her eye, and she scratched his face badly. The quarrels became more and more frequent about who was going to cook dinner, do the shopping, throw the trash out the back door, wash clothes at the local Laundromat, kill the snakes, and all the other chores that living on even the most basic level imposed. Gradually, though, they stopped doing one chore after another and spent more and more time in the cantina at the foot of the path, where pulque and tequila were cheap. Sex was also cheap, and Earle, when he had any money, began to frequent the local *putas,* who would play any games you wanted, and sometimes when he was very drunk he went with the teenage boys who hung around the plaza. Chancie began to take men back to the trailer or, when she was really drunk, took them just to the brush at the edge of the plaza or to one of the benches under the single dim light that burned there, while the scratchy music box in the cantina blasted "La Paloma" through the streets.

After a while Earle didn't really mind very much when some of the local caballeros fondled Chancie while dancing with her, but once she responded to them they became proprietary and made threatening gestures and scornful speeches to the gringo *borrachón* who couldn't hold on to his woman. There was one particularly loathsome-looking fellow with a big smile named Muy Pistole, or something like that, who wore red ostrich-skin cowboy boots, a huge hat, and long, black mustaches. He was always grabbing Chancie by the breast or the ass and spitting on the floor near where Earle was sitting at the bar. His teeth were huge and white—for some reason they reminded Earle of those his little brother Somerset had described as seeing in his nightmares—and he laughed a lot with his mouth wide-open when he looked at Earle or Chancie in the cantina.

When Earle saw the red boot sticking through the trailer floor, he wanted to run away, but it was too much effort, and when the screen door opened with the screech of metal on metal, Muy came out stretching lazily in the sun, looked at Earle, laughed loudly, and said, "Hey Gringo, go ahead in, you're the next in line. She'll do it any way you want it. But don't take too long, Gordo and Julio will be along any minute for a doubles match. Ha, ha, ha!"

These were fighting words, Earle vaguely remembered, but he couldn't raise enough energy even to answer the Mexican, so he simply sat down in the shade of the trailer and fell asleep. When he woke, the sun had worked around the sky and was baking him. Dry-mouthed and feeling like hell, he made his way into the trailer and fell asleep again on the rumpled, dirty bed. When he woke it was dawn, and while stirring about looking for something to eat, he noticed that Chancie's clothes and her knapsack were gone. He should have felt something, and he did, relief. He rummaged through the mess in the trailer and found a few pesos in an old coffee can, took them, and went down the path to the cantina. The children yelled insults he didn't understand at him as he walked along the shit-covered path, and the young girls raised their skirts and showed him their oversize, hairless, raw pudendas, taunting him with what he had followed to perdition but which now only disgusted him.

Chancie had moved in with Pistole, and he took her around in an old, battered car from one village to another, keeping her drunk on tequila and high on Mary Jane and selling her for whatever he could get to peons who dreamed of a blond gringa with big tits. Earle saw her from time to time in the cantina, but they never spoke, as if they had never known one another, except when the monthly interest on his T-bonds came in from Merrill Lynch, and she demanded some of the money. Sometimes he gave her a little, sometimes he did not, unless Pistole threatened him.

One day he fell off the bar stool with a glass of tequila in his hand. It smashed on the tile floor and cut him badly. He staggered out of the door and sat in the plaza on a bench in the sun, holding the artery in his wrist to stanch the bleeding. The hand went on dripping blood until a tourist passing through town took a scarf and bound the wound tightly, but she said he needed to see a doctor and have it stitched. Since he continued simply to rock back and forth on the bench, she offered to take him to the doctor, and on learning that there wasn't one in Santa Ynez, got him into her car and drove him to a clinic in Durango, where she was doing research. Nothing was said, but Earle moved in with her.

Taffy Spreadeagle, when she was unable to get an academic appointment, had worked for a time for a TV news program, but now she was back at her fieldwork as a feminist anthropologist studying the different styles and poses of masculinity and their psychic, cultural, and sociopolitical implications. The strutting cocks who hung around the Mexican bars were grist for her academic mill. She didn't know what to make of Earle, who had no interest whatsoever in sex and no pretenses to conceal his deficiency. She tried from time to time to test him, but he remained inert to all her clumsy moves. Not surprising, since he was still drinking heavily with money he panhandled on the street.

The days passed with Taffy playing around the edges of sex in the cantinas with the Mexican studs. Earle sat mostly in her room alone having hallucinations in which he visualized exploring various terrains through which sex might become intelligible. In his dreams he moved through a desert covered with millions of dried condoms leading to libidinal investments across visual and discursive practices, corporeal enactments, and virtual identifications. His sexual *jornada del muerte* passed through an infinity of provisional locations, implying a constitutive and reflexive negativity of absences, repulsions, failures, and banalities.

Taffy had to go north to begin the teaching year at Greasewood Community College, where she had recently been appointed as a part-time, temporary lecturer to give a course based on a monograph she was working on, *The Hogtied Phallus: Misogynist Themes in Cowboy Poetry.* Not knowing or caring what he was doing, still stoned, Earle rode with her. When they got to Mesquitopolis he stayed in her apartment, but when she caught him stealing money for drinks from her purse, she threw him out.

For a time he drifted, more often abusing one substance or another—*How do you abuse a substance? Hold it down and hit it with a baseball bat? Seems more like it's abusing me*—sometimes in jail for a few days, doing odd jobs here and there, sleeping on park benches on newspapers. One day he found himself staring at the personals on the bench under his face, reading an ad for work in the alumni office at Greasewood Community College. *Good old Greasewood, "through the greasewood the candlelight is gleaming, Across the fields there comes the smell of new cut greasewood" what the hell, I'm sure not getting anywhere this way.* He cleaned himself up a bit in a gas station and soon found himself working as a file clerk in the Greasewood alumni office. When Smithers, '07, became CEO of American Nuts and Screws, Earle saw to it that the information went into *The Greaser: The Alumni Review of Greasewood Community College.* He did the same for the guy who won a country-club golf tournament or was honored as Christian of the Year, in Tombola, Mississippi. In time Earle became a fixture on campus, "Good old Joad," and one of the favorites of the *Greaser* staff, famous for knowing the names of all the alumni.

Nine

Operation Gulliver

"Outage is just the person for the job, tenacious, smart, a real fighter. Stopping the genocide in Tbongo with its green-hell jungles, its people-swallowing swamps, its vicious Tongo and Bongo tribes, and its fearsome diseases is not a task for your ordinary general. Tbongo has been the center of the African World War for years, and the land is filled with hostile armies. Someone with real fighting instincts and abilities is required, and Outage stands firmly in the shoes that Burnside, Custer, and George C. Scott once filled."

T. Bullit Fullstop, secretary of defense (DEFSEC), slammed his fist on the table to emphasize his words and glared at the Joint Chiefs of Staff, the director of the CIA, and their aides gathered around the table in the Pentagon war plans room. Doctor Alice Dashiki, who sat at the State Department desk on central Africa, had been invited but had not shown up because of a prior commitment to the campaign to pay reparations to all descendants of former slaves.

Those present all looked out the windows and up at the ceiling, and as he looked at their bland faces, DEFSEC's face got purple. *Goddamn President Thud, anyway, why the hell can't he keep his hands off those young girls who work around the White House? This Triola Joad—where the hell does a name like that come from?—was probably asking for it anyway with a skirt up around her ass and nearly bare boobs. The son-of-a-bitch has barely gotten through one scrape, and now, here he is, back at it again. She's going to sue, dead certain, and the attorney general, that fink, Ellen Barratri, will sure as hell appoint the special investigator that her old boss, Senator Brightgrin, is screaming for. So now we've got to have another nice little technological war, Operation Zip Up, with correspondents broadcasting from inside the target area, Goddamn it, and all to get the country's attention off this bimbo. Here I am,* DEFSEC, *expected to somehow run a war with these geeks. If I can get Outage out of the country as commander of the expeditionary force, maybe Chameleon and the FBI will drop his molestation investigation, and we can avoid another scandal.*

The secretary of defense began to speak again. "We have the most democratic army in the world, no doubt of that. Gender parity has been achieved in every rank, except buck private, and in some specialties there are more women than men, they tend to reenlist more often than the men. The 'tell, and tell, and tell' policy has been a really big success in getting the homos to enlist. And while all this has led to a considerable amount of 'grab ass'—it is impossible to ignore it—so long as it is consensual apparently it is okay. The population is 10 percent blacks, and the armed forces are 37 percent, so no discrimination there, or among Latinos or other races, except whites, and nobody bothers to count them. Yes, Sir, the Democratic Armed Forces of the United States, DAFUS, are fighting fit."

But there is that damned business of the union. If the fucking Congress hadn't made it legal for the armed forces to organize, to make the frigging unions happy, there never would have been this army strike over low wages, long hours, and dangerous work-

ing conditions. But just now the entire United States Army is out on strike, and how do we get the bastards to return to duty and bring democracy and human rights to Tbongo?

"Well, there is no doubt that Outage is a good man, the very best, in many ways." It was Lieutenant General Nancy Grinder, commandant of the United States Marine Corps, a black glove over her prosthetic hand, "but I've sometimes wondered if he has, to put it crudely, big enough balls for fighting a hot war in difficult circumstances. He never scored above the 95th percentile in the Military Goniff war games. My own candidate would be General Candy Bellicose, who regularly scores in the 99th percentile on aggression games and has never had a breath of scandal attached to her name. She is the kind who will give the Tongos and the Bongos what for, get right down in the ditch and engage in a pissing contest with them, and win."

Her sentence finished, General Grinder dropped her artificial hand on the table with a mechanical clank to emphasize her point. *If they are going to fight this lousy little war and kill a lot of people just to distract the attention of the media from another of President Thud's gropings, then it's only fair that the women should for once run things. Besides, old Outage has a bad reputation for harassing his female staff and the wives of other generals. No one has ever openly accused him of extramarital affairs, right, but Freddy Ananias, the new head of the CIA, has a file on him a foot thick. One report says that he has been visiting kiddie-porn sites on his computer and that he has set up meetings in New Jersey motels—what a state—with some of his contacts. Those goddamn men know better than to mess with me, though. When old Rugby Portface tried to use me as a human shield at Dry Tortuga, I may have lost my hand doing it, but I took the steam out of that old fraud. And when General Nukem groped me I gave him the back of my hand, the false one, he lost two teeth. A man with a moral character like Outage's is certainly not fit to lead the cream of democratic women into battle.*

DEFSEC was annoyed but had his feelings under control. "I know what you are insinuating, Nancy, with that world 'scandal,' that Outage has had, may God forgive him, adulterous affairs with the wives of fellow officers. There may be just a little truth in the rumors, I'm not saying yes, I'm not saying no, but nothing has ever been proved. Besides, just here in this room, I have always wondered whether real fighting men and women don't need a little extra testosterone. I know, I know, whenever some woman charged them with harassment, whatever that dreaded word means for sure, we have fired more generals than Stalin and the KGB. Just the other day we demoted General Nukem one grade, broke his sword, cut his pension, and retired him, all for patting a colonel on the butt. Okay, that's what the code of military conduct says we have to do, but we are at the point where our officers would be more at home at a church social than on a battlefield. Who thought up this crazy rule anyway that officers couldn't look at a woman other than their wives? The Chaplains' Corps? As I read history, the old warriors have almost always been hell on the women. Julius Caesar, Alaric the Hun, Napoleon, Eisenhower, they screwed their heads off, and it never seemed to hurt their ability to deploy their weapon systems against the enemy."

Everyone at the table, embarrassed at this macho display, doodled away on their scratch pads. General Grinder was clearly pissed but said nothing. After a time the air force chief of staff, General Jetaway, ventured, rather nervously, "Well, the air force is ready for whatever task our commander-in-chief may order it to undertake. The cost of hardware—over a billion dollars for a fighter plane, and cheap at that price—has forced us to cut back a bit, but we still have almost a squadron of F-38 fighters, made out of solid platinum, and two or three old B-2 bombers. They cost a lot but they have lasted a long time. All the longer since we never took them out in the rain where the paint would have peeled off."

"I wonder," DEFSEC said, if the general configuration of our armed forces is such that we can with confidence take on the Tongos and the Bongos. Very tough fighters, I hear, and masters of their terrain. It may be hard for even a fully democratic armed force to engage them effectively. Somebody is sure as hell going to have to go in on the ground, or the swamp, and winkle them out. We haven't fought a war in the last twenty-five years, and I hear that some of our units are markedly under strength. I should tell the group, in confidence of course, that the army is on strike."

The deputy secretary for procurement and manpower flushed, knowing that DEFSEC was breaking it off in him. *Of course there are serious problems. Some of the assault divisions, despite all the recruitment efforts, lack a racial and gender mix that matches the composition of the national population. Though, God knows, it's not my fault.*

"Don't blame me," he burst out, "once Congress raised the armed forces pay scale to equal civilian rates for the same kind of work, it was necessary to cut back on the manpower a bit. You can't pay buck privates over a hundred thousand dollars a year, plus benefits and golden parachutes, and send them to Harvard after one enlistment, and still run a big army. Unless, that is, you are willing to spend the gross domestic product on soldiers, and the war on disease is already spending the GDP."

"Maybe we better have an unofficial nose count right now," DEFSEC said. "Just how big an armed force do we have? Jetaway has told us about the air force, about a squadron altogether. There are some Apache helicopters in the army, but I hear they are so complicated that no one can fly them, and besides they are so vulnerable to handheld surface-to-air missiles that the army won't risk them in combat. But what about the marines, Grinder?"

"Semper Fi, DEFSEC. [standing up and saluting smartly] We're up to strength and raring to go, as always. Specially now that we have our full complement of the modified Gooneybirds that rise like a helicopter and then flap their wings to fly like a bird. The 32d Deep Penetration Battalion has just been reinforced by a bunch of women with lower-body strength equal to any men. They may not scare the enemy, as the duke of Wellington said about his troops at Waterloo, but they sure as hell scare me. The Lavender Berets, our elite seek-and-destroy group, are also up to strength. Yes, I can say, with great satisfaction, that the United States Marines are ready once again to fight our country's battles on the land and on the sea. Our enlistments fell off for a time, but the new uniforms designed by Ralph Lauren took care of that handily and also helped us achieve male-female parity in the shock troops. Full democracy now reinforces the fighting spirit of the old corps."

"Well, that's just great, Nancy, *now every marine has someone to screw,* since you're supposed to be the first to fight, just how many combat-ready divisions can you field by, say, next Wednesday?"

"Shit, DEFSEC, I haven't heard anyone talk about divisions since Nam. Combat teams are all the thing now."

"Well, [snarling] combat teams then, how many goddamned marines have you got ready to go in and kick ass in Africa?"

"Don't raise your voice to me, DEFSEC, just because the goddamned army is on strike. I don't know why you are always picking on me and my Marines, DEFSEC. You turn everything I say around and twist my meaning until I don't know what we're talking about. But I do know that I am not going to take this sexual chauvinism any longer. You men want the armed forces to be a testosteronic phallocracy again, and when the Congress makes you run a truly democratic, gender-blind outfit you get mad and try to hegemonize the women. Submission is what you really want, but you are not going to get it from General Nancy Grinder, USMC. My lawyer will file a class-action gender-bias suit against you tomorrow in the name of the entire corps. Good-bye." [an exaggerated salute]

General Grinder swept out of the room, followed by several aides in lavender berets and Gucci jump boots. DEFSEC was holding his head in his hands, but he had one more arrow to his bow. He had been in the navy when a young man, and he still tended to think of the fleet as the first line of defense. *Let's see, does Tbongo have a seacoast? No, can't count on that. Seacoast of Bohemia. Ha, ha!!! Goddamned Harvard education. Cruiser lobbing shells into the jungle in Conrad's* Heart of Darkness, *hopeless. "Mistah DEFSEC, he dead." Yes, by God, there is water there, the Tbongo is a river, a big river, maybe not aircraft carriers or nuclear submarines, but surely a destroyer, maybe even a missile cruiser, show those damned Tongos and Bongos to fool around with the democratic armed might of the United States.*

"Well, Admiral Keelhawl, is the navy prepared to put the troops ashore in the upper Tbongo, just like the good old days, Guadalcanal and Omaha Beach, providing forward air support and clearing the landing beaches, maintaining a steady flow of supplies to our boys, and to our girls, too, it goes without saying? The navy has in recent years gotten the largest portion of the defense budget to build a fleet that would have astounded John Paul Jones and Admiral Farragut. And now you have a chance to use it."

You could talk to Keelhawl about Guadalcanal and Omaha Beach because he had been in the navy that long. Since the Equal Rights for Soldiers and Sailors (ERSS) bill had been passed, the armed forces had had the same rights as civilians, including the right not to be retired because of age. If ageism was forbidden in colleges, then it was out on the navy's poop decks as well. So Keelhawl was permanent CNO, seniority took care of that, but his staff did most of the talking, particularly the bluff Commodore Bowditch Bulkhead, who was the real power in the navy these days.

Keelhawl, who hated the democratic all-gender navy, had a little speech that he always used on such occasions as this. He used it now. "Once we used to know how to fight a war because we knew that the purpose of the armed forces was to fight, and we did the things that made us better fighters, not more democratic wimps. Will we ever be able again to do what we did in the war, World War II? We put fourteen million men in uniform, supplied the rest of the world with arms and money, and fought in two oceans. During one week in 1944 an American army occupied Rome, the American navy destroyed the Japanese fleet in the Philippine Sea, and another army invaded northern Europe. That is power, and after that we won a cold war with a nuclear superpower, bankrupting them in an arms race that made us rich. But now we just piss around, making sure the troops have plenty of ice cream factories and worrying about whether someone deprived somebody of their democratic rights by propositioning them."

Bulkhead took over at this point, with his engine-room indicator on full confidence. "Sir, America rules the waves now, not Britannia. But the upper Tbongo is not an ideal operational locus for aircraft carriers three thousand feet long, guided missile cruisers that can destroy half the earth with one launch, and atomic submarines with doomsday capacity. The United States Navy is a battle force second to none, Sir, and since it is fully integrated, it can go anywhere in the world and annihilate any enemy. So long as he is big enough, so long as he is big enough, Sir."

Heavy silence descended on the polished mahogany table around which were assembled the leaders of the mightiest war machine the world had ever seen, DAFUS.

Clearing his throat, DEFSEC spoke again: "Let me see if I can sum this up. The United States has enough firepower to waste the world many times over, to obliterate every living thing on the face of the earth, and yet we are a muscle-bound giant. Our weapons are so complex that people need doctorates to load and fire them. And so costly that building even one absorbs all the dollars that once were spent on entire armies. So large and powerful have we become that we cannot bend over and crush the small enemies who plague us and thwart our will everywhere. The air force planes are so fast they will be halfway out of Africa in the time it takes to say 'Tongo' or 'Bongo.' The navy's ships are so big and so powerful they can't get at the enemy, the marines are suing the Department of Defense, and the army is on strike. Does that about take care of it?"

Again silence descended on the table, a few glasses of ice water were poured and drunk, Jetaway lit a cigar by nervous mistake, and hastily stubbed it out on his palm. The smoking lamp was always out, smoke had joined drink and sex in being forbidden to the American armed services.

Bulkhead, always alert and knowing that things couldn't be left in this state, raised his hand and began confidently:

"Sir, it would perhaps be more suitable for this particular task to outsource it, hire someone, say the Cubans, to undertake the Tongo-Bongo democratic independence expedition (TODIE). The Cubans are short, damned short, on technological warfare, but have lots of small boats they use to take refugees to Miami, and three or four brigades of their troops are armed with rifles and light machine guns. Then, too, they are renowned for their fighting spirit, and they are also very hungry just now. They have been sitting down there on that little island, refrying the beans, getting madder and madder at the Yanqui Capitalist Pigs for continuing to embargo them, and Castro—he's still in control—might be very relieved to blow off this steam in some place far from home. He's been to Africa before and is nimble enough to deal effectively with the Tongos and the Bongos, Sir."

[Long, thoughtful silence, everyone looks around to see how the idea is being received, then big exhalation of collective breath]

"Well, it has merits, he might come cheap. How would we pay him?"

"On a cost-plus basis, surely. Meet his expenses and guarantee him 10 percent over his actual outlay. He will need to buy the food, ammunition, fuel, and medical supplies that our embargo has kept from him these many years, and we can provide these out of our stores, with a profit margin that will cover all expenditures to him."

"There's really no sense in thinking about it. Miami would raise holy hell, and President Thud can't afford to lose the Cuban exile vote. He ran on a platform of no deals with Cuba and would find it difficult to wiggle out of this one. But, what do Director Ananias and the CIA have to say about all this, [sarcastically] after all, they know a good deal about Cuba."

"That's right, DEFSEC, the agency *didn't* distinguish itself at the Bay of Pigs, but that was long before my time and my present staff's. The days of poisoned beards and explosive cigars delivered by the Mafia are long gone, and we now rely on long-range, state-of-the-art, cutting-edge communications technology, of the same kind just installed in the Pentagon, fed into a vast data base and analyzed by computers as big as boxcars. Our information is nowadays scarcely touched by human hand, so to speak. And by simply punching the appropriate code into my handheld wireless computer [he holds it up] no bigger than Dick Tracy's [incomprehension all around]—ha, ha, that's what we call it in a kidding way, a Dick Tracy, the old funny-paper detective?—I can instantly give you the latest gin on Cuba and things Cuban."

"Ananias, I haven't believed a word from your agency since Saddam Hussein took over Israel without a word of warning from you, and Afghanistan went nuclear, but let's hear what your machine has to say."

"I protest, DEFSEC, those were not on my watch, and at that time the agency was working out some bugs in our new supercomputers. But, here, I have "Cuba" on my Dick Tracy. Look! The latest *beisbol* scores, the price of sugar on the world market, the current cigar production rate, the number of refugees in route to Key West, ah, here it is, under 'R,' 'readiness of armed forces.' It's all pretty technical, DEFSEC, but what it comes down to is that half the population is in the army and that they are considered among the finest jungle fighters in the world."

"That's pretty high-tech information, Mr. Director. I don't suppose you have a link that will allow you to tell us just who are the very best guerrillas."

"Yessssss, I think so, DEFSEC, I heard the other day they were working on something called links, they're in blue, and, damned if here isn't one. I just double-click on the blue words, GorillaWarfare@CIA.Guv, just like that, see [pointing], and here on the screen are tables of effectiveness of irregular freedom fighters from various countries."

"And, pray tell, Mr. Director, who is at the top of that list?"

"Well, ten minus one plus four, yes, that looks like it, thirteen. King Kong, Inc., no, that can't be right. Let's try another spelling. Yes, here it is. The agency estimates that the Tongos and the Bongos are the finest guerrilla fighters in the world, with, let's see, a note that reads—some of this print on the Dick Tracy is pretty small—a note that reads, 'if only spears and bows are counted.'"

"And if guns are counted who are the best fighters? Can you give me that?"

"Yes, I think so, just a minute, here it is, 'if firearms are weighted, then the Cubans are the world's best mano-a-mano fighters. So, it's okay, DEFSEC, you have the expertise of the CIA for it, make sure all the Cubans have rifles and they can beat the hell out of the Tongos and the Bongos, so long as they don't get any guns."

Murmurs of approval around the table, a few smiles break out and a little conversation, until DEFSEC bangs the gavel for order.

"It looks like we've done a pretty good morning's work here. It's not foolproof, and we still have the strike in the army and the class-action suit from the marines, but we can handle those in time. I don't know if I can sell Thud on this, or if he can sell Castro, who must be a hundred and ten. But if we get the Cubans on board for this expedition to restore freedom to central Africa, we will be able to say once again that the armed forces of the United States have the know-how to get any job done. I have on my desk a sign saying, 'The difficult we do at once, the impossible takes a little longer,' and, by God, we are going once again to do the impossible. Now, who's got a good code name for this shindig, Operation? Operation? What? Come on."

"Groper."

"No nasty jokes now, a lot of people, not Americans, thank God, are going to die to avenge that little White House bimbo."

"Coconut."

"No, too primitive, sounds as if we were disrespecting the natives."

"Gulliver, Operation Gulliver, and the enemy can be Lilliput." Commodore Bulkhead had come up with exactly the right name, and there was a round of quiet applause.

"Mr. President," DEFSEC had his phone in hand, "the code name is 'Operation Gulliver.' No, no, I was just as nice as I could be to General Grinder, you know I really am very fond of her, and I wouldn't do anything in the world to hurt her. Yes, yes, that's right, a wonderful woman, and a fine general, a little sensitive, but so understanding, not a trait always found in marines. No, no, she won't sue; I will personally cut her legal budget to zero this afternoon. Yes, 'Gulliver,' we are going to land the toughest bunch of rojo combat teams you have ever seen in the upper bend of the Tbongo, and wham! . . . 'Rojo?' it's Spanish for 'red,' a common way I believe for designating Cuban assault troops. Yes, I know they are communists, that's why they are called 'rojo,' and of course they are our enemies, but what better way to get rid of them than to send them up the Tbongo without a paddle, so to speak? One hell of a tough place, I can tell you, Mr. President. I certainly wouldn't want to send any of our boys, and certainly none of our girls, I mean women, into the heart of darkness. Oh, you like the phrase, 'heart of darkness,' just something I thought up for 'Operation Gulliver,' we might use it to define our objective, 'a mission to bring light to the heart of darkness,' something catchy like that, of course all these terms will have to be vetted by public relations.

"The gender mix of the rojo brigades? I don't believe we know that just yet, but we can negotiate any mix we want, I would suppose; and race, too, though it's a bit complicated in Cuba. Castro is going . . . Of course, Castro, who else runs Cuba, Elián Gonzalez? And of course it is going to take some sweet talk to bring him around, but I have the feeling you are just the man to do it. At the same time you will make your name in American history as the statesman who brought to an end the long and painful divorce between two nations that have so much in common. Yes, yesss, yesssss. It will go over big, and no one will remember old indiscretions in the Oval Office, Mr. President, I promise you."

"Nearing target. The green light is on. On your feet. Hook up your lines. Over drop zone. The door is open. First woman out. Pocohontas!"

Corporal Triola Joad of the Lizzie Borden Independent Women's Parachute Combat Team (LBIWPCT) felt the yank of the chute above her and looked down at the green jungle stretching for miles in all directions, unbroken except for the wide curving line of the river. Around her, other chutes blossomed white, and now the equipment chutes began to open, red for heavy weapons and ammunition, green for food, blue for, *oh my God, medical supplies. How did I ever get into this anyway?* She had only signed on for the internship program at the White House during the summer, and when President Thud had groped her in the Oval Office, she had been so shocked that she had blurted out something about the law against harassment. And then before she could say Jack Robinson, that nice black guy, the president's best friend, had offered to be her lawyer and get her a golden parachute. She thought that meant a big settlement of some kind, like the executives got when their companies went bust, but it turned out to be a real parachute in the LBIWPCT. *Oh, God, the ground is coming up so fast. What do you do? You flex your knees, land lightly, and roll over. Shit, what a messsssssss.*

Triola came to, lying on a big lily pad, floating on a shallow pond covered with gunk. She unbuckled her chute and slid into the water, made her way through the mud to the bank, where several of the other paratroopers were drying their hair and opening some of the equipment drops to see what was in them.

"Where's Captain Sharpspur?"

"Damned if I know, I saw her jump, but I haven't seen her or Lieutenant Dollop since. None of us are going for sure to look for those mean bastards, they have been pounding our asses ever since we trained at Fort Custer. Corporal is the highest rank we've got, so I guess you're it, Triola."

"Whaddya mean, 'it'? I don't know any more about this crazy expedition than you do. I heard just what you heard, how we were the vanguard of Operation Gulliver and that we were being landed ahead of time to take Idi Amin International Airport so that the heavy weapons troops coming after us could land and deploy."

"What's 'deploy'?"

"I think it means 'blow the hell out of them,' it's what the troops always do, but we better get our asses moving toward IAIA. Saddle up and move out, column of twos, your left, your left, your left."

The sound of a roaring motor came out of the bush, and the Lizzie Bordens dived for cover. But it wasn't a tank, or even an armored car, just an old rusty bus with a smiling black driver who pulled up and offered cold Mazo Lite Beer from an ice chest for a dollar apiece.

"Howdy. My name is Jack Robinson. Cold beer, get your cold beer here. Where you all going with those great big guns?"

Triola spoke up, "To Idi Amin International Airport to pacify those goddamned Tongos and Bongos who are defying the armed might of DAFUS and the ultimatum of POTUS, the president of the United States."

"My, my, you sure are rough looking, and those are mighty big hatchets you are waving about, but how come they sent a bunch of good-looking girls like you—those combat fatigues do a lot for you, and I sure like that big shoulder patch, an ax is it, with '40 more' underneath?—to do a big job like taking on the Tongos and the Bongos? They're mean bastards. I thought they were paying some real macho Cuban men, the rojo brigades, to do this job, the U.S. Army being on strike, the navy unable to get up the river, and the marines in court."

"Well, Castro wouldn't play, or I guess he wanted too many pesos to take on the Tongos and the Bongos, so the only combat-ready outfit available was the Lizzie Bordens. It turned out that when an all-woman combat parachute team was formed in response to the nonnegotiable demands of the Million-Woman March on Washington, the authorities, for some reason, never got around to officially inducting the unit into the regular army. So we are not legally on strike like the army, or suing like the gyrenes, on the contrary we are in a high state of readiness, and when Castro said 'nyet,' they rushed us onto the plane, and here we are."

"And none too soon, either. They've been waiting for days at IAIA with the welcome wagon. Every hour another plane loaded with correspondents and TV folks arrives, and the Portapot facilities are beginning to fail. You don't dare put your foot down in the bushes anywhere around the field. The Trans-African Bagpipe Band has been practicing The 'Star-Spangled Banner' night and day, about to drive everybody crazy with all those high notes. You better hop aboard; it's a hot day. Have a nice Mazo Lite, only a dollar U.S. I'll drop you just before the airport so that you can rush in, looking like you've been on a desperate march through the jungle, wave your axes around, and give somebody forty whacks. Then we can all have a nice barbecue and try out the latest native dances before we sign the new treaty. Don't worry about the parachutes loaded with supplies, my associates are already picking them up and delivering them to the central warehouse."

"Some of them are booby-trapped if you don't know the code."

"That was that loud boom we heard a minute ago? Well, let's hope nobody got hurt. Get aboard and we'll motor up to the airport."

The pictures were one of the TV triumphs of the century, won the Pulitzer and every other journalism prize. Hard-looking women, their clothes torn here and there, revealing some white flesh, war paint on faces, screaming their fierce battle cry, "FORTY MORE!" Hatchets raised, hair loose below their helmets, rushing out of the jungle at the spears of the massed formations of Tongos and Bongos, who gave their blood-curdling native war cry in return—something that sounded like "FORGIVE FOREIGN DEBT!"—and rushed headlong at the LBIWPCT.

The two warlike formations didn't get at each other, however, because of the crush of camera operators, reporters, media types holding microphones on long poles, paparazzi, and the anchorpersons of all the major networks dressed in foreign-correspondent bush jackets and safari pants tucked into high snake-proof boots.

Buzz Mordant, with his red suspenders over his bush jacket, talked excitedly into his mike while his camera crew ground away:

"Buzz Mordant, Nebbish News, folks, there are some of the toughest paratroopers you ever saw coming out of the jungle at us, full speed. We can see their hatchets in the air, so we know this is the famous Lizzie Borden women's parachute combat team, feared far and wide for giving America's enemies forty whacks, and then giving them forty more. A blond corporal with JOAD T printed on her combat fatigues leads them with a battle light in her eyes. Uncle Sam can be proud of the women who represent him here today, standing tall, like Custer at Little Big Horn and MacArthur in the Philippines. Corporal, would you be willing to say a few words to the folks back home who are sitting with bated breath in front of their TVs, their hearts and minds with you gals?"

"Joad, Triola. Corporal. 372–29–08."

"No, no, I'm not the enemy, I am a friend, an American television commentator, everybody loves us, we make people famous, you can tell me everything freely, where you come from, what you were thinking when you jumped into this green hell. But first, before we do an in-depth interview, a message from our sponsors, the makers of the only beer that never lets you down or blows you up, Mazo Lite, who are supplying the airship *Spirit of Tbongo* to film these events from high overhead today."

By this time, Triola and the Lizzies had gotten through the media crowd only to find the Bongos and the Tongos selling some nice souvenirs, a few tribal masks but mostly T-shirts and sweatshirts, printed with Bongo, or Tongo, with crude drawings of fierce lions, snakes, and crocodiles. The fires for an authentic native African barbecue—ALL YOU CAN EAT FOR 2 DOLLARS US—were already burning and great oxen were turning on the spits, with grease drops hissing on the coals. Here and there dances had begun and the Trans-African Bagpipe Band had put away their bagpipes and taken to steel drums and to more fundamental beats that everybody could sing and dance to. The Lizzie Bordens were drawn into dancing circles, clapping hands and trying out new steps, and soon disintegrated as a fighting force. As Triola was stripping off her camouflaged fatigues to dance the latest craze dance, the wild fandango, in her G.I. khaki skivvies, she caught sight of a familiar figure coming toward her through the crowd.

"My God, Calista."

"Triola. Oh, my, my, my little sister, and a big soldier come to save the queen of the Tongos on the eve of her being sacrificed to appease the wrath of the Great God Torque."

"No, Sis, that isn't what we're here for at all. What a gorgeous costume you have, that short grass skirt suits you particularly well. I always envied your legs. President Thud and the United States of America are intervening in the name of humanity and the United Nations to keep the Bongos and Tongos from genociding one another. But as long as we are here, we might as well save you, too, from a fate that is no doubt worse than death. What does the old god Torque have to be pissed off about enough to require the supreme sacrifice of a Valley Girl?"

"Well, we don't quite know, but it's a long-standing custom to give him a virgin queen every year at the end of the dry season."

"But, Calista, you're not a . . ."

"Shh, let sleeping dogs lie, so who knows the difference any more? Surely not old Torque."

"Aren't there tests conducted by witch doctors with dirty hands, ugh, who cackle, paw your smooth white body, and probe your tender parts?"

"You've been reading too many adventure-romance novels, but so have the Tongos and the Bongos. They are just mad for Primal-Scream Comic Books like the new best-seller, *Queen of the Phallic Women,* by someone who calls herself Drusilla Fury, the World's Angriest Woman. I wouldn't want to be related to her."

"So, what are you going to do? We can get the Lizzies together, if we can find them in the middle of this carnival, and make a stand to protect one of the fundamental rights of an American woman, not to be questioned about intact hymens, but we probably couldn't hold out."

"No, no, don't make a fuss now. It's all arranged, and I have made lots of friends here, people who know how to handle these little things. It's not New York, but, hey, what is? It's okay except for the telephone system."

At that moment a messenger from Cleftstick Overseas Express arrived with a high-priority message:

> commander, us intra-african expeditionary force stop: agreement with the un to keep peacekeepers in place at idi amin until tongos and bongos work out satisfactory means of controlling ancient enmities stop lbiwpct pentagon choice for this critical duty stop remain on site and keep peace until further orders stop use american express card for expenses stop keep in touch by new pentagon privatized telephone customer service center, a modern electronic marvel stop defsec fullstop.

Calista had been swept away into the crowd by the time it took Triola to read the message, and so she made her way to the public telephone and using her card dialed the Pentagon to get some clarification of exactly what they had in mind for Operation Gulliver and how far they should go in keeping the peace. She got through only after a lot of buzzing and explaining to operators in Bangkok and Valparaiso.

"This is the Pentagon. Thank you for calling. We value your business. Please hold." For a time all she heard was a medley of the marches of John Philip Sousa. Then after a silence a voice came on: "This call may be monitored to ensure that it is being used for official business and that your concerns are treated courteously and promptly. If you want to report a war, press 1, followed by the pound sign. If you want to start a war, press 2, followed by star. If you want to stop a war, press 3, followed by pound and star."

Oh hell, Triola thought, *which is the star and which is the pound, I can never remember. Besides, am I here to start or end a war?*

"Your time limit has expired. Please hang up and dial again."

Triola swiped her AmEx card through the telephone and went through the routine again. *Well, 3 sounds closer than anything else,* and so she punched 3 and hit both pound and star.

"You have punched 3, if this is correct please punch 1, followed by the pound sign. If it is not correct please punch 2, followed by the star sign.

"Listen carefully to the following choices as the menu options have recently changed. Are you authorized to stop wars? If so, press 1. Are you merely an interested party who thinks he or she can help out? If so, press 2. Are you a peacenik of some kind? If so, press 3.

I just got orders to stop this war from DEFSEC, *so I must be authorized, and so I have to press 1, I think.*

"You have punched 1, if this is correct please punch 1 again, followed by the pound sign. If it is not correct, please punch 2, followed by the star sign.

"If it is a naval war, press 1, if air war, press 2, if land war, press 3, if ballistic war, press 4, if all of the above, press 5, followed by pound, star."

Well, it seems to be mostly on the ground, at least just now, though we are paratroopers, so 3 it is.

"You have punched 3, if this is correct, please punch 1, followed by the pound sign. If it is not correct, please punch 2, followed by the star sign.

"How would you describe the war? If brushfire, press 1, if guerrilla, press 2, if superpower, press 3, and if third-world, press 4."

Guerrilla seems about right, though the Tongos and the Bongos do seem to be well organized, and 4 certainly fits, but you can't select two, so 2 it is.

"You have punched 2, if this is correct, please punch 1, followed by the pound sign. If it is not correct, please punch 2, followed by the star sign. Hold on the line until our next peacemaking expert is free. Please be patient, this is a busy time of year for us."

The strains of the "Washington Light Infantry March" began to play in the background.

"Thank you for holding. All of our experts are still busy serving other customers."

More marches.

"Thank you for holding. One of our representatives will be free shortly."

"My name is Bulkhead, how may I help you? First, give me your full name and serial number, if any, and then identify the continent on which you want to stop a war."

"My name is Corporal Triola Joad, 372–29–08, and since all our officers are missing, I am the highest-ranking trooper in the Lizzie Borden Combat Team, and we have just jumped into darkest Africa to keep the Tongos and the Bongos from slaughtering one another, which they are busily getting ready to do over the souvenir concession."

"What is your present exact location?"

"We are at Idi Amin International Airport."

"Bully for you, Joad, my computer says that that is exactly where you are supposed to be and that DEFSEC has just sent you a secret order to stay there for as long as necessary to serve as a peacekeeping force for the U.N. Good luck, and thank you for calling the Pentagon."

The Lizzie Bordens moved into an old French fort, Fort Zinderneuf, on a little hill overlooking Idi Amin, and there they waited, where so many French Foreign Legionnaires before them had waited until they had been unable any longer to remember what they came there to forget. Everyone puzzled over graffiti carved into the barrack's wall, like the copperplate "Adjutant Lejaune Eats It, B. G.," and below it in ragged legionnaires' argot, "Beau Geste, vous batard, nous nous rongeron ici—Achille Lejaune."

But now the Stars and Stripes flew overhead, representing America's commitment to keeping world peace, though orders telling the Lizzies just what to do never seemed to come. There had been a plane or two with rations and other supplies, and Captain Sharpspur and Lieutenant Dollop, a little the worse for wear, emerged from the jungle and began making everyone salute and practice routine drills, until they both came down with malaria and were invalided home. The friendly bus driver, Jack Robinson, who had picked the Lizzies up after they jumped, seemed to run everything and was arranging all purchases at very reasonable prices, charged to their American Express cards.

Life there in the tropics could have been really quite pleasant, except for the constant ominous beating of the drums in the jungle. The Tongos and the Bongos were inclined to make trouble whenever they felt like it, and rained rocks on the troops whenever the Lizzies tried to prevent them from raping, mutilating, and murdering one another.

When Triola asked about Calista she was told that she had indeed been taken into a cave and ravished by the Great God Torque, who must have been satisfied because it had been raining ever since. But one day Triola got a cryptic postcard from America that said only, "Torque a disappointment. New York still Big Apple."

There would be a new election in the United States in two years, and the candidates were already campaigning hard in Iowa and New Hampshire. Culpable was promising to bring our troops home from Africa, promising that America would never again intervene in civil wars, while Thud, who was running for a second term, promised to keep them there until the ancient enmity between the Tongos and the Bongos was at last at an end and peace reigned in Tbongo.

Ten
Virtual America

The in-depth focus group, funded by Nebbish Network, 51 percent of which was now owned by American Nuts and Screws, was under the direction of Dr. Emma Pessary, Ph.D., whom Somerset Joad vaguely remembered from high school days. The topic was, interestingly enough he thought, since he had had some experience in this matter, the connection between television watching habits and early toilet training. Somerset had been looking for work after his booth in the Religion USA Mall had been closed down, on a strictly bottom-line basis. Business had been dropping off for some time, and the Right Reverend Retrofit's successor was less than friendly. The pay for the new job was fairly good, and since no heavy lifting was involved, Somerset made an appointment to be interviewed by Dr. Pessary.

"What do you do when you watch the news on TV?" Emma Pessary, who didn't remember him, glared at Somerset and bit off her words as if she had something against him. *What does she want?*

Something to do with toilet training the ad said, so, okay, smart-ass, let's try this one.

"Well, I don't know if I ought to say so, but I usually watch the news while I'm sitting on the can."

"Did you have a TV in your bathroom when you were a child?"

"Not exactly, Ma just left the door open, and I could see into the front room and hear what was said if she turned the volume up."

"It doesn't sound very sanitary, but let's let that go. Does the news have any effect on you?"

"Oh, yeah. I'm normally pretty tight, you know, but I begin to loosen up once I hear the announcer's voice, 'This is the Nebbish Network, WNIT Bodybag News, with Buzz Mordant and the Channel 666 news team. Sitting in tonight for Buzz is Angelica Semicolon, and sitting in for Angelica is Ronald Ampersand.' When the traffic helicopter comes on and shows the bottlenecks on the highways, it clutches me up, but by the time I have seen two or three fire victims, a police brutality or two, a madman who has pushed a young girl in front of the subway, and am getting into sports, I begin really to relax. But it's the weather that finally does it, 'Partly cloudy tomorrow, temperature in the 90s, showers in the evening,' and everything lets go."

Emma Pessary's lips steadily tightened and her eyes grew narrower as Somerset really put everything he had into it, thinking that he was giving her a connection between anality and the news that would enable her to write half a dozen articles for *Sociological Niches*. It didn't work quite the way he planned, though.

"I think you must be some kind of pervert or something, I've never heard such a load of you-know-what. But I suppose your mother must have let you watch the TV to keep you on the potty, and you got hung up on that phase, never moving on to the genital level."

Somerset wanted only to please her, so, remembering what he had learned from Dr. Transférans about anal and genital, he blurted out, "No, no, I get an erection every time it happens, and sometimes when certain kinds of weather are being described, like, 'heavy precipitation with winds at twelve knots from the northwest,' I just . . ."

"Enough, stop right there. I know everything I need to know. You are obviously deeply neurotic, the 'void-loop syndrome' I would hazard a guess, or you may have a 'downward displaced glossolalia dysfunction.' Whatever, you need a good psychiatrist and some heavy tranquilizers, but in the meantime we can use you. You provide a real base, a rock-bottom base, on which to begin constructing an image of what goes on in the limbic brain in response to the TV news. The network is funding a long-range study of this psychic linkage in the population at large, and we are going to workshop the question by setting up a focus panel to test how items in the news affect the autonomous nervous system, and we might as well begin with certain primal minds like yours. We would pay you a living wage, enough to provide you with a place to live and meals to eat."

Even though the idea of becoming one of Emma Pessary's white rats running through her maze did not appeal to Somerset, it was at least worth trying. Lots of things were going on in television, and something really interesting might turn up.

Somerset was right, there was lots of activity in TV at the time, most of it generated by the disappearance of Seamus O'Hoopla. The major fault line running through television, and electronic communications in general, is "too much," and true to the nature of their medium, the stations had been showing, twenty-four hours a day, seven days a week, pictures of the fence around the O'Hoopla Ranch in West Texas, pictures of the family hugging one another while saddling their horses, and endless discussions of the latest link in "The Tragic Chain of the O'Hooplas, America's Royal Family."

Young Seamus had died in the prime of life, soon after graduating with honors from Lone Tree State University, which, with his democratic instincts, he had preferred to Ivy, where most of his family had gone. In the spirit of adventure and risk-taking that had marked his family from the days when Himself O'Hoopla ran illegal booze and bucket shops, the O'Hooplas had always sought adventure, and found it. Senator Codswallop O'Hoopla, the "old lion guarding the family," as *The New York Smirk* perceptively called him, in his youth had driven cars off bridges at high speeds and swam a bay alone in the dead of night. Other reckless O'Hooplas played fatal football games on ski slopes among trees and rocks, chased fleet-footed young women down unlighted beaches, and flew aircraft at night without instrument training.

Young Seamus had heard in one of his courses at Lone Tree State, "Restoration and Eighteenth-Century Drama," of "headstrong allegories on the banks of the Nile," and nothing would do but to seek out and wrestle one of these monsters, just like the Seminole Indians he had seen on the Tamiami Trail. Presumably he realized, the moment he tried to put a full nelson on a ten-foot-long headstrong Nile allegory, that he had missed something in class that fatal day.

The search for his body had been long and unsuccessful. The New York branch of Abide with Me, the chain that had made a fortune out of the many national remembrances of this and other public tragedies, ran out of yellow ribbon, teddy bears, candles, children's drawings, and flowers the first day. Tons of these items and other testimonies of a nation's sorrow blocked the doorway to the New York condo—not far removed from the famous *Wall of Hope*—in which Seamus had lived out his joyful bachelor existence among ordinary citizens. Television interviews with folks on the street showed a sorrowing people in tears. "He worked for the people, like all the O'Hooplas," said a homeless man from his pasteboard box at Lincoln Center. "I think it will turn out all right if we just pray to God and have faith," said a mother of seven, hastily crossing herself in front of Saint Patrick's Cathedral.

Meanwhile, other big news was getting short shrift on TV. The Tongos and the Bongos were at it again, united for once to attack the Lizzie Bordens holed up in Fort Zinderneuf. The Supreme Court had just found unconstitutional the congressional declaration of war on disease; and a new and very controversial book about the media, *Tell It Like It Isn't* (Three-Holer Press), by Buzz Mordant, the news anchorman for Nebbish and one of the new communications arts intellectuals, had just appeared.

As a young man Mordant had gone to Ivy University, where he had majored in deconstruction, writing his senior thesis, "Blank Spaces and Acts of Silence," with Professor Pierre de Hors. His studies at that time provided the base for what he now told his readers, including the Suits who ran big networks like Nebbish: "The time has come to treat the news as symptoms of a desire for forms that function as praxis, through their elimination of the distance separating the historical real from its conceptualization."

Despite his fame, Mordant had had souring troubles lately. He had been accused by a girlfriend, Callista Joad—whom he had met in romantic circumstances at Idi Amin International Airport while covering the Tbongo debacle—of biting her severely on the buttocks and breasts in her hotel room. When the house detectives broke the door down in answer to her screams, Buzz was clad only in garter belt, brassiere, silk stockings, and high heels. He had just barely escaped prison when the eccentric Judge Momus put him on probation on the condition that he have his front teeth pulled and not replace them with a denture. The extraction and pictures of him with a goofy smile had done nothing to improve Mordant's already touchy personality, and while waiting for his gums to heal he worked off his resentments by writing a seminal book about television.

Tell It Like It Isn't began by pointing out that the press had always claimed that its sacred mission was to tell the people the truth in order that democracy might flourish. Thomas Jefferson was often quoted in this regard, "No people can be both ignorant and free." "But," Mordant hastened on, "the press has fulfilled this democratic function in an uninspired manner over the years. The face of a mother when told that her children perished in a fire while she was at the corner bar, the cigar that a former president had used to excite an infatuated girl, the distraught woman describing how she had been penetrated by a purple alien with six testicles from outer space, these are the kinds of truths daily made available to the American people. A world of violent drug busts, serial killers loose in the street with assault rifles, flood and drought, murder and mayhem, and countless other disasters that otherwise would not be known are served up daily to the folks. No effort is spared to inform them that the ozone layer is disappearing, that genetically modified food is poisoning the land, and that global warming is about to melt all the ice at the poles and inundate the East Coast.

"But no matter how the news industry strains," Buzz went on, "they, as everyone knows, just can't hack it. The public always wants more excitement. Reality, whatever that might be," said the old deconstruction major, "will always disappoint, is always ontologically deficient. Virtual reality ought to be the true goal of the news, and until everyone accepts the superiority of fiction over fact, the news will remain dreary and disappointing, unworthy of a real democracy." This led to the Mordant Principle: "Fiction is always superior to fact in every way."

In private, the media people in the TV stations and the newsrooms responded with incredulity. "What does this guy want? Picasso would get a migraine from the imagination we burn up every week. Come on, now, Buzz baby, give us a break, we do a lot better creative-wise than most folks. This is a bum rap. We may look like we are telling the truth, but actually we make sense out of a senseless reality. An aborted billion-dollar rocket with only two white rats aboard, launched to see if they will copulate when weightless, we show as the cutting edge of modern science and a bold adventure into the unknown of the universe. We do offer the audience a lot of junk fact, sex, and scandal, but we regularly make the best out of the worst.

"Take, for example, American politics, which most folks know is a colossal sham in which an oligarchy of wealth and power wears the disguise of a folksy democracy. But if it were to become public knowledge that the ordinary citizen has no power whatsoever in the nation's affairs, that they are in fact run by a cabal of politicians, lawyers, Fortune 500 companies, communications moguls, and other power brokers for their own benefit, the whole democratic show would collapse. Without us not a citizen would bother to leave the house on the first Tuesday in November. We construct the democratic scenery that legitimates the act that the pols perform on the national stage. 'Get out and vote for the candidate of your choice,' 'Every vote counts,' 'The price of freedom is eternal vigilance,' 'All people are equal at the ballot box,' and so forth.

"We do a lot more, too. We create for the people the omniscience of modern medicine, the justice of the law courts, and the effectiveness of the educational system. We make the nation believe that God is in his heaven and all is right with their world."

But the old deconstructor wasn't having any of it. He had mastered the art of speaking effectively without any front teeth, some even preferred his toothless talk, and in a nationally televised interview with Regis Goldbrick, he urged the TV industry to forget altogether the ancient and empty distinction between fact and fiction that crippled effective communications and instead turn their imaginations free to create positive news programs worthy of a great nation. "Go for the jugular," he shouted at a grinning Regis, "let it all hang out. Front page a cure for cancer, life on other worlds, flying saucers that penetrate our air space regularly. Tell the folks that only 3 percent of husbands and wives have been unfaithful to their spouses, that 98 percent of the people believe in God and in Santa Claus."

"But, Buzz," Regis exclaimed, "won't people lose faith in us if they think that we say the thing which is not?"

"So, who will know the difference? How many times will there ever be a real test of who believes in God or whether there are flying saucers whizzing around interfering with TV reception? And as for cancer cures and such, no one will check up on you the next day, let alone the next week. History is stone dead. Television doesn't provide information, it provides interest, excitement, action. It provides NOW.

"If you look at TV today," Buzz concluded his argument, "as all of you will, the only really creative and imaginative things on it, you will have to admit, are the advertisements. This is so because the wizards of Madison Ave long ago learned that their business was not to tell you the truth about their products, bulldozers or deodorants, but to stroke you and make you believe that you and the world are interesting, that problems can always be solved, that things are fun. The ordinary ad bubbles with life, with sex, with charm, with good nature, with invention. Advertisements point the way to putting life and meaning into the news. And if you are worried about going too far you can always add, 'If the problem persists, see your doctor.'"

Buzz went on to demonstrate with charts and graphs that advertising was already the raison d'être of all the media, including television. Advertising paid for the news, and the news's final purpose was to get the folks to look at the advertising. So, Mordant continued, "why not forget the artificial barrier between facts and ads, choose the ads every time."

Tell It Like It Isn't was an instant best-seller, and President Thud was prevailed to declare National Media Week and ask all Americans "to join with me in celebrating the work of our communications experts who keep the wheels of this blessed land from spinning in the mud of ignorance." It was a Book-of-the-Month Club selection, and it rose to fourth on the national best-seller list, just behind Alice Dashiki's new blockbuster, *A Big Paycheck for Slavery*. *The New York Smirk* praised *Tell It Like It Isn't* in a long editorial, noting that Mordant was once a *Smirk* stringer who had learned much from his newspaper days that had stood him in good stead in his meteoric career in television.

Everyone was very respectful of the Mordant Principle, but nothing really changed. Cynics said that Mordant had only described what was already going on. Pictures of O'Hooplas and headstrong allegories gave way in time to chronicles of a serial killer shooting his girlfriend, their children, her boyfriend, her mom, and then himself. Sports headlined salaries that made professional athletes rich as Croesus, the business news told how executives of bankrupt companies floated to soft landings in their golden parachutes, while the NASDAQ passed 20,000. Incest, sodomy, serial murder, clitorectemy, rape, torture, oral sex, mixed with fascinating items about necrophilia, ritual cannibalism, dismemberment, bestiality, infanticide, the birth of dectuplets after using fertility drugs, and movie stars cloning exact duplicates of themselves.

Overseas, tyrants old and new continued their relentless assaults on their own people, "ethnic cleansing" assured that the ancient inhabitants of lands from Palestine to Timor were exterminated, and dollar loans to "developing nations" were diverted to numbered accounts in Swiss and Cayman banks.

In the boardrooms and the executive suites, however, the Suits read Mordant and sent memos to one another to cover their behinds:

> From the Desk of C. S. Moosebugger—
>
> Say, J. C., I think this guy Mordant's got something. I've always wondered why we didn't ginger up both the news and the ads by mixing them together. It's hard to tell them apart, anyway. Just a state of mind, Mordant's right. Let's workshop it,

> maybe use the gal who was doing that survey for us, Emma Pessary, with a few assistants, give her a few bucks and let her run a couple of focus groups. She's supposed to be tracing the linkage between toilet training and response to the news, but we won't lose anything if we shift her team over to working on a seamless mix of ads and news. Maybe, just maybe, Nebbish TV is on its way to overtaking CBS, NBC, Turner, Fox, and ABC in the ratings.

The scientific testing of the Mordant Principle began in a suite of dingy rooms on the top floor of Nebbish House. Team Pessary consisted by this time of Emma Pessary; Somerset; a black man who had been directed to the project by the welfare agency's threat to cut him off if he didn't take a job; and Olga Moosebugger, the obese blond ex-wife of CSM, whose job allowed him to cancel her alimony. All the team members were issued white scientist jackets with the Nebbish logo. Any scenarios they came up with were dramatized on tape by pickup actors sitting around waiting to speak their lines in one of the soaps.

The Suits came up one day to see how Team Pessary was getting along and were shown some examples of what Emma considered the most promising approach to the problematics of newsmaking, INSERTS, folding the ad content into the news so that one became indistinguishable from the other. Her first exhibit was a lumpish item about the police breaking in a door to arrest some sleeping drug sellers—"Why are they always in bed?" "They must be very tired"—and stopping just before the arrest to discuss how fast they had gotten to the crime scene in their new eight-cylinder Ford Excrescence, its new tires after the big recall, what great pickup it had, the safety of its antilock brakes, the comfort of the seats when you had to sit in them all day long, the roomy area in back where the seats could be adjusted in any number of ways to fit the particular kind of perps you were hauling to the station.

Team Pessary's prize exhibit, however, was a high-quality in-depth news program, something like *20/20* or *Nightline.* The title was *Spousicide: America's Hidden Shame,* and it dealt with a growing social problem in middle-income, highly stressed executive families.

After an intro citing statistics, the scene opens in a typical American kitchen with all the gadgets. The Smithers family is around the breakfast table. One of the kids is gloomily feeding his oatmeal, the "ugh" brand, to the lovable dog, but perks up when his mom says, "I know what you want, you want some of that new cereal-coated sugar, Dextrograin Yum-Yums!" She pours out a twelve-pound economy box of Dextrograin Yum-Yums, empties a bottle of milk on them, and the kid slurps it up. The noise annoys Pop, unshaven, with dark circles under his eyes and a harassed look, who growls, "When you eat I can't tell you from the dog. Why don't you try to act like a human being for once?" The kid and his sister, and the dog, take one look at the old man and beat it out the back door.

Mom isn't daunted, however, she knows the wimp she is dealing with, and has put the old boot in many a time before: "If you had taken two of those Wooly-Sheep-Counter™ tablets, like I told you, you wouldn't have lain awake all night with that big rod of red acid running from your fat stomach up to your big mouth, twisting and turning, worrying about your difficult executive-level job. But you are always Mr. Smartypants, you won't listen, so you get up in a foul mood and spoil a nice quality-time family breakfast."

At this point Pop begins to look like Jimmy Cagney about to push a grapefruit in Mae Clark's face, as he says, "Hey, kiddo, I got something for bright girls like you. Yesterday I went down to Mort's Friendly Weapons Emporium, at 2301 Charlton Heston Boulevard, and bought this shiny new Colt Allegory .357 Magnum." He takes a huge nickel-plated revolver out of the table drawer where he has stashed it, spins the cylinder a couple of times, like Clint Eastwood, with real satisfaction, and shows it to her. [voiceover, "Make my day."] She laughs, and says, "How did a wimp like you get a gun permit, you don't even know which end the bullet comes out." He grins at her, looking even more like Cagney at his most manic, and says, "Yeah, but I got smart, I took a course on self-defense and the exercise of my second-amendment constitutional rights to keep and bear arms offered free by the National Rifle Association—contributions to PO Box 1776—and the instructor said, you just hold it in your hand, like this, aim it like this, and pull this little thing." Mom exits at high speed as Pop begins firing. When the police come to get him, he breaks down and cries that he was redundantized yesterday and the thought that he can't give his little American family the things they are entitled to, like all the Dextrograin Yum-Yums they need to build strong bones, had driven him crazy.

"What a story," the Suit in charge of the project jumps up as the lights brighten again, "it will tear their hearts out, explain the spousicide epidemic, and at the same time sell Dextrograin, Wooly-Sheep-Counters, and Colt Allegories by the boxcar, as well as raise some much-needed dough for Charlton Heston and the NRA. This is what you get when you mix ads and reality, pow, blast, bam, dynamite!"

But the other Suits were not so sure. Most of them left without saying anything. One mumbled something about how this project had maybe gotten off the train at Bridgeport rather than Darien. Another said it might *miss* the audience they were *aiming* at, and everybody had a good laugh that relieved the tension. After the Suits were gone, Team Pessary went back to work, and the lights burned late in the Nebbish TV Scientific Research Center. Work was progressing on a dynamite series called *Mortuary* in which a degenderized bunch of go-go yuppie postmortem docs, with oodles of hair and mouthfuls of white teeth, talked about the diseases that had killed the bodies on their slabs and recommended medicines and health plans that would have saved them.

The Suits knew that the project wasn't really working well, and they began to look glum when they came up to check on things. The advertisements were great, but the stories about real people were dragging them down. "What we need," one of them opined, "is ALL advertisements, you know, one right after another, or if not that, then a narrative line built around the ads, not the other way." They floated the idea with Team Pessary, encouraging them to say what they really thought: "Come on, guys, you are the real people, that's why you're the experts, speak up, let's hear your ideas."

Olga only unwrapped another candy bar, but Somerset, who had been biding his time, sensed that this was his moment. He now wore a sincere tie, and he had read a few on-line e-zines about what the future holds for advertising. Out of what he read he had cobbled together a collage of what seemed the right words. He hung back for a time, and then began in a kind of stumbling fashion.

"Uh, uh, say, I just maybe got this idea of how by now it is clear that topographies of power and representation have emerged in the wake of the profound popularity of postmodernist discourse and theories of cosmopolitanism. Right? [gaining speed] Right! The new global order of intensified flows and accumulations of capital and labor—displacing old forms of racism, nationalism, and hetero/sexism—has reconfigured the relationship between identity and space in the twenty-first century. Got it?"

This was a language the Suits understood, and after a moment of respectful silence, they all began to babble.

"Right on."

"That's just what we've been looking for, a radical conceptualization of the problem."

"This gives us something solid to build on, don't you think, J. C.?"

"Yeah."

They all gave Somerset, but only Somerset, a high five or a low five as they left.

By the next day all of Team Pessary had, except for Somerset, received pink slips. Out of Team Pessary's ruins, Team USA, consisting of Somerset, had been set up and commissioned to undertake a long-range search to "seek out new methodologies and conceptual tools in the disciplinary diagrams circulating around transnational cultural studies and advertising modes, with a view of basing TV programming 100 percent on ads that showed 'dynamite potential.'" "Dynamite potential" was not spelled out, but Somerset intuitively knew that it meant those ads that had symbolic energy, that glowed as if irradiated with an inextinguishable fire, ads with icon status that soared into the empyrean. "Sweets for the Sweet," "Don't Give Her a Present, Give Her a Gruen," "I'd Walk a Mile for a Camel," "Less Filling—Tastes Great," and "Don't Leave Home Without It."

Team USA moved to a single office among a number of storage rooms on the tenth floor of Nebbish House. Day after day Somerset culled, from nine in the morning until late at night, clips of old ads on VCRs that were brought to him in big boxes, the long-forgotten masterpieces of the Michelangelos of Madison Avenue in ancient times.

Washing powder, automobiles, cereal, beer, aspirin, hair dye, stocks, second and third mortgages, tires, toothpaste, tropical cruises, houses, soap, more and more soap, the treasures of America flowed from a bottomless cornucopia onto the screen before him. He had little curiosity about what happened to the ads he winnowed, but the kid who brought the new boxes of film in and took the old ones out told him, "Joe Camel really has his nose under the tent." A little more questioning revealed that this meant that the ads he sent downstairs marked with five stars got a lot of use. Some became "breaking stories" in Buzz Mordant's Bodybag News, or sometimes they were retrofitted into a collage of old ads, skillfully combined to create a panorama of American life, a special report on one aspect of society or another. Sometimes, he heard, when one of the ads was particularly dramatic, it would become the germ of a new "made-for-television movie" or a sitcom or soap opera that could run all season. Television ads had with Somerset's guidance become the mother lode of imagination from which all American entertainment was being manufactured.

He didn't think about it much, but as he watched, a shiny new America took shape in front of his eyes, something very different from the painful world that the Joads had left a hundred years before in Oklahoma, something very different even from the disappointments they had found in California.

The primary social organization was still the family, but a family of an odd kind. There were young people who for a brief time fluttered in the sunlight between the darkness of one family and that of another, but they were always doing or wearing something that would soon propel them into another family, their own. Inside the primary family, Mom was the paramount figure. Her children were healthy and clever, but careless, and required a lot of good-natured, if slightly exasperated, tending, like driving them to some kind of sporting event, washing recurrently soiled clothing, or instructing them in what to eat.

Pop was there, but he was, it had to be said, marginal. When he did appear, he was bumbling and dim. Mom had to straighten him out about almost everything, see that he took his medicine, maintained the car and the lawn, and didn't burn the hamburgers at the frequent outdoor barbecues where he did the cooking. Pop worshiped Mom, brought her frequent presents, and never forgot an anniversary or birthday. Pop was 100 percent faithful to Mom, and his only other girlfriend was his daughter, Young Mom, in training to become Big Mom. With her, his relationship was a bit intense. She was crazy about riding, and he bought horses for her and spent his vacations taking her places where she won championship sporting events like ski races and tennis matches. They went golfing together, and Pop was at times maybe just a bit too familiar.

At work Pop was a minor executive who made a lot of mistakes, was in danger of being fired, and came home exhausted and inflated with a persistent, nasty acid-gas. The people who worked for or with him thought him an insensitive boob. He forgot to take his daily aspirin and had heart attacks every time he tried to play basketball with his son or tennis with his wife.

All of the family and their activities were faithfully recorded in photographs, both still and moving. No occasion was quite real unless someone got the camera out and took lots and lots of colored photos or moving pictures complete with soundtrack.

"Say something."

"O, my Gawd . . . !"

The virtual family was a nuclear family, in every sense. It extended only to children, grandchildren, and grandparents—Mom's parents, not Pop's—who looked as if they were in their forties, rode horses a lot, took a barrel of vitamins everyday, fastened their false teeth to their gums with a kind of cement that made it possible to eat apples, and had lots of money and a consuming desire to take care of and spoil their grandchildren.

TV America was middle-class land. Everybody had an upscale lifestyle. For a time Somerset couldn't figure out how a "lifestyle" differed from a "life," but he finally realized that you could buy a lifestyle, whereas a life was just something that time loaded on you for free. Buy the right big-ticket items, the right tennis shoes, a house in the suburbs with a cathedral ceiling in the living room, a vacation in the Caribbean, and especially the right automobile, preferably two. *It takes a heap of buyin',* he thought, *to make a lifestyle.*

Television adland didn't have many really rich, and the poor were invisible, therefore no class warfare. There were some young working-class people, men for the most part, who spent all their time drinking beer, going to football games, and driving pickups at breakneck speed through deep mud and snow. Otherwise, the scene was the middle-class house complete with every labor-saving device ever invented, from the electric toothbrush in the vast bathroom to the radon exhaust system in the cellar, all set in the middle of a huge green lawn that Pop fertilized and mowed with a huge tractor every day.

Mom's hair, vagina, and bowels were the lares and penates of the virtual family, but the great gods were the cars. Everybody had one: sports cars to humor an aging Pop; big sports utility vehicles that put Mom in the command seat and allowed her to run over the top of smaller vehicles in case of an accident; heavy luxury sedans that brought the family safely home from trips on dangerous highways, where wild animals and rapist-murderers screamed with frustration along the roadside, while the children and Mom slept comfortably; pickups to go to the dump on Saturday when you wore your cowboy boots and ten-gallon hat and gossiped with old friends.

The family did not smoke or drink, except for the young men and women who consumed gallons of beer. But despite being abstemious, the postmodern family's health was worrisome. They looked great, but they spent a lot of real time in doctors' offices being told to have tests, take medicines, get through the CAT scan, join a health maintenance group, give up something that is bad for them. To judge from the frequency of ads for medicines, "doctoring," as the old people of the land like the Oklahoma Joads used to call it, was the main occupation of the family, after driving cars. There were a lot of small aches and pains, backaches and migraines were daily occurrences, menstruation was frequent and painful, teeth required lots of special fluorides and whiteners, and dentures were forever falling out unless held in by "Locktite—They Will Never Know." But there were big time diseases, too. Mom had to spend a lot of time feeling her breasts for lumps, but the various tests she took for all kinds of cancers, cervical to brain tumors, kept her in tip-top shape so long as she conferred regularly with her doctor, went to the numerous specialists he, or increasingly she, recommended, and got prescriptions for the many miracle pills advertised by the pharmaceutical companies so that you could tell your doctor you needed them, in case he/she forgot.

Pop had to do a lot more than treat his jock itch. He was particularly subject to blocked arteries, palpitations, prostate cancer, heart disease, and stroke, and it was important for him to remind his doctor that White Rat Pharmaceuticals had just brought out a new zeta-blocker and a nonoleaginous cholesterol suppressant that would stop these dangers cold.

Virtual America was an equal-opportunity, affirmative-action place, and the percentage of black families in TV ads was much higher than in the census. All the blacks were remarkably happy people—nobody talked about reparations for slavery on televsision—200 percent participants in the American TV Ethos. Other minorities were visibly there as well. No group of kids gathered in Mom's kitchen to eat her delicious prebaked choco-chip cookies without an Asian, a Latino, and one free choice, an Indian or an Eskimo, usually. Plus, of course, a lovable puppy or two. Feminism was very okay, and Somerset figured out after a time that homosexuality was accepted as a standard deviance without dwelling on it any more than the occasional tart remark or limp wrist here and there.

Politics was a strictly forbidden subject in the home, though there were numerous political attack ads that revealed the sinister intentions of one party or the other. In its lifestyle the virtual family was just a bit liberal left of center, like the college grads who created the ads. Its members were tolerant, they gave to charities and did volunteer service happily, they voted and cheered for their candidates. They rarely traveled abroad, they spoke no foreign languages, and when they tried a word of Spanish or French they got the pronunciation amusingly wrong, just to show that they were real Americans; but they were interested in the people of other lands and supported the U.N. They were church people, which church was of course not specified, but God meant a lot to them, and they respected all beliefs, from totemism to the *I Ching. No wonder,* Somerset thought, *that Religion USA had been so prosperous.*

Were there villains? In the political ads, of course, but everybody expected politics to be something like all-in wrestling. The garage mechanic who cheats you, the grouch who yells at your children in the backyard, the motorist who risks your kids' lives running a red light, maybe even the Mafia don running the labor union and carting away garbage, though there was a deep admiration for ethnics who had made it the hard way. But television people were a surprisingly amiable lot with few enemies. Terrorists and mad bombers may be around, but they didn't shoot their way into TV Land very often.

Above all, Somerset observed, TV Folks were patriotic. Grandpa was likely to have served in the military, though his uniform sadly no longer fit him. Virtual people voted, they paid their taxes without whining, obeyed the law, supported public works, and attended town meetings, which seemed to be the government of choice in nearly every TV town, even the South Bronx.

Education did not play a very big role in TV Land. The kids studied reluctantly and went off to school without enthusiasm, but they were crackerjacks with computers. They would go to college, as Mom and Pop did, but it would be a social, not an intellectual experience. Theirs was not a world of ideas.

What *were* the TV Folks interested in? Well, in things. Theirs was a *totally* materialistic society. People were concerned only with automobiles, junk food, houses, bowels, cars, beer, and on and on and on. Even those things that had once been spiritual or conceptual were now commodified in TV Land. *Could the commies have been right, that capitalism puts a price on everything? Well, THEY didn't produce anything to put a price on.* Love was the right hairdo, fresh breath, ultra-thin maxipads, and a bright smile. Friendship was watching TV football together while eating pizza and drinking Coke. Well-being was the right brokerage firm and the solid insurance policy from your friendly agent, who stops to pick up your dog at the vet's on the way to discuss updating your coverage. Religion was going to church together and saying hello to the minister afterward. Education was having gone to a high school and a college and using standard English, but nothing too heavy.

Television ads showed Somerset a new America he had never really seen before, a post–Cold War America, a postmodern, post-Y2K America, virtual America, a self-fulfilling America. It was an uncanny place, this virtual America, at once fascinating and repellent, simple and sinister, folksy and deeply perverted, totally fake and at the same time potentially real. Somerset was troubled and confused by what he felt, but he reasoned with himself, *Nothing really wrong, is there, with the TV society that the ads create? A real paradise compared to less happy lands where you can get your hands chopped off for just standing by the side of the wrong road, or where some mad dictator can send millions to concentration camps to relieve a childhood neurosis. TV America is a decent, healthy, and happy place by comparison.*

But Somerset could not avoid feeling disappointed as day after day of looking at the ads went by, and he began to think that looking at old television ads was not maybe where he wanted to spend the rest of his life. On one occasion he actually quit and took a minimum-wage job washing dishes in a Chinese fast-food restaurant. It was a tough, hot job but he found a friend, Cholly, the counterman, and from time to time when there weren't any customers they would philosophize.

"Ah so, Cholly, how's it going?"

"Hey, Somerset, boy, you know how it is, here today, here tomorrow."

"How come, Cholly, that only the poor like us, never the rich, are good-natured *and* smart?"

"Somerset, you just don't know enough poor people, most of them are as bad as all the rest. Some of them are a lot worse. You should live in China. But you're right to this extent, the more money you have, the bigger asshole you are."

"But everybody believes just the opposite, 'If you're so damned smart, why ain't you rich?' That's what Pa used to always say to me."

"I'll tell you, Somerset, I guess if people are having trouble making it, it keeps them a bit uncertain and humble, but when you reach lifestyle country, your rear aperture enlarges exponentially. Still, rich or poor, something is speeding up the assholification of America, and I've been meaning to ask you, the expert, if it couldn't be all those television ads that are the alpha and the omega of all of TV. You can't turn the set on without someone blatting or whining at you to buy this or buy that."

"But, Cholly, sweetheart, ads are only a small part of what's on TV. There's sports, and there's the news—how would we know what's going on in the world if we didn't watch Buzz Mordant and his Bodybag News every night? And there's made-for-TV movies, and soap operas that keep teenage girls and lonely housewives and old people amused, and talk shows where politicians tell us what we need to know about the state of the nation, and interviews with famous people, and quiz programs on which real folks can become millionaires. There are even public service programs like the one on the disappearance of the sea turtle, or how to rewire your house, or dramatizations of classics like the new Masterpiece Theater production of *Remembrance of Things Past* that shows its hero, the Baron Charlus, in a new light. It's a big medium, Cholly, you spend too much time in here boiling rice."

"No, no, no, Somerset. The ads are Anthrax letters, they infect everything they touch. Politics is all TV exposure nowadays, and look at the attack ads that are obvious lies, and the costs that drive the pols to do anything for campaign funds. Sports, well, the ads lengthen the games to the point where the audience can't remember whether they are watching football or hockey. The advertisers pay the zillions of dollars the athletes get now. And does that improve the game? Fugeddaboudit, as we used to say in Shanghai. You don't agree, huh?"

"No, Cholly, baby, I don't. I've had a rough life, Cholly, and no one, I'm sorry to say, has seen more TV ads than I have, but I'm glad to say that I'm not a rotten cynic like you. Must be because you're a foreigner, not to the manner born, as one of our native bards put it. How much for the eggdrop soup?"

"A dollar fifty, just like always, Somerset, but for you it's on the house. But look, paisano, you're a sensitive kid and you will figure things out one day, so when you go back to Nebbish—and you will—look for what is 'rotten in the state of television.'"

"No, Cholly, I won't go back to that dull job. But if I did, say, what would I look for?"

"Look to the ads, kid. The ads will themselves tell you not only that something is wrong, they will tell you what it is. Even the biggest, flashiest, most successful lies ever told always show somewhere just a flicker of truth. I don't know why, but the truth will out; as Confucius used to say, 'There's no rope long enough to hang the truth."

Cholly was right. Washing dishes in the steamy kitchen of a Chinese restaurant was too much for Somerset after a while, and he crept back to Nebbish House, where his old job was still open. He retired again to his high lonely tower and watched more TV ads. After a time he moved in a cot and a microwave and pretty much lived there. No one seemed to notice.

Cholly's view that television ads carried some fatal social disease had disturbed Somerset more than he had admitted. He found himself looking for that breakthrough that Cholly had insisted he would find somewhere in the ads. Then, one Sunday, late in a long afternoon, something remarkable happened. It was not as overwhelming as the teeth that had obsessed him as a youth, but Somerset shuddered with some kind of sixth sense when a long chain of ads he was listlessly watching all focused on Mom having trouble with her stomach and lower intestinal tract, as she so often did. White Mom dosed herself with buckets of Soft Stooler™, and a wonderful old black Mom, bowed with the wisdom of the ages, pressed either a very blue or a very pink laxative on her husband, her children, her neighbors, passersby. A yuppie-queen Mom threw herself on a bed in a fury because her stomach was so distended that it would no longer fit in her skin-tight designer jeans. Then, a grandmother vamped the groom at her daughter's wedding, all in good fun, of course, after she used Blowzit™, to get rid of a blockage that was making her look cross and old.

"*Mom is full of shit.*" The horrid idea was in Somerset's head before he could defend against it. He rejected the dreadful thought at once, but could not shake it off entirely, and it forced him to ruminate on what he had seen. *Is Cholly right? Is there an indelible reality, inscribed so deeply in things that it expresses itself in some way no matter how completely the surface has been hyped and sanitized? A long reach, and a direct contradiction of the reigning metaphysics of deconstruction, but still conceivable.*

As Somerset went on watching more and more ads, day after day, he couldn't avoid seeing that Mom wasn't the only American having trouble with her fundament. There were scenes, for example, in which some poor wimp sits in a movie, or in a jury box, or at a meeting of the school board, some place where he or she is in full public view, and twists and writhes, trying desperately to keep tormenting rectal itch (TRI) under control, smiling broadly all the while in a vain effort to deny that life is a nearly unendurable pain in the ass:

"Something wrong?"

"With me? No, Sir, ha, ha."

Somerset told himself he shouldn't make too much out of this evidence, but then came the ultimate ad where Santa Claus in his red suit and bushy white beard was unable to sit on his chair and listen to America's children tell him what they wanted for the most sacred of holidays, Christmas, when the gross domestic product lives or dies depending on how many presents folks bought. Only when he rushes out and applies some Old Soothy™ to his rear end is Santa able to give full attention to the major public service he is engaged in. This was it. If Santa, the giver of gifts, the myth of myths, is suffering from TRI, why then there *is,* has to be, something wrong at the bottom of Virtual America.

And one day confirmation came through, unmistakably and absolutely *en clair,* like the vision of a saint, right out of the tiny screen in an ad for a diarrhea control pill, Pucker Up™. A gigantic Excresence SUV taking commuters to work is stuffed with fleshy, crude Philistines, who looked to Somerset like some of the great men and women of the world. Buzz Mordant, the toothless Nebbish Network anchorman, helped Alphonse DaGunto, the porn king, get his wheelchair on the bus elevator. There was the politician Senator Amos Brightgrin and the intellectual guru Professor Pierre de Hors. There was the great scientist Dr. Angelo Circulari, who harnessed rotary motion, and the PR genius Stanley Moosebugger. Saint C. Beecher Retrofit, whom the pope had recently canonized in a fit of ecumenicism, sat intently trying to read yesterday's closing price for ANUS on the Big Board in *The New York Smirk.* There were generals and lawyers, Outage and Rattenkrieg, in this very crowded van, as well as tycoons and an artist drawing Thurber dogs in the mist on the window, and they were all jeering the wimp of the group—who somehow reminded Somerset of a picture he had seen of his maternal grandfather, old Muley Graves—as he begs them to make stop after stop at service stations to relieve himself. At each stop they hoot in derision as he waddles ducklike at high speed toward the bathroom, trying to keep his arse tight enough to avoid befouling himself, while his face registers a mixture of clenching embarrassment, griping agony, and cheerful insouciance, in a frantic simultaneous revelation of his plight and a denial of his desperation.

Selected Items from the On-Line Biography of Great Americans

Abime, Meece N.: Foucault Professor of Deconstruction, Ivy University; murdered by student determined to prove the reality of reality.

Allen, Ethan: Green Mountain Boys Socialist Labor Party; U.S. Representative, Vt.; dairy and maple sugar subsidies.

Ananias, Fredson: Certificate, Delta Bible College; chief of police, Los Angeles Police Department; deacon and SWAT leader, Cathedral USA; director, CIA, under President Thud.

Barratri, Ellen: Lone Tree State University, Non Sequitur Hall; associate, Cease & Desist; called to New York bar, Pegasus, Parnassus & Culpable; legal assistant, Senate Majority Leader Amos Brightgrin; counsel committee on WJC politics gene; U.S. attorney general.

Brightgrin, Amos: B.A., Lone Tree State University; banker, Brightgrin National Bank; U.S. senator, D–Calif.; Senate majority leader; best known for Klutz-Brightgrin H.R. 1984, the John Quincy Thud On-Line Biography of Great Americans; m. Senator Pomona Hardstones shortly before untimely stroke.

Bulbous, Lemuel: Greenville State University Law School; U.S. senator, R–N.C.

Bulkhead, Commodore Bowditch; U.S. Naval Academy, 1995; service in wars in Taiwan, Greenland, Antarctica, and Miami; chief of staff to CNO Admiral Keelhawl, Tbongo incident; court-martialed for loss of the Lizzie Borden Independent Women's Parachute Combat Team.

Casy, Jim: itinerant Oklahoma preacher; traveled to California in 1930s dust bowl exodus from Midwest; founder, Chapel of Lost Spirit, Scorpion Springs, Calif.

Chameleon, Boris: b. Absolute Zero, Deep Siberia; KGB Bureau of Counterterrorism; Hero of the Soviet Union; defected to U.S.; director, disinformation section, CIA; appointed director, FBI, by President Thud.

Circulari, Dr. Angelo: Italian-born physicist; head of NERDGO (New Research and Development Group); applied rotary motion to new areas of human activity; inventor ROD (Rotary Orgasm Device); Public Committee on WJC politics gene; long-listed for Nobel Prize.

Clitterhouse, Ginger: San Fernando Valley High; cheerleader; choir, Cathedral USA; high priestess, Religion USA; charged Right Rev. Dr. C. Beecher Retrofit with statutory rape, later married him; divorced; jailed for attempt on life of her lover, Fredson Ananias.

Crankshaft, Frank: Michigan State University; executive, Excresence division, Ford; U.S. senator, R–Mich.

Culpable, Honorable Elmore: Harvard Law; partner, Pegasus, Parnassus & Culpable; U.S. representative, D–N.Y.; Speaker of the House.

DaGunto, Alphonse: publisher *Puss Magazine;* shot and paralyzed below the mouth by Father Rugby Portface; sued by Right Reverend Dr. C. Beecher Retrofit for portraying him as hermaphrodite; diagnosed with acute satyriasis; confined to hospital for incurables.

Dashiki, Doctor Alice: B.A. and Ph.D., Harvard, Afro-American culture; Huey Newton Professor of Black Culture, Ivy University; Pulitzer Prize for *Laboring Together* (Three-Holer Press); assistant secretary of state, central Africa; leader of the militant Reparations for Slavery movement.

De Hors, Pierre: Collège de France, Vincennes, deconstruction; Derrida Professor of Anomie, Ivy University; author of many works, especially *How We Became Post Human: Virtual Bodies in Cybernetics,*

Literature, and Informatics (Three-Holer Press) and "Manifesto for a Democratic Art."

Disputandum, N. E.: professor of forensic rhetoric, Non Sequitur Hall.

Dungan, Ralph: B.A., Lemming College; Fort Wayne, Ind., auto dealers' used-car salesman of the year.

Fallopian, Dr. Karl: cell biology, STASI research center, DDR; prominent in Freedom of Choice abortion movement; National Medicalization Committee; long-listed for Nobel Prize; Krafft-Ebing Professor of Sexological Studies, Manatee Institute of Social Technology.

Firewall, Rex: son of a bishop who became a deacon at early age; LL.D., Non Sequitur Hall; in-house legal adviser, Lone Tree State University; famed for skill in guiding neophytes to highest peaks.

Fullstop, T. Bullit; B.A., Harvard; banker; DEFSEC (Secretary of Defense), war on Tbongo.

Fury, Drusilla: nom de plume of Drusilla Joad, née Grunge; m. Earle Joad, two children; author of *Jane Breaks It Off in Dick, Queen of the Phallic Women,* and other popular feminist romances (Primal-Scream Comic Books).

Grinder, Lieutenant General Nancy, USMC: U.S. Naval Academy, 1992; service in Timbuktu, St. Helena, French Frigate Shoals; warden, Hardtime Dry Tortuga Federal Prison; Purple Heart for loss of arm at Hardtime stopping break by desperate felon, Rugby Portface; commandant, U.S. Marine Corps; chief of staff after Tbongo debacle.

Happenstance, Benedict: B.A., Ivy University; inventor, "The Better Mousetrap," a wildly popular cheese spread; philanthropist; famous for nearly cornering gold; died indigent.

Hardstones, Senator Pomona: homecoming queen, Lemming College; Miss Georgia and runner-up, Miss America; hostess, Washington Entertainment Agency; appointed U.S. Senator, R–Ga., to fill out term; m. Senator Amos Brightgrin; envoy plenipotentiary without portfolio, Paris.

Heavy Thinker, Barbara: professor, Ivy University; dean of faculty, Lone Tree State University; U.S. representative, D–N.Mex.; honorary chief, Amalgamated Indian Tribes of America, Inc.

Holofernes, Judith: dean of counseling and harassment officer, Lone Tree State University; president, Association for Democratic Sex; early victim of AIDS.

Illwill, Chancie: descendant of Mayflower Illwills; B.A., Ivy University; Feminist Cybernetics Movement; adviser on feminist digital systems to bellyup.com; foreign travel; mutilated body found near Santa Ynez con Cojones, Mexico.

Imus, Max: political and social activist; director, Save the Children; charged with molestation but copped fondling plea.

Inhouse, "Nails": four-time offender, sentenced to life as incorrigible; TV interviews about famous people he knew in prison.

Joad family: traveled with Oglethorpe to Georgia to escape debtors' prison; moved to cotton plantation, Mississippi; settled on Indian land, Oklahoma; driven out by drought, 1935; moved to California, led by Old Tom Joad and Grandma Joad, née Hazlett, accompanied by sons Noah, Tom, and Winfield, daughters Rosasharn (the pregnant Rose of Sharon) and Ruthie, and son-in-law, Al.

Joad, Calista: second child of Winfield Joad, III, and Elspeth Graves Joad; mother of Lowrider Joad; art-law expert, Pegasus, Parnassus & Culpable, New York City; common-law wife, Dimitri Parnassus; resided and practiced law in Tbongo; filed complaint against newscaster Buzz Mordant for indecent assault; proprietor, Bosom Buddies Lounge, Las Vegas, Nev.

Joad, Earle: first child of Winfield Joad, III, and Elspeth Graves Joad; B.A., Ivy University, deconstruction; Ph.D., Manatee Institute of Social Technology, deconstruction; part-time, non-tenure-track lecturer, Lone Tree State University; m. Drusilla Grunge, two children; dean of remedial studies, sex counselor, Lone Tree State; resided in Mexico for a time; file clerk, *The Greaser: The Alumni Review of Greasewood Community College,* Mesquitopolis, N.Mex.

Joad, Ellsworth: fourth child of Winfield Joad, III, and Elspeth Graves Joad; associate's degree, Ethicists' Training Program, Lone Tree State Extension; resident ethicist, Little Sisters of Misery Hospital; special committee on WJC politics gene; assistant ethicist, Step 1, GS-1, Surgeon-General's office.

Joad, Elspeth Graves, Ma: granddaughter of Muley Graves; associate's degree, Lone Tree Community College, social work; m. Winfield Joad, III, six children; later in life became famous for being militant Gray Panther.

Joad, Somerset: third child of Winfield Joad, III, and Elspeth Graves Joad; *wanderjahren* during his twenties and thirties; employment at Cathedral USA; briefly led millenarian breakaway sect; manager, faith healing booth, Religion USA Mall; leader, Team USA, at Nebbish Network for analysis of TV ads; murdered outside Nebbish House by deranged tramp.

Joad, Thompson: fifth child of Winfield Joad, III, and Elspeth Graves Joad; B.A., Lone Tree State University, and LL.D., Non Sequitur Hall; associate, Pegasus, Parnassus & Culpable; won famous case *Poshpenny v. Lone Tree State;* assistant claims collector, Squeeze & Grind; m. Linda Statutory, four children.

Joad, Triola: sixth child of Winfield Joad, III, and Elspeth Graves Joad; White House volunteer training intern; corporal, Lizzie Borden Women's Independent Parachute Combat Team; killed in action in defense of Fort Zinderneuf; posthumous Tbongo Pacification Medal; Purple Heart.

Joad, Winfield, III, Pa Joad: grandson of original Oklahoma Joads; m. Elspeth Graves, six children; A-One Rockets assembly line, thirty years; End of the Trail Managed Care Home; testified before House committee considering the on-line database of all Americans; trampled to death by angry crowd in Washington protesting the passage of the John Quincy Thud On-Line Biography of Great Americans.

Keelhawl, Admiral Bluewater: U.S. Naval Academy, 1941; Midway, Philippine Sea, Okinawa; commander destroyers, Atlantic; chief of naval operations, Tbongo incident.

Kernan, Alvin: B.A., Williams; Ph.D., Yale, English; professor Yale and Princeton; blotted copybook; part-time, off-tenure-ladder lecturer in satire, Manatee Extension Institute.

Klutz, Solon: served thirty terms in U.S. House of Representatives, D–S.Dak.; chair, Appropriations and National Information Committees; noted for Klutz-Brightgrin H.R. 1984, joining with the Democratic Senate Majority Leader to pass the John Quincy Thud On-Line Biography of Great Americans; oldest member of the House for many years; d. in House restaurant.

Knockoff, Sergei: sculptor, site-specific works *Batterer 2* and *Wall of Hope,* ten-foot-high wall of solid brass running full length of Broadway, without portals, separating East and West sides of NYC; *Wall* destroyed in uprisings against privileges of art by frenzied mob of handicapped and homeless demanding gates.

Lamprey, D. Buster: B.A. and Ph.D., World Wide Web Institute of Cognitive Studies; director, Program of Post-Digital Cognitive Studies (POPS), Ronald Reagan Research Center for the Study of Higher Cognition; consultant to plaintiff, *Poshpenny v. Lone Tree.*

Lasher, Simeon: de Sade Professor of Sexology, Lemming College; president, Association for Democratic Sex.

Load, Lockin: ELF Certificate in Activism; U.S. senator, Idaho, Anarchist Party; killed by federal agents in siege of mountain fort for refusal to file National Identity Database form.

MacAdder, Fiona: B.A., Vassar; LL.D., Katherine Gibbs School of Jurisprudence; crossexamination specialist, Pegasus, Parnassus & Culpable; lifetime companion of Kendra McFacile.

McFacile, Kendra: U.S. representative, Green Party, Oreg.; sponsored bill to remove all dams from Columbia and Snake Rivers; CEO, Upriver Indian Entertainment Centers.

Marauder, Jeff: peripatetic artist of uncertain origin and name; believed to combine styles of Goya and Thurber; Rose Window, Cathedral USA?; attack grafitti, 116th St. Station, New York subway?; murals preserved on trailer wall in Santa Ynez con Cojones, Mexico?

Momus, Judge Anthony: Second Circuit Court of Appeals; presided, *Retrofit v. Puss;* remembered for Mordant decision, in which he required sexual predator to have his front teeth removed.

Monorail, Ida: Radcliffe Institute; Ph.D., Harvard, body studies; professor of women's studies, Ivy University; Alzheimer's, early retirement to Sans Joy Extended Care Hospice.

Moosebugger, C. Stanley: premier public relations expert of early twenty-first century; life trustee, American Nuts and Screws; advised National Medicalization Committee on WJC politics gene; Committee on Political Genetics; consultant to Pegasus, Parnassus & Culpable in *Poshpenny v. Lone Tree State;* adviser to President Thud on sodomy charges; consultant, Nebbish Network; choked on steak when companion could not get arms around him to execute Heimlich maneuver.

Mordant, Ethelred, "Buzz": B.A., Ivy University, summa, deconstruction; for many years anchor, WNIT-TV Bodybag News, Channel 666; best-selling author, *Tell It Like It Isn't;* foreign correspondent in Tbongo incident; probation for mutilation revoked and imprisoned for buying set of false teeth; d. fit of impotent rage, Hardtime Dry Tortuga Federal Prison.

Nano, I: descendant of French painter Henri Toulouse-Lautrec?; B.A., Lemming College, art; known for patriotic native paintings; director, Museum of Ancient American Art; academician, American Academy of Arts and Letters.

Nolo, Judge Anthony: LL.D., Yale; tried *Poshpenny v. Lone Tree State;* landmark finding established American students not dumb, only badly educated; author, *Not So Dumb After All;* commissioner, Bureau of Federal Prisons.

O'Banshee, Father Sean, S.J.: Borstal School for Irish Boyos; Clongowes Wood Seminary; chaplain to IRA; cut Devil dead on Roman street; director, Vatican Office of Infernal Authority; translated to Cathedral USA as resident exorcist-in-chief; numerous articles on casuistry.

O'Hoopla, Seamus: scion of distinguished O'Hoopla political family; B.A., Lone Tree State University; disappeared wrestling allegories (alligators?) on banks of Nile, body never found.

O'Hoopla, Codswallop: B.A. and LL.D., Harvard; U.S. senator, D–Tex.; long-distance swimmer in youth; proposed moral rights of artists.

Outage, Major General Hannibal: West Point, 1980; Desert Storm, Kosovo, India-Pakistan peacekeeping force; procurement officer, Pentagon; found guilty by court-martial of indecent proposals to minors on Internet; cashiered and pension rights revoked.

Parnassus, Dimitri: b. into wealthy Greek shipping family; LL.D., Sophistic School of Law; founding partner, Pegasus, Parnassus & Culpable, New York City; common-law husband, Calista Joad, whom he supported at her life's end.

Pessary, Emma: sex activist; Hungry Hollow School for Wayward Girls; B.A., Lone Tree State University, sexology; sex counselor, Have It All Valley High, Calif.; Ph.D., extension program, Columbia Teachers' College; focus group leader, Nebbish Network.

Pistole, Muy: Mexican bandit of Santa Ynez con Cojones; shot for traffic in drugs, prostitution, and suspected murder of American *puta*.

Portface, Father Rugby: B.A., Lemming College, D.D., Princeton Seminary; chaplain, Manatee County jail; seconded, Episcopal Church Chapel, Religion USA Mall; defrocked for marrying parishioner to her weimaraner; life sentence for shooting and crippling Alphonse DaGunto, publisher of *Puss Magazine;* d. in desperate attempt to escape from Hardtime Dry Tortuga Federal Prison while holding warden, General Nancy Grinder, hostage.

Poshpenny, Peter: B.A., Harvard, body studies; failed Ph.D. general exam in body studies, Lone Tree State University; sued Lone Tree State on grounds he was improperly prepared, lost; served long jail sentence for failing to wear crash helmet in auto.

Potsherd, Buffo, "Jungle Jim": B.A., East Keokuk Junior College; Ph.D., Princeton, anthropology; editor, *American Ethnophobe;* specialized in cannibalism; eaten by Tongos or Bongos in Tbongo.

Proudfoot, Henry: U.S. senator, R–R.I.; Senate jogging champion for many years.

Rattenkrieg, Emmit Shuldig: Yale Law; partner and chief litigator, Pegasus, Parnassus & Culpable; known for his tenacity in closely contested cases.

Redskievic, Professor Ilya: B.A., Red Star University of Perpetual Revolution, Beijing; Karl Marx Medal for dialectic; Mao Tse-Tung Professor of Revolution, Ivy University; board member, American Nuts and Screws and numerous other corporations.

Retrofit, C. Beecher: American evangelist; b. Jack Pudge, Bideawhile Trailer Camp, Geeks' Hollow, W.Va.; compensatory high school certificate, Young Offenders' Institute, Wheeling, W.Va.; D.D., Hallelujah Bible School; missionary to Tbongo; called to Cathedral USA; primate of Religion USA; sued *Puss Magazine* for portraying him as hermaphrodite; charged with statutory rape of minor female, Ginger Clitterhouse; m. and divorced Ginger Clitterhouse; chair, Committee on WJC politics gene; chaplain, U.S. Senate; papal appointment to sainthood as part of Vatican Great Apology to All Pagans.

Robinson, Jack: b. Abou-bin-Adam; Beirut School for Practical World Revolution; Comintern apparatchik; sales manager, Mazo Lite Brewery Tbongo, Ltd.; native informant for Jungle Jim Potsherd;

leader of Tbongo freedom movement; extradited and hanged by International Tribunal, The Hague, for massacre at Fort Zinderneuf.

Savage, Richard: B.A., Yale; professional writer; author *Making It Up: The Authorized Life of C. Stanley Moosebugger* and many other "with-the-help-of" biographies; soi-disant illegitimate son of Norman Mailer and Lillian Hellman, both of whom strenuously denied any responsibility.

Slinker, I. Harrison, III: b. Ignace Slinkowycz, Poland: LL.D., Lvov Law School of Polish Jurisprudence; partner and trial leader, Retrograde, Replevin, & Persiflage, in landmark case *Poshpenny v. Lone Tree State.*

Spreadeagle, Taffy: studied anthropology, Pow-Wow School of Native American Culture; leader, WNIT-TV, Channel 666, news team, *Here's the Lowdown*; independent scholar, research on macho rituals; author of *The Hogtied Phallus: Misogynist Themes in Cowboy Poetry;* lecturer, Greasewood Community College, Mesquitopolis, N.Mex.

Surdstein, Dr. Arnold: South Bronx Boys Choir; M.D., Catscan New Order Research Center; chair, National Medicalization Committee; codiscoverer of WJC politics gene; tax evasion, ten years; escaped New Alcatraz Federal Prison; eaten by sharks?

Thud, John Quincy: All-American football player, Fighting Manatees; pro All-In League; Hall of Fame running back, Manatee Maulers; U.S. senator, D–Ark.; vice-president U.S.; POTUS, two terms; impeached for molesting White House aide but not convicted; sent expedition to pacify Tbongo; signed the John Quincy Thud On-Line Biography of Great Americans bill.

Torque: ancient god of Tbongo people; requires annual sacrifice of virgin.

Transférans, Dr. Toussaint: M.D., Port-au-Prince Outpatient Clinical Center; trained as psychoanalyst, New World Bedlam Hospital, Jamaica; practiced in Hollywood, Calif.; National Medicalization Committee, Little Sisters of Misery Hospital; honorary doctor of science, Lone Tree State University; clinical professor, voodoo medicine, Lone Tree State Medical School; appointed Surgeon-General by President Thud.

Uncas, Rodney: lone descendant of sole survivor, Mohican genocide; leader Indian affairs; casino investor.

Undone, Ralph Waldo: Fustian Professor of Anthropological Rhetoric, Ivy University; nearly eaten by Tbongo tribe in Africa; in latter years spoke and wrote only pidgin English.

Whitewater, Naomi Guccibagger: Radcliffe College, summa; Harvard Law; m. & FLOTUS President Whitewater; famous for immortal words, "Let's hear it for the POTUS, the man I love"; U.S. senator, D–N.Y.; political career ended by panda coat scandal, in which two CIA agents killed pandas at National Zoo with poisoned bamboo to obtain pelts.

Yell, Thurible: known as "Rebel"; U.S. senator, R–S.C.; life member, Confederate Diehards of America; leader, Right to Life movement; sponsor of Stars-and-Bars law requiring Boy Scouts to carry Confederate battle flag; president, Stars and Bars Association; d. heart failure reenacting Battle of Gettysburg.

www.ingramcontent.com/pod-product-compliance
Lightning Source LLC
Chambersburg PA
CBHW060759310726
48980CB00002B/163

* 9 7 8 0 3 0 0 0 9 2 9 0 5 *